# FORGIVE ME, FORGIVE ME NOT?

"Have you ever considered how strange it is that we are on our way to Gretna together at last?" Morland asked Harriet. "Can you believe it took twenty years after the trip was first proposed to you for you to finally agree to it? Don't you find that ironic, ma'am? I do!"

Harriet wished he had not mentioned that long-ago time; after his first outburst she was grateful he had pretended to forget it had ever happened. She wondered what made him refer to it now.

"I have been trying to forget," she said when she realized he was waiting for a reply. "And I thought we agreed never to discuss it again."

"So we did. But no matter what we agreed, you must admit our past will always be part of our memories. And whether we speak of it or not, it refuses to be disregarded. And those things we never said to each other, whose omission we can only regret now, clamor to be revealed at last. And those things we did say, and regret even more, beg to be forgiven."

"If it will make you feel better, know I forgave you for them long ago, m'lord," Harriet told him. Her throat felt so tight she had trouble swallowing. "Yes, I forgave you with all my heart," she heard herself repeating. "I hope you in turn can forgive me for all the pain I know I caused you . . . ?"

# The Runaways

by

Barbara Hazard

A SIGNET BOOK

SIGNET
Published by the Penguin Group
Penguin Books USA Inc., 375 Hudson Street,
New York, New York 10014, U.S.A.
Penguin Books Ltd, 27 Wrights Lane,
London W8 5TZ, England
Penguin Books Australia Ltd, Ringwood,
Victoria, Australia
Penguin Books Canada Ltd, 10 Alcorn Avenue,
Toronto, Ontario, Canada M4V 3B2
Penguin Books (N.Z.) Ltd, 182–190 Wairau Road,
Auckland 10, New Zealand

Penguin Books Ltd, Registered Offices:
Harmondsworth, Middlesex, England

First published by Signet, an imprint of Dutton Signet,
a division of Penguin Books USA Inc.

First Printing, July, 1997
10  9  8  7  6  5  4  3  2  1

# One

"The Earl of Morland has called, ma'am. He requests a few minutes of your time."

Mrs. Harriet Winthrop-Bates did not betray any emotion at this announcement. Instead she took the earl's card from the tray her footman was presenting and studied it carefully. But behind her placid exterior her heart had begun to beat faster, and her breathing had quickened. He was here! What did he want? What could he possibly want?

The slightly adenoidal breathing of the footman reminded her he was awaiting a reply.

"Very well, Biggs," she said. "You may show the earl to the sitting room. Tell him I shall be with him presently."

As the footman bowed and hurried away, she added, "Offer m'lord wine."

She did not wait for her order to be acknowledged but turned instead toward the library windows. It had been threatening rain all day, and now that threat was a reality. A steady downpour lashed the windows, doing its best to clean the cobblestones and gutters of the quiet street on the outskirts of Mayfair. Mrs. Winthrop-Bates hardly noticed. Absently, she inspected the elegant carriage waiting before her door—the matched team, the earl's smartly liveried attendants. Through the streaming glass the image of them wavered until it resembled a child's watercolor.

He was here, she told herself. She had never thought to see him again. What could he want? Surely not to renew an acquaintance that had ended so bitterly and finally more than twenty years before. No, it could not be that. She closed her eyes, but she could not shut out the memory of how he had looked so long ago, how wounded and disbelieving he had been and how that disbelief had been replaced by scorn, and worse, by a fury icy and searing at the same time. He had lashed out at her, his savage words accusing, and even now, all these years later, she remembered how she had felt as if she had been flayed.

He must have seen her at one of the London parties she had attended this spring. Could he have come here to gloat? She moved a little restlessly. She did not think that could be the case. When she had known him, Marsh Pembroke had been passionate and possessive and wild to a fault, but he had never been petty or vindictive.

The brass clock on the desk struck the half hour and she was reminded he was waiting in her inadequate sitting room. She was sure he must be sneering not only at its size but its old-fashioned furnishings. At least the wine he had been served was excellent. Her husband had prided himself on his cellar. She had brought two dozen bottles of Madeira to London to save the expense of purchasing wine here.

She turned from the window. As she put her hand up to smooth her hair she realized she was still holding his calling card and she had crushed it in her fingers. She was surprised. She did not remember doing that.

She found the earl leaning against the mantel, staring down into the small empty grate. He straightened and bowed as she came in. After a quick glance she was glad the business of curtsying allowed her to lower her eyes, for a little pulse in her throat had begun to pound at an alarming rate. How different he looks, she thought. I would hardly have known him!

"M'lord," she said, pleased the hand she held out was so steady. "Won't you be seated?"

As she took a chair she saw his hesitation and was sure he was about to refuse. At last he shrugged and obeyed, and as he did so, she studied him. His hair was still dark except for a hint of silver in his sideburns, and he was dressed in an elegant style. How different that was too, she thought, recalling the impatient young man she had known, striding about in muddy boots and careless riding dress, and more often than not displaying a spill of torn lace at his cuff and laughing away her offers to pin it up for him.

He was frowning now, his heavy dark brows almost meeting over his arresting blue eyes. Those had not changed at any rate. His square jaw had firmed in maturity and there was a small scar above his left eyebrow. She wondered how he had come by it. His shoulders were broader than she remembered, and if he were not still boyishly slim, at least he had kept his waistline. The hands that rested now on his knees were larger and more powerful and she could see the long thick muscles of his thighs acquired from years of bruising riding. Marsh had always been hard on both himself and his horses and obviously that had not changed.

"No doubt you are wondering why I am here, madam," he said and she hoped he would not notice her confusion. His voice was so changed! Then it had been light, musical. Now it was deeper and harsher and devoid of every bit of sentiment or animation.

"Indeed I do wonder," she replied, determined to be as cool as he.

"I believe this is your first visit to town for the Season, madam," he continued. It did not sound like a question, but still she nodded.

"Your husband died a year and a half ago, did he not?"

"Why—why, yes, he did."

"And now, having observed the required period of mourning, you have brought your only child to London. No doubt you did so for the purpose of seeing her creditably established. Am I correct, Mrs. Winthrop-Bates?"

She was so startled she could only stare at him. The

earl seemed to know a great deal about her and her affairs. She wondered why and for what purpose.

"Permit me to wish you every success in this worthy endeavor. But you must also permit me to tell you your daughter has no hope of being so creditably established as to become the future Countess of Morland and the wife of my son and heir. Yes, that is plain speaking indeed but I do so to make myself perfectly clear. I am not a devious man and I am known to speak my mind. You may believe I mean what I say."

His hostess continued to stare at him in shock. Her mouth was so dry she knew she could not reply. Instead, she went to the decanter placed on a side table against the wall. The earl rose as well, punctilious in his courtesy, quite as if he had not just roundly insulted her and her daughter.

As she poured herself a glass of wine she struggled for control. She told herself she must be calm. He must not see how he had wounded her.

As soon as she was seated again she sipped her wine. Only then did she speak. "I cannot imagine what possessed you to come here and say such a thing, m'lord," she remarked. "It was very rude."

"Although I am often rude, in this instance I beg to be excused," came the swift retort. "You see, I came to spare you and your daughter pain, madam. You should be grateful to me. I am so seldom kind and hardly ever caring.

"But now, being forewarned, you can make sure your daughter looks elsewhere for a suitable connection. If you do not set your sights too high, I am sure you will find one in London. Although the nobility is above your touch, there are many other young men from genteel families like yours. I suggest you make a push in that direction and forget any fond dreams you might have entertained of one day being the mama-in-law of an earl. Believe me, I would never permit such a thing. Never."

He looked around the little sitting room as if to remark its meanness, and his mouth tightened. He could not have told her what he thought of her surroundings more clearly if he had spoken and Harriet Winthrop-Bates stiffened, her wine forgotten.

Many years ago she would have lashed out at him, her voice as strident as his as she matched him insult for insult. But he had not been strident today. She remembered then how their arguments had always ended, but she was not tempted to smile. Instead she told herself that time was long gone and better forgotten.

"I was not aware my daughter had even met your son, sir," she forced herself to say in a mild voice. "Indeed, I did not know you had one, so you see I can hardly be accused of setting my sights on him. In fact, you may be sure I would find such a connection a thousand times more repugnant than you."

For a moment a ghost of some little amusement danced in his eyes and he raised his glass to her. "*Touché*. My compliments. But how can it be you are so negligent you have not noticed how often our children converse and dance and even, I daresay, arrange to meet alone? By chance, of course."

"Lark is lovely and charming. She is often surrounded by various young men. But as for secret assignations, no. She would not be so abandoned, so careless of her good name and reputation. I know my daughter. I trust her."

Ignoring the latter part of her speech, he grimaced as he put his empty glass down. "Lark!" he said in a voice rich with scorn. "How came she by such a ridiculous name? Surely it cannot have been your choice."

His hostess felt her face grow warm. "My husband claimed he heard a lark begin to sing just as she was born," she said.

The earl stared for a long moment. "But how touching, to be sure," he drawled. "And did you hear this, er, bird too, madam?"

His blue eyes held her captive until she was forced to say, "I did not. I was rather preoccupied just then."

He ignored her suddenly heated face and nodded. "I can imagine you must have been. But over the years you must have been grateful that it was a lark. Only consider how unfortunate it would have been if a donkey had chanced to bray at the crucial moment."

When his hostess refused to dignify this pleasantry with a reply, the earl rose and returned to his position by the fireplace, to lean once more on the mantel above it.

"You have said you trust your daughter to behave as she ought. May I remind you, madam, that even the most carefully reared young ladies can forget everything they have been taught when they are in love? Or think they are? Surely you remember how it was for you when you were young. It was not that long ago, after all.

"You also say you are not aware of my son's growing regard; his close attentions. I suppose I must accept that, even that you do not know how your daughter welcomes them. However, having now been made aware, surely you will watch the minx more carefully; order her to give Andrew up. Surely you agree such an order will only spare her grief, even though young love, so consuming and fervent at the start, soon dies.

"I do not know if you share my views, madam, but I have found age brings wisdom. And I have come to see parents are right to insist on an arranged marriage between those of equal birth and estate."

Mrs. Winthrop-Bates's face was now as white as it had been rosy only moments before. She stood, determined to terminate this distasteful interview without delay. "I thank you for coming and warning me, m'lord," she said. "You may be sure I shall be on my guard from now on. Lark has never been disobedient. She will certainly agree to discourage your precious heir if I suggest she do so." Aware she had let a little temper show, she was quick to add, "Surely you will be able to control your son as well. You do command his filial respect, do you not?"

"Of course I do," he said, his lips compressed. "But Andrew is young, and typically idiotic. He is all high-flown ideals and impractical dreams. Eventually he will steady into a sober maturity and it is only then I would have him wed, when he has seen enough of the world to choose, with my assistance of course, his life's partner well.

"What I would deplore is for him to be swayed now by rampant virility and the heat of the moment. Ah yes, those heated moments nature provides in such abundance to ensure the continuation of the species. Surely as the mother of an impressionable and physically mature daughter, you are all too aware of them and their power?"

She did not bother to answer. Head held high, she went to the sitting room door.

"Give you good day, m'lord," she said, forcing herself to look into his arrogant face without flinching.

"My compliments and my best wishes for a most successful and satisfying London Season for you, and of course, for your beautiful, charming daughter, madam," he said. "And since it is most unlikely we shall meet again, I shall not say good day, but rather good-bye."

Harriet Winthrop-Bates remained by the door as he accepted his cane, gloves, and top hat from her footman. Only when the street door shut behind him did she re-enter the sitting room.

She did not waste any time thinking about the earl as she poured herself an unprecedented second glass of wine. Lark would be home soon. She had only gone to the shops on Bond Street with her maid for some new ribbon to refurbish her second best ball gown. The driving rain would probably bring her home sooner rather than later, and her mother knew she must have herself well in hand before then.

Putting her visitor firmly from her mind, she considered what he had told her. Had Lark been singled out by his son? Had she even encouraged the young man as he had claimed? She thought hard but try as she might, Harriet Winthrop-Bates could not recall Lark ever mentioning an Andrew Pembroke. She had talked about a number of beaux on occasion. Freddy Colchester—Alastair Stone—Sir Roger Beaton, and yes, a Viscount Byrn.

It did seem to her now she thought of it, the viscount was the most favored by her daughter, in a very casual way, of course. Lark was only seventeen, heady with the success of her first triumphs in the six weeks since their arrival. But surely she was not in love. She had shared her triumphs with her mother, even told her of the compliments she had received, her green eyes full of laughter and delight as she did so. But she had given no sign of any fixed interest, no great urge to settle for the one man rather than the many. It had even worried her mother a little for she could ill afford another Season.

Harriet sipped her wine pensively. It should all have been so different. When she had married James Winthrop-Bates he had been a wealthy man, or so she and her parents had been led to believe. Of course they had resided quietly in the country all their married life. James did not care for the racket and bustle of town. He had been a poet and a scholar, and although Harriet had missed London, she had adjusted. It was only after his untimely death that she had discovered to her horror that he had invested in a number of schemes that had only one thing in common—their quick and inevitable decline. The ship he had bought for trading had been lost in a typhoon in the China Sea, the mines he had sunk so much money into had become unproductive and closed down, and the mortgages he had taken on the estate to raise capital had proved impossible to repay.

His man of business had told her stiffly these schemes were none of his advising. Indeed, he had claimed he had tried every way he knew to get Mr. Winthrop-Bates to give them up. Harriet shook her head, remembering. James had been the most stubborn man she had ever known, one who hated to listen to advice and one who refused to admit he was ever wrong.

And so, after he had died in the riding accident, she had discovered she was as good as penniless. Of course her daughter's portion was safely guarded and she herself had a small legacy from her grandmother, but Moor House had had to be sold. After the debts had been paid she had little left to launch her daughter in society. Yet she was determined Lark would marry not only well but for love if that were at all possible.

The Earl of Morland's stern face, those powerful dark brows and determined jaw invaded her mind. He had been so sure of himself and his facts. She would have to question Lark about this Andrew Pembroke—discover just where she had met him and how far their flirtation had gone. For she had meant it, she told herself as she heard the outer door flung open and Lark's gay laughter in the hall. She did not want her daughter to have anything to do with the Earl of Morland's son. Certainly she did not want her to marry him! For if such a thing happened, she and Marsh Pembroke would be thrown together again, this time into a parody of family life, forced to attend Christmas gatherings, christenings, even birthdays together. How unpalatable such an alliance would be.

No, not Morland's son. *Anyone* but Morland's son.

# Two

"Dearest."

"Oh, do take care! Someone might hear you."

The tall young gentleman rose from his bow, at the same time releasing the young lady's hand he held. "Shall we stroll, Miss Winthrop-Bates?" he asked politely in a normal tone of voice.

"If you would care to, m'lord," she said demurely, opening her fan and waving it languidly before her face. "How warm it is this evening, to be sure."

"What has upset you?" he asked in an undertone even as he remembered to bow to old Lady Mainwaring and her bosom bow, Lady Boothby, seated together against the wall, quizzing glasses raised in unison.

"The most dreadful thing! Did you know your father called on my mother yesterday afternoon?"

"He did? I was not aware they were acquainted. Are you sure?"

"Good evening Mrs. Deering, Lord Carson. A delightful party, is it not?

"But I like squeezes, m'lord. No, you shall not tease me. I do, truly I do!

"I was quite sunk when I returned from shopping and Biggs told me of our exalted visitor," she went on as the pairs separated. "Surely he came to tell my mother about us, don't you think?"

"But did he? M'father has said nothing to me, and I can assure you he has never been what you would call reticent. Lord, no. Comes right out and blasts away whenever he's displeased. Been doing it all my life."

"I don't know. My mother seemed nervous some-how—upset. But she did say they had known each other many years ago, why, even before she married my father."

"I say, how marvelous. They must have liked each other, and when they discover we're in love, they'll be all smiles."

"Hush! Do be more careful, Drew. I'm sure Mr. Jeffers overheard you. He turned so suddenly."

"All this sneaking about is intolerable. When am I going to see you alone? And when are we going to be able to announce our betrothal?"

"You know we cannot, not yet. You're not of age yet, and if you remember, you were the one who said it would be better to wait, for your father might kick up a dust because . . . why, good evening, Mr. Colchester. I am so happy to see you."

Freddy Colchester, a slight young gentleman sporting a head of flaming curls, smiled sweetly at the two of them.

"I am delighted you say so, Miss Winthrop-Bates," he said. "Especially when Byrn here is looking daggers at me. Do fetch the lady a glass of lemonade, there's a good fellow. You've had her to yourself far too long."

The viscount was prepared to argue any separation, but a glance at his beloved's face showed she was in favor of such a course of action, and even though he did not understand her reasoning in the least, he bowed and obeyed.

When he returned, he found Lark seated on a sofa beside Mr. Colchester. Two other young gentlemen also formed her court, and he had difficulty getting close enough to hand her the glass of lemonade he had procured. It was well over an hour later before he was able to be alone with her again, this time on the terrace with a number of other couples come out to escape the heat of the Marquess of Gaines's drawing rooms.

Andrew Pembroke was desperately trying to think of a way he could whisk Lark unseen around a dark corner so he might kiss her, when she said, "I am afraid we are about to be discovered, Drew. If my mother and your father become close, they are sure to find out about us. And I don't know why, but just the thought of it makes my blood run cold."

She shuddered and he wished he might put his arm around her to reassure her.

"It is not that my mother will try to keep us apart," she continued. "She is the sweetest, dearest thing! But your father frightens me. He is so hard-looking, so severe. I am sure he intends you to marry a duke's daughter, or someone fabulously wealthy, not poor little Lark Winthrop-Bates from Suffolk with nary a lord or lady on her family tree, and only a pittance of a dowry to commend her."

"He will never be able to keep me from marrying little Lark Winthrop-Bates, so don't you even think it!" the viscount whispered fiercely. "I don't want a duke's daughter; why, the only one I know is old, at least thirty-five. And I don't need any more money.

"Oh, Lark, I do love you so. How am I ever going to wait a whole year and a half for you?"

Even in the faint moonlight he saw her blush and he put his hand over hers and squeezed it where it rested on his arm.

"Darling, darling Drew. I know, I know. It is so hard! But we must be circumspect. For some reason my mother has been watching me all evening. I cannot remember her ever doing so before. Perhaps your father does know about us. Perhaps he went to tell her because he disapproves. He will keep us apart, I know he will, and my mother will be forced to bow to his dictates, and unable to help us. I am so afraid!"

"But how could he know?" the viscount asked, his brow furrowed in thought. "No one could have been more prudent than we, and no one knows of our secret meetings but your maid. You can trust her, can't you?"

"Oh, yes! I've known Fanny all my life. She was our head groom's daughter and we played together when we were little. How she envies us. She says this is the most romantic adventure she ever heard of, and she has sworn not to betray us even if she is threatened with torture or death."

"My father is a hard man, that's true, but I don't think he'd go that far," the viscount protested.

In spite of her fears, Lark gurgled with laughter. "Of course not," she agreed when she could speak again. "But Fanny does love to dramatize."

"Then I am to continue giving her my letters to you every morning when she comes out for the milk?" he asked. "I wish we could make some other arrangement, Lark. You know I'd do anything for you, my darling— anything at all—but getting up and leaving the house before eight is raising some suspicion. I don't wake easily. Sometimes my man has had to shake me—hard. He's been looking at me so oddly these past few weeks."

"Oh, he may have told your father," Lark whispered, her green eyes wide, and her mouth forming a circle the viscount was hard pressed not to kiss and hang the consequences.

"M'lord, Miss Harwood, give you good evening," he said instead.

"I must not stay," Lark whispered when they left the other couple a few minutes later. "My mother will be wondering where I am. But perhaps we could find some other way to exchange letters?"

"If only you had a garden. I could put them in a hollow tree. Any time of day, even afternoon," he added, his face brightening at the thought.

"Or under a stone," she elaborated. "I once read a book where a couple did that. Alas, we live in that horrid little place and the houses on either side are so close. Of course there's the mews, but it's not much bigger than an alley. I can't see you there, Drew, with the grooms and horses. You'd be sure to be noticed and remarked."

"I'll think of something," he told her as they reached the doors of the drawing room and prepared to rejoin the company. "Trust me."

Her eyes assured him of that, and he felt his heart swell until it felt too big for his chest. How he loved her, this slender girl with the clear green eyes, the glossy hair that was a hundred shades of honey, the skin like alabaster. He had tumbled in love with her at first meeting a month before, and now he was forever lost.

As he bowed over her hand, he whispered, "We meet next at the Colchester ball. How the hours till then will drag. I adore you!"

"And I you, dear love," she murmured before she slipped away to join her mother.

Harriet Winthrop-Bates had seen enough this evening to realize the Earl of Morland had not been mistaken in his belief his son and her daughter were, if not in love at the moment, only a heartbeat away from that happy state. For of course Andrew Pembroke *was* Viscount Byrn, and Morland's heir. She wondered she had been so dim as not to know that immediately.

Now her heart sank. She had not questioned Lark after the earl's visit for she had not wanted to confront the girl until she had seen the state of affairs with her own eyes. But now, without hearing them exchange a single word, she was sure, too. One had only to watch them together to know; the eager way the viscount took Lark's hand in his and held it perhaps a moment longer than necessary, even how he bent close to her when he spoke—the touching look of complete concentration he gave her when she replied. As for Lark she alternately sparkled and gentled in his company as she had never done before. Her laugh was gayer, her smile for him softer. Her mother felt an encompassing ache deep inside just looking at them for she knew no matter how much they thought they loved each other, it would all come to nothing. She herself might be brought to approve eventually, if their love lasted a year or so, but she knew the earl was not so softhearted. He would not be swayed by sentiment. She had seen how any tenderness and concern for others he might once have had was gone now. He would do just as he promised and separate them, and he would do it ruthlessly.

As Lark sat down beside her with a little smile and began to ply her fan again, Harriet wished she could spirit her away this very night, take her far from London and keep her from being hurt as she had been trying to keep her from hurt since the moment of her birth. Of course she knew how impossible that was. Children did not remain children. They grew, went out into the world to forge their own lives far from any mother's tender care. And, she reminded herself, they had to make their own mistakes. No safeguards, no amount of warning could prepare them for the rocky places—the hardships, the grief, and the pain they would find in the paths they chose to walk. It was too bad it had to be so, but it had been ever thus.

She made no attempt to speak to her daughter when they returned home from the soiree. It was very late, and Lark could hardly contain her yawns. But as Harriet went up the stairs with her, she resolved to bring everything into the open first thing the following morning.

Unfortunately, the kitchen maid scalded herself badly helping the cook prepare breakfast, and as a result of the ensuing chaos and the upset of normal routine, it was almost eleven before Harriet asked the footman to send Lark to her.

"Miss Winthrop-Bates has gone out, ma'am," Biggs told her. "Left at ten she did, to join a party of young ladies, I believe."

"I see," Harriet said, hiding her annoyance. Yes, she recalled Lark had mentioned something about a walking party if the weather were fair. But now, influenced by the earl's suspicions, she wondered if such a party even existed. Perhaps Lark and the viscount were locked in each other's arms this very minute at some secret trysting place, even though she had no idea where such a place might be found. London was so crowded, there were so many thousands of people, she would have said

it was impossible. She was, however, well aware young
men in love could often show dangerous ingenuity.

She dismissed the footman, wishing, not for the first
time, she had been able to afford someone who did not
constantly wheeze and sniff. Then she was ashamed of
her pique. Poor Biggs! It was not his fault.

Later, she received a hand-delivered letter from the
Earl of Morland. She recognized his handwriting immediately. That was something else about him that had not
changed, she thought as she broke the seal and unfolded
the single sheet.

She was frowning when she finished. He began
abruptly, telling her he had learned of the meeting of his
son and her daughter at the soiree the previous evening.

> I was informed Andrew danced attendance on your
> daughter, all but fawning over her. It was also re-
> ported she did nothing—nothing, madam—to dis-
> courage such a sickening display. Obviously you
> have not spoken to her. I suggest you do so without
> delay. You may be sure I shall have words with my
> son this morning.
>
> I would also suggest you make sure any communi-
> cations that come for your daughter are delivered to
> you first for your perusal. I shall forbid Andrew to
> write to her. Of course he will not obey me. We must,
> you and I, be vigilant. Yours, etc. Morland.

Harriet folded the letter and tapped it against her lips.
Yes, she must intercept any letters from the young man.
That was her duty even though she hated to think of herself as Lark's jailer. They had had such a wonderful relationship, the two of them, till now.

She had been invited to a loo party that afternoon, and
did not like to send her regrets. Instead, as she dressed
carefully for it, she told herself she would talk to Lark
later at tea. Surely there was no need for this frantic
haste to confront the young couple the earl seemed to
feel was necessary.

Had she known what was to occur that afternoon, Harriet might not have felt so calm, for Viscount Byrn wrote a hurried note to Lark after a painful interview with his father at Morland House on Park Lane. Not daring to entrust it to a Morland footman after his father's ultimatum, he paid an urchin a penny to deliver it.

Lark read the note as soon as she returned from her walking party, and she left the house only moments later, accompanied by the faithful Fanny. Biggs screwed up his mouth in disapproval. He wasn't a green 'un, not he. There was something havey-cavey going on, he'd bet his last farthing on it.

Andrew found the wait wearisome even though he had appointed a particular bench near the Serpentine in Hyde Park for the trysting place. When he reached it, he found it occupied by two nursemaids, and they did not leave until one of their young charges got his feet wet.

It was well over an hour later before Lark appeared and he was tired of sitting and watching the quiet water, the children playing, and the commoners who strolled by, undeterred by the unspoken decree no aspirant to fashion would ever be seen there before the fashionable hour of five.

But he forgot his boredom when he saw Lark, and he jumped up to clasp her gloved hands and kiss them passionately. Her maid, a few steps behind her, sighed gustily, and Lark ordered her to go and wait for her back at the gate.

"What is it, Drew?" Lark asked as she pulled her hands from his and looked around nervously. "Whyever did you say you must meet me and here of all places? Anyone might see us, and then we would be undone."

"No one here this time of day but a bunch of cits. Not that it matters. We're already undone, sweetheart."

"What do you mean?" she demanded. "Come, we had better walk. We will be less noticeable that way."

Eyeing a little copse of trees some distance away, Andrew was quick to agree. When they reached it they could slip inside and exchange an embrace, he thought, brightening considerably.

"Well?" she demanded.

"My father called me to the library this morning," he began, all thoughts of dalliance fled.

Looking sideways, Lark saw his frown, and wondered with a stab of apprehension why he could look so pale. "What did he say?" she whispered.

Andrew frowned even more fiercely, wondering how he was to phrase it. He had no desire to tell his beloved his father had called him a chuckle-headed cork-brained flat with more hair than wit, a damned fool, and several other equally unflattering names he would rather she did not associate with him. After thinking a moment, he said, "He has learned of our love for each other and he is adamant he will never give his approval to any marriage between us."

"I told you so," Lark said glumly. "I told you he wouldn't want you marrying an untitled girl with no fortune."

Actually the earl had said he'd be damned if he permitted his only son to wed a little nobody from the country who bore the ridiculous name of Lark, but Andrew knew better than to say so.

"What are we to do? Oh, what are we to do?" Lark cried, now as pale as her escort.

"I will not give you up," Andrew growled. "I don't care what he says or how he threatens me, I will never give you up."

"He—he has threatened you?" she echoed, stopping dead in the path and turning toward him, her green eyes huge with terror.

"Well, I daresay he didn't mean a word of it," Andrew told her, trying to appear manly and in control of the situation. "He may be a hard man, a cold 'un as well, but I am sure he is fond of me, you know, under that gruff exterior. And he's never beaten me."

"I should hope not," Lark was quick to say. "The very idea!"

"Yes, well, but according to some of my friends, their fathers take a strap to them regularly, or at least they did so when they were younger."

His companion waved an impatient hand. "I do not see what your friends have to do with our problem. I must go home soon and we have so much to talk about and decide. What are we to do? Tell me!"

They walked on for several steps before the viscount said, his voice a little petulant, "I don't have a clue. I only know I will not let you go. I can't. I love you too much."

"I love you too, my dear, but you do see just repeating that over and over will not get us very far, don't you? Will we be able to meet somehow do you think? Will you still write to me?"

Andrew remembered then the idea he had had while waiting for her, and he brightened. "Of course we shall write," he told her, patting her hand where it lay on his arm. "Your mother patronizes Lackington's bookstore in Finsbury Square, doesn't she? I am sure you mentioned that to me once."

As Lark nodded, he hurried on, "Then it is simplicity itself. I shall place my letters to you in a certain volume in the store. When you are able to go there, you can retrieve it, replacing it with one of your own."

He paused as if for applause of such an ingenious plan, but to his surprise, Lark was frowning. "Suppose someone else takes out the book?" she asked doubtfully. "Suppose I can't escape the house, or someone sees me exchanging the letters?"

It seemed to the viscount his love was raising all kinds of objections without even acknowledging how stunning his plan was, but he stifled any criticism and said, "Never fear! I'll choose a volume no one ever takes out. And I'll find a spot that's dimly lit and easy for you to reach without help. I'll tell you of it at the Colchester ball. Trust me, darling. All will be well."

Lark tried to smile. "I pray you are right, Drew," she said. "But even if we can exchange letters, how does that help? We will still be separated and unable to wed. Of course, I suppose if we show we are willing to wait until you are of age, your father might be brought to have a change of heart. Surely such devotion for well over a year will prove our love is constant."

The viscount nodded but he was not so sure—of himself now, not his father. Before he had come up to town he had fancied himself in love with a pretty dairymaid and he had been horrified at how quickly he had forgotten her. He could not even remember the color of her eyes. Would not the same thing be likely to happen if he and Lark were apart for a long time? He did not doubt his father would do his best to make sure there was no contact between them, and bully her mother into keeping Lark close. How cruel parents were, he thought, and he did not cheer up until they reached the copse. There, safe from prying eyes, he reveled in Lark's sweet kisses. The feel of her in his arms made him almost dizzy with desire. He would have lingered for hours if she had not protested and made him take her to the gate where her maid waited.

They exchanged one last, searing glance before she fled, and as he watched her out of sight Viscount Byrn told himself his Lark was a priceless gift, and he would strive to be worthy of her no matter what. But as he turned toward Morland House, he hoped it would not take too long or be too difficult.

# Three

Lark was glad her mother was not at home when she returned there. She ran up to her room to change her gown and spend a few quiet moments alone. She also washed her face in cold water for she knew the viscount's kisses had brought a glow to her skin that could not be attributed to the rather languid weather.

Her solitude did not last long, for barely fifteen minutes had passed before Biggs came to summon her to the library.

She thought the footman's voice sounded stiff and unctuous, and taking her cue from that, she knew the next few minutes were bound to be extremely unpleasant. She did not hesitate, however. She loved Drew, she told herself as she went down the stairs. She would not be a coward now, not when their whole future was at stake. And somehow, *somehow,* she must win her mother to their side.

That lady was not behind the desk where Lark had expected to find her. Instead she was seated in a comfortable wing chair to one side of the fireplace and she waved her daughter to the chair opposite.

Nothing of any consequence was said until Biggs had brought in a tea tray and bowed himself away.

"You have something you wish to discuss with me, Mama?" Lark asked as she took the cup her mother had prepared. Although she had never been an impatient child, now she could not bear to wait to learn her destiny.

"I do, and I am sure you know the subject very well,"

Harriet Winthrop-Bates said as she poured another cup of tea. "I was not aware you had formed an attachment for a certain young peer, Lark, and I am a little disappointed you kept that news from me. Why didn't you tell me? Why were you so secretive?"

"I wanted to be sure myself, first," Lark said before she sipped her tea. She began to relax. Her mother had not sounded angry, only a little sad.

"That was commendable. And now you are sure?"

"Yes, yes, I am. I love Drew, er, Viscount Bryn and he loves me. We intend to marry."

"I am sorry to hear you say so. Such sentiments can bring nothing but pain and disappointment to you both."

"I know his father the earl does not approve, but why should you dislike it, Mama?" Lark asked, bending toward her. To her surprise, her mother did not answer at once.

"In the eyes of the world it is a splendid match for you, my dear," she said at last. "And yet I cannot give you my blessing. I would wish you to marry anyone but Morland's son."

"You do not care for the earl? You would keep Drew and I apart because you don't like him? But that is not fair, Mama!"

Her mother seemed to recall that she was not on trial here and she was quick to take charge of the conversation again. "My feelings for the earl are of no significance. What does matter is that he disapproves of any match between you and his son. He will never let his heir marry you, Lark. He will do everything in his power to keep you apart, and I assure you, he has a great deal of power. Viscount Byrn is not even twenty yet. He must obey his father. I have no doubt he will."

She paused to stare at her daughter's bent head. A stray sunbeam touched it and brought her honey-colored hair to vibrant life. Harriet felt sadness clog her throat and she swallowed.

"You have not known the viscount for very long, my dear," she said gently. "It is entirely possible this love you have for each other will not last. And you are very young, too young perhaps to know your own mind. I fear your successes have dazzled you. Falling in love seems wonderful and right and inevitable to you, but I think you are more in love with the idea of it than truly loving."

Lark raised her head and stared at her, her pretty lips set in a pout. "You don't understand, do you, Mama?" she said. "You have never loved as I do now, you *couldn't* have or you would not speak as you do."

"I will not tolerate impertinence, Lark."

"I do not mean to be impertinent, but I must try and explain how things are with me and with Drew. He loves me too, Mama. We are prepared to wait until he comes of age and even if that does not convince his father our devotion is real and lasting, we intend to wed anyway."

Her mother shook her head as she put her cup down. "A viscount and heir to an earldom is not free to choose his bride as other lesser men do," she said. "He must be guided by his duty to his name and title. The future Earl of Morland will wed a girl of his own station, one who brings him an ample dowry, perhaps lands and other wealth."

"Drew doesn't care for any of that, he doesn't! He only wants me!" Lark exclaimed, her words tumbling out in her effort to make her mother understand.

"I am sure he thinks so now," that lady agreed. "But when he is of an age to marry, say in five or ten years, he will feel vastly different. Trust me, Lark. I do not say these things to hurt you, but to help you. You must be realistic. Furthermore, it will not matter how long you are prepared to wait. The earl does not care about your devotion. He doesn't want his son to marry you. You must accept that."

Lark jumped to her feet. "I won't!" she said passionately. "I think you are horrid not to want to help us, and as for the earl, he is monstrous!"

Harriet rose as well to look up at her slightly taller daughter. "If you do not moderate your words and be-

havior, I shall take you back to Suffolk just as soon as
our trunks can be packed. Do you understand?"

There was a tense silence in the library. Then Lark
turned tear-drenched eyes to her mother and said, "I—I
beg your pardon, Mama. I was much at fault. I shall not
lose control of myself again. You have my word on it."

"Thank you. I must also have your word you will not
attempt to meet the young man alone again, and that you
will make every effort to avoid him at any party you
both attend."

Again there was silence, and at last Harriet was forced
to add coldly, "I will have your promise, Lark. Now."

"Very well. I promise," the girl said so softly her
mother had to bend forward to hear her. "May I be excused, Mama? I prefer to be alone just now."

Harriet nodded and Lark left her without another
word. She held her head stiffly but her mother could not
tell if it was to show defiance or to keep her tears from
spilling over and disgracing her.

Once alone, she sank back into her chair and wiped a
tear away herself. She would never have suspected her
daughter had been as involved as she was. Almost she
felt she was discovering Lark for the first time. Growing
up she had had few moments of rebellion, yet today she
had spoken in a shocking way that showed she was not
the obedient, pliant daughter her mother had always believed. Of course there had been little reason for her to
rebel. An only child, adored by her father and mother,
she had been indulged in every way they could afford.
But now, forbidden for the first time to do something she
wanted, she had been strident and determined and thoroughly disrespectful.

Harriet Winthrop-Bates wondered if it might not be
wiser to go back to Suffolk immediately. Or would such
a course only fan the flames between the two? Convince
them they were indeed star-crossed lovers, and pitch
them all into a boiling broth of tragedy and high emotion?

She could imagine how the earl would react to that, all

cold contempt and bitter condemnation. No, they must remain in London and hope the enforced separation would serve to confirm that the love that the viscount and her daughter thought they shared was only infatuation.

As it was for you? her conscience inquired. Have you forgotten you loved once like Lark does now? And it was real and true and the most beautiful thing you had ever known? Have you forgotten?

No, I have not but I survived it, she thought proudly. Lark will survive, too. She is only seventeen and still a child in so many ways. And I do not think I was ever that young even when I was only seventeen myself.

Two evenings later, the Winthrop-Bates ladies were among the throng who attended the Colchester ball. Mrs. Colchester was one of London's most revered hostesses, and when she opened her doors all society clamored to enter them.

Harriet Winthrop-Bates had been glad her daughter did not pout or sulk the two days before the ball, although no one could have said she was lively or gay. Still, she spoke when spoken to, even initiated the conversation on occasion, and she made no effort to leave the house. Her mother did not make the mistake of thinking she had forgotten her lover, not in such a short time, and she was aware she must watch Lark carefully this evening. It was all too possible Viscount Byrn would also be attending the ball.

He was there indeed, for when she inquired, an acquaintance pointed him out to her. But he made no effort to come to Lark or to ask her to dance. Her card was filled quickly even so and Harriet was delighted when Freddy Colchester honored Lark as his partner in the opening set. She sat back and began to relax.

But sometime later that evening, she looked up to see the Earl of Morland approaching, and her heart gave a funny little skip. She had not seen him come in—she wondered why he strode so purposefully toward her after he had said good-bye to her in such a final way.

"I see you have taken the chit to task at last, madam," he said as he bowed over her hand.

"Did you come tonight to make sure I had, m'lord?" she asked.

He did not smile. "I came to be sure my son obeyed my orders, and to catch a glimpse of this paragon he claims to adore to distraction."

"For some reason I find I do not care if Lark meets with your approval or not, sir."

"And why should you? But she is lovely. A little too quiet and contained for real beauty—yes, yes, I know my decree has made her so and it is all my fault her legendary charm is in abeyance this evening.

"I believe she shall survive."

"Her hair is not as blond as yours."

"My husband had light brown hair," Harriet said even as she wondered why she bothered to explain.

"So he did. I recall Mr. Winthrop-Bates. I heard him recite his poetry once at a salon in London. He carried a rose. A large pink rose, as I recall. He, er, waved it as he recited, quite as if he were afraid his audience would not be able to follow the meter if he did not. Strange is it not I remember that so clearly yet cannot recall a word of his poetry?"

Before Harriet could retort, he went on, "Of course he was young then and as callow as all young men. Yes, your daughter is lovely, madam, but she does not soften my heart."

"I don't believe you have one," Harriet was horrified to hear herself say.

"If you think back, you will recall I did. Once. Your servant, madam." He paused and hesitated before he added, "Your daughter cannot hold a candle to you when you were her age. And not now either."

He went away then. When Harriet felt the eyes of many of the guests nearby studying her face, she schooled herself to smile slightly as she turned to a couple and began to chat with them. What they said or she replied, she could not have told you later. But for a long time the final words the earl had spoken so casually before he went away echoed in her mind. It was a strange compliment to give her, and it had sounded almost grudging, as if he had been forced to an admission he would rather not have made. What it could mean she had no idea.

During her conversation with the earl, his son had seized the moment. Passing close to Lark where she stood with some other young people, he tapped her arm, then pressed a sheet of paper folded small into her hand before he sauntered away. Lark hid it behind her fan and excused herself shortly to repair to the small room that had been set aside for ladies who wished to retire. Only there, safe from prying eyes, did she open and read it.

To her disappointment there were no words of love or rage or loss. Instead, the viscount only wrote tersely, "Second floor back on left. Large volume, dull red binding. *Moral Lessons from Antiquity* by the Reverend Tobias Cruthers. Bring handkerchief. Very dusty."

Lark read the note twice while the maids in attendance looked at her strangely. Catching their expression of interest she folded it again and slipped it into her glove.

Even if the viscount had not written a romantic note, the evening seemed full of promise to her from then on. He had not forgotten her—he loved her still. She would go to Lackington's tomorrow and find his letter, and she vowed he would have hers in return if she had to stay up all night to write it.

It was afternoon before Lark could make her escape from the house. She had overslept, not only as a result of her exertions at the ball and the late hour they had finally come home, but because she had sat up writing to Drew almost to cockcrow. She thought her mother looked at her a little strangely when she announced her intention to visit the library and it made her uneasy. As she and Fanny left the house, she maintained a decorous pace in case Mrs. Winthrop-Bates was watching. She had told

her maid all about the plan to exchange letters and
Fanny had clasped her hands to her bosom and declared
it was so touching she could hardly bear it.

The bookstore, called The Temple of the Muses, was
crowded this brisk spring afternoon, the flag on its dome
that snapped in the breeze proclaiming Mr. Lackington,
the proprietor, was there in person. Lark's heart was
beating fast as she made her way past the large circular
counter on the ground floor up the wide staircases to the
second level where the slightly damaged books were
kept.

It took her quite a while to find the Reverend Mr.
Cruthers's tome for there were several dusty old books
bound in dull red. Fanny hovered behind her, but since
she had never learned to read, she was no help in the
search. Lark was sure an old woman nearby was staring
at her suspiciously it was all taking so long, and beads of
perspiration dotted her forehead. She dared not wipe
them away lest she soil her gloves.

At last she spotted the book. It was on a lower shelf in
the middle of the row. She stooped quickly to take it out,
turning her back on the inquisitive woman watching her
as if she intended to scan it. The viscount's letter had
been placed in the middle and she handed it to Fanny before she replaced it with the bulky letter she had spent so
long writing.

Lark waited until Fanny had put Drew's letter safely
in her pocket before she replaced the book on the shelf,
just as if the Reverend Cruthers's worthy moral tales had
proved of little interest. As she did so, the dust on the
book made her sneeze, not once but several times. Dirty
handkerchief to her scarlet face, Lark beat a hasty retreat. She did not leave however until she had chosen a
book for her mother and one for herself for she knew she
must have some excuse to visit the library frequently.
Lark was not a studious girl who enjoyed reading; she
chose the slimmest book she could find with no regard
for its contents.

During the next week she managed to visit the Temple

of the Muses twice, but in order to do so she was forced
to excuse herself from a number of delightful excursions
so she could read the books she had brought home. She
would not have bothered except her mother often asked
her about them.

Surely there could be no greater proof of my devotion
than this, she told herself as she settled down one glorious, breezy afternoon with a book lecturing on the
proper etiquette for young, unmarried ladies. She was
prepared to be thoroughly bored, especially when she
knew she might have been getting dressed to go driving
with Freddy Colchester in Hyde Park later, or even now
transported a short distance from town with Sir Roger
and a party of his. They intended to fly kites and enjoy
an alfresco tea. How she would have enjoyed that!

But of course her love for Drew overrode all other
considerations. She sighed a little. She wished he wrote
a more exciting love letter. To tell the truth she found
him rather dry and uninteresting, although he never
failed to remind her of his love at the end. How dear he
was. How exciting it was when he held her in his arms
and kissed her so fervently. A letter, even one retrieved
in such daring fashion was not at all the same as being
together in person. If only her mother had not made her
promise she would not try to see Drew alone again.

She wondered how long she would be able to keep
that promise.

# Four

Lark was still asleep one morning when the Earl of Morland called on her mother again while she was still at breakfast. Harriet was startled for a moment when Biggs announced him, but she quickly recovered and asked the footman to bring the earl to the breakfast room. As he went to do her bidding, Harriet smoothed her hair under the widow's cap she occasionally wore, and wished she had thought to wear her new morning gown of pale green muslin with its lace trim at the bodice and short puffed sleeves. Then she scoffed at herself for her foolishness.

When the earl came in, she inquired if he had had breakfast, and when he waved a careless hand, she asked him to be seated while she poured him a cup of coffee.

"And to what do I owe the pleasure of this visit, m'lord?" she asked as she handed it to him and indicated the cream and sugar.

"I felt I had to confer with you, madam. Perhaps it is only my suspicious devious mind, but my son's behavior this past week has given me pause."

"He has attempted to see Lark?" Harriet asked, her muffin forgotten.

"No, he has not, and that is what concerns me. He is behaving much too well. He is invariably pleasant and as meek as any lamb. He comes home at an hour that would in the past have made me sure he was sickening for something, and he appears to have forsaken all his former cronies and their madcap schemes. Such saintliness is most unlike him, and I find it unnerving."

Harriet had trouble hiding her smile. "He is a handsome young man. Those dark curls, his high color and chiseled profile. You must be proud of him."

"For his looks? He had nothing to do with them, he got them from his mother."

"My condolences. I only learned recently of her death."

The earl paused for a moment, staring down into his coffee. Those dark brows met in a ferocious frown across his forehead as he said, "It was a long time ago. Ten years to be exact.

"Tell me, what did you think of Andrew's behavior last evening at the theater?" he said abruptly, as if loathe to speak of his late wife anymore.

"I thought it strange how studiously he avoided catching Lark's eye. I would have expected a lovelorn glance on occasion."

"And your daughter did not favor him with so much as a yearning pout either. I know for I was watching her the entire time."

"So that was why she seemed so distraught. I wondered," his hostess murmured.

The earl ignored this remark. "What has she been up to, madam?"

"Why, nothing to remark, I swear."

"Have any letters come for her?"

"Nothing unusual. A letter from a girl in Suffolk, various notes enclosed in bouquets from some of her beaux. I read them all. They are unremarkable. There has been nothing from your son."

"And you don't find that passing strange, madam? I mean when you consider they shared the love of a lifetime together? And yet now they accept our conditions and ignore each other so quickly? I smell a rat, madam. A large sly rat."

"It does seem odd now you mention it. But how could they possibly communicate?"

"Could her maid be helping? Carrying letters between them? I must tell you before I discovered what Andrew

was up to, he had formed the habit of rising very early
and leaving the house. And before you tell me how commendable that was for him to seek exercise in the fresh
morning air, permit me to disabuse you of the notion.
Bryn never rises early if he can possibly avoid it. Sometimes it has even been necessary to drench him in cold
water to rouse him. Why do you suppose he went out so
early? I suspect to deliver a letter to your daughter,
handed in secret to her maid."

Harriet thought for a moment. "I suppose it could
have happened that way. They are close, and Fanny goes
everywhere with Lark."

"And where does she generally go?"

"Why, occasionally to the shops on Bond Street on an
errand for me. But mostly she goes to Lackington's
bookstore in Finsbury Square. I have had to scold her
lately for staying in on bright afternoons to read. It is
quite a new comeout for her, to be so industrious. I have
even thought it a blessing for it is no doubt taking her
mind from Byrn."

The earl snorted as he rose. "Yes, and pigs may fly,"
he said, his voice harsh again. "What do you call that
ridiculous thing you have on your head, madam?" he
added.

"Why—why, it is a widow's cap," Harriet told him as
she rose too, one hand going up to make sure her cap
was secure.

The earl's frown grew marginally darker. "Take it off
and don't wear it again. You look like a child pretending
to be her grandmama. Good God!"

"I remind you, m'lord, what I do is none of your concern," Harriet managed to get out. "I often wear a cap. It
is customary for a widow, no matter her age. It shows respect for the deceased."

"Not sitting on spun gold curls it doesn't," he threw
over his shoulder as he strode to the door.

The door closed decisively behind him and Harriet
took several deep breaths to calm herself before she sat
down and resumed her neglected repast. The earl was in-

sufferable! He had been so when she had known him long ago, and age had not mellowed him in any way. How unfortunate they were thrown together this way because of their children's attachment.

Still, when she rose from the table later and prepared to begin her morning routines, she paused for a moment to look into the mirror over the buffet. The charming little confection of lace and pale green satin ribbons pinned to her gold curls complimented green eyes much like her daughter's. But as for making her look like a child, obviously the earl's eyesight was failing. She was hardly young. She was a mature woman, thirty-seven years old. She told herself she was quite prepared to see wrinkles at any time now.

The earl reappeared three days later. The footman had barely shut the door of the sitting room before Harriet said, as if to herself, "For someone who bade me goodbye at first meeting, you do seem to keep popping in, don't you, m'lord?"

He went to the decanter and poured them both a glass of wine without so much as a by-your-leave she saw indignantly. Only as he handed her a glass and took a seat opposite did he say, "It has been necessary. And when you see what I have brought, you will be glad of it. That is, you will if you are still of the opinion any connection between your family and mine is not to be considered? Well, madam?"

"I hold that opinion more strongly than ever," she said.

His grim smile was gone almost before it lit his face. "As do I," he said, nodding to her. "Between us we may yet pull the thing off, and it is going to be easier than I thought. You see, I have discovered although they do not see each other anymore, they are in constant communication."

"But how on earth—Fanny?" she asked a little defiantly.

"No, not this time. It is really quite an ingenious

scheme, and someday I may even compliment Andrew—er, years from now, that is."

"How do they contrive it?" Harriet prompted.

"The Temple of Muses, of course. When you told me your daughter was not a reader yet was suddenly passing up all the Season's pleasures to peruse various books, I became suspicious. Yesterday I followed Andrew. Fortunately he did not spot me for the streets were crowded as were Lackington's premises.

"What a conceited fellow he is, flying that flag when he is there, quite as if he were the king."

"Yes, yes, but what happened?"

"Andrew went right to the second gallery without even looking around and took a book from one of the bookcases. He extracted papers from it and replaced them with others. I waited until he had gone before I retrieved them."

He reached into his pocket and drew out a sheaf of papers. "I also returned yesterday to fetch the letter your daughter had written to him. I was sure you would want to read both of them."

He handed the papers to a suddenly reluctant Harriet Winthrop-Bates. Yes, it was all very well to say it was her duty to read her daughter's correspondence, but quite another when she knew she was to read love letters. For no matter how misguided, willful, and disobedient the two had been, they still deserved some privacy.

"Well, read them," the earl urged as he settled back and prepared to enjoy his wine. "There is nothing to alarm you. It is just the usual nonsense."

Harriet read her daughter's first. It surprised her for it was not only fervent and resolute, it was almost shy in tone, as if Lark could not believe even now in the good fortune that had come her way. As for the viscount's, he wrote of his daily activities and even commented on the weather, but Harriet was not tempted to smile at his poor excuse for a love letter. Byrn was young. No doubt he found it impossible to put his yearnings and desires down in words. Besides, he did end the letter pledging his eternal love.

"Sickening, are they not?" the earl drawled as she folded the letters carefully.

"How can you say such a thing? They are touching— dear. To be sure, both of them are very young—"

"Your daughter has a good ten years on my son, madam," he interrupted.

She must have looked a question, for he went on, "Compare their letters. She writes of their future, how she misses him, what it will be like when they are together. *He* on the other hand is barely articulate. He spends half a page regretting the showers that suddenly plague London. Idiot!"

"I will grant you Lark *seems* older, but she is very naive."

"I was not referring to any loss of virginity, madam," he said his blue eyes intent on her face. Harriet swallowed a gasp.

"No, I am sure there has been nothing like that. Andrew would not dally with a girl from a good family, no matter how many dairymaids he tumbles."

"Sir!" Harriet protested, outraged now.

To her indignation, he chuckled. "Come, come! There is no need for us to tiptoe around the situation muttering platitudes. They are in love, and love inevitably results in passion. Can it be you have forgotten that?"

Harriet made herself meet his eye. "Of course I haven't," she said. "My husband has not been gone from me that long."

The earl's face darkened and she saw him clench a fist on one knee but she was not afraid. For all his bluster and black looks, she knew Marsh Pembroke would never hurt her. And she was not about to sit here and listen to him say the most outrageous things, things she was sure he would not say to any other lady, without retaliating.

"I fear we stray from the point, sir," she said, delighted her voice was so even, so calm. "What are we to do with these letters?"

"My first thought was to confront them both, raining thunder and lightning down on their heads. Hah! That would be a weather situation Andrew would tremble to describe," he said, completely in control of himself again. "But I have had another idea, and that is that we do nothing. We do not, either one, indicate we even know about them. I shall go to Lackington's every day or so to intercept future communications. What do you think they will imagine when all their frantic queries go unanswered? It might well speed up their disenchantment with each other."

Harriet had a vision of Lark desperately searching the book they had been using as their post, perhaps even the ones nearby. And putting her latest letter in it in despair when she did not find one from the viscount. But what must she think when she returned a few days later and discovered her letter gone and no reply waiting for her? And the viscount would suffer the same way. There would be no conclusion they could reach but that the other wished to end the relationship and did not know how to say so. Yes, it might well serve. Still she hesitated. It seemed so cruel, so backhanded.

"You must not allow your compassion to blind you to the fact the sooner this fiasco has been resolved, the better," the earl reminded her.

"Yes, you are right, of course," she admitted. "Very well. I shall say nothing."

As he rose, she held out her hand to him. "May I ask a favor, sir?"

He nodded curtly, his eyes intent on her face. "Then I would beg you to destroy the letters you intercept without reading them," she said simply.

She thought she detected a sneer on his face and she added quickly, "I feel it is the least we can do, to allow them some privacy and the remnants of their dignity."

"Ah, you were always softhearted," he replied, his own face softening slightly. Then he frowned. "Almost always, that is. Give you good day, madam."

Harriet did not move until he had left the house. She

knew what he had meant by that last statement, and she felt she had no defense. He was right, and he had every reason to be scornful of her. Her green eyes turned stormy. Why couldn't she forget those long ago, distant days? They were history and dwelling on them over and over, wondering what might have happened if things had been different did no good at all. She and Marsh Pembroke were no more suited to each other than they had ever been; perhaps even less than his son and her daughter were now.

She thought of Lark then. Surely after the first frantic black days she would begin to recover. Surely she would forget Viscount Byrn. And surely someday there would be another man for her. Lark was not made for a solitary life. She had too much passion, too much verve. No, she would marry and no doubt revel in the children playing around her. Someday.

Harriet busied herself putting the wineglasses she and the earl had used on the tray and replacing the top of the decanter. If he kept coming here so often, she would be forced to seek a vintner. The thought of it made her smile until she remembered that if this scheme of his should work, there would be no need for him to come here ever again.

She felt as if she were holding her breath for the next few days. The suspense was so unnerving she almost wanted to urge Lark to go to the bookstore. But when the girl announced at last she intended to change her book that afternoon, her mother found herself biting her lip lest she beg her not to go. She was sure no one could be more contrary.

There was nothing on Lark's face or in her conversation when she returned to show a casual observer anything out of the ordinary had occurred, but Harriet found herself intercepting the little frowns, the puzzled air, when her daughter did not suspect she was being watched.

She had not brought a book home that day so Harriet was not surprised the following morning at breakfast when she was informed another trip to the bookstore was imminent.

"The clerk said a delicious new novel was expected, and he assured me I would enjoy it," she said, not looking at her mother as she spread marmalade on her toast. "Is there anything I can get for you, Mama?"

Harriet assured her there was not and went up to dress for a visit to her late husband's great-aunt. Mrs. Selma King had lived in London most of her life. It had been she who had introduced her Suffolk relatives to those in society she knew. Mrs. King was an elderly woman who, Harriet suspected, was delighted when the two began to receive their own invitations, a state of affairs that allowed her to retreat to her cozy rooms, her cats, and her needlepoint, feeling smug her duty had been done.

As she went to her in a hackney cab, Harriet wished Mrs. King was a friend. There was no one in all London she could confide in, and she felt she badly needed advice. But James's great-aunt was very hard of hearing and any remarks made to her had to be conveyed at the top of one's voice. Hardly ideal for confidential matters, Harriet thought, her lip curving in amusement in spite of her troubles. Of course she had several acquaintances now, but not a one with whom she cared to share secrets. The mothers she knew with daughters Lark's age looked at her askance, as if they were all in some sort of fierce competition for the available, suitable males. If she were to tell one of them that far from reveling in the catch her daughter had made, she was doing her best to extricate her from it, they would have thought her mad. Cast off the future Earl of Morland? Was she insane?

She supposed she would just have to muddle through herself.

That evening at dinner, Harriet saw the remains of the tears Lark had shed in her slightly puffy red-rimmed eyes. She accepted the girl's explanation of an incipient cold and did not inquire for the delicious novel her daughter had supposedly gone to fetch.

The rest of the week was much the same. Lark visited

the bookstore again, they attended the theater one evening, went to a small tea party one afternoon, and drove out with Freddy Colchester and his mother on another day.

Harriet wanted to hug her daughter close to her when she saw the valiant effort she was making to smile and appear happy on that occasion. She wondered if the Colchesters suspected it was all a sham.

Of the viscount there was no sign, and Harriet told herself it was just as well when she saw the eager way Lark inspected the occupants of other carriages, and those people strolling along the walkways. Perhaps he had left town. Perhaps his father had given him a trimming after all, and sent him to the country in disgrace. She seemed to recall the earl's principal seat was in Derbyshire.

She wished the earl might call on her so she could inquire if Byrn was taking the loss of his love as much to heart as Lark was. But of course he would not do that. Now that his plan to separate the two was turning out so successfully, why would he bother?

# Five

The Earl of Morland received a call from an old friend at ten one morning shortly after his discovery of his son's ingenious solution for getting around parental edicts. He was at the breakfast table at the time, Byrn still slumbering in his room two floors above, when Viscount Webster was announced.

"Early hours for a call, Douglas," he remarked after they had greeted each other and the viscount had selected a large plate of food. "Your servants are not feeding you any longer?" he added as his friend took a seat. "Time you married. Past time, now I think of it. A wife would take care of you."

"No, thank you very much. But I've only just arrived from Derbyshire and the place is at sixes and sevens. Besides, I knew your buffet would be groaning with food. Just look at that sirloin. It could feed a brigade."

"May I suggest the kippers? The whitefish is excellent. And don't neglect the ham and shirred eggs. Ah, I see you have availed yourself of them already. I cannot tell you how delighted I am my cook has been of service."

His friend, his mouth full of food, only waved his fork. When he could, he said, "Tell me everything that's been happening. I feel I've been away this age, but I couldn't leave the Hall until the new cottages I'm having built were well underway, and the crops planted."

"Change your agent," Morland said brusquely as he poured them both another cup of coffee. "You shouldn't have to fuss over such things."

"I'm not easy if I don't. Perhaps there is more than one serf in my background. I never did believe we were all descended from French nobility anyway."

"I'm as sure as you are of that. No doubt there have been archers, swineherds and the occasional hangman somewhere on my family tree. As for the season, let me see. The Duchess of Norfield has been most indiscreet. When was she not? I understand the duke is considering a crim. cons. case now her latest affair is being caricatured in all the print shops. Well, he has his heir. No one can say she played him false there. Poor boy looks just like Norfield, beak of a nose and all. As for the others, all twelve of them, better not to ask who their papas might be. Oh, the new lover is a groom."

"Stamina, Marsh. Stamina, I'm sure."

"The Prince of Wales is in debt again which will come as no surprise. I understand his household is trying to keep news of it from the king. And to keep Mrs. Jordan's name from him as well now her star is in ascendancy yet again.

"There have been the usual betrothals among the young, but you can't possibly be interested in them."

"Not particularly. How is Byrn?"

His fond father shrugged. "As idiotic as ever. I shudder, I positively shudder when I consider that someday he will stand in my place. Heaven help Morland when he does."

"You are too severe, Marsh. Byrn is just young, something he will outgrow as we all did. And you won't be sticking your spoon in the wall for years. By the time he does come into the title, he'll be a sober middle-aged man with a wife and grown children."

"He'd like to have a wife now," the earl growled. As his friend stared at him, a query on his long, tanned face he explained, "Fell head over heels for some pretty little chit from the country. Most unsuitable, to say nothing of the folly of marrying before he reaches his twentieth birthday. Puppy! Not that I would permit such a thing.

By the way, don't give him any sympathy when you see him. He is taking this hard."

"But this sounds very serious," Webster said. "Who is this girl? Do I know her?"

"I don't think so. She is only seventeen, in town for the Season. Her name is Lark."

"No, you must be jesting! Lark?"

"As the bird," came the dry retort. "Her father—you may remember him, James Winthrop-Bates?—claims he heard a lark singing when his daughter was born."

"Winthrop-Bates? Hmm. I seem to remember—no, it escapes me."

"Silly ass. A poet or some such thing. They called him Stuffy at Eton. He was ten years or so older than we."

"Was?"

"Yes, he died over a year ago."

"Harry!" the viscount exclaimed. "By all that's holy, Harry!"

"There's no need to sound so gleeful. Yes, it is indeed Harry. The Harry who married Winthrop-Bates at her dear parents' urging."

"And her daughter and your son are in love? Marsh, my dear fellow, I am finding this coincidence hard to believe."

"*You* are! You can imagine how confounded and furious I was when I discovered it. But they are not going to marry. I have seen to that."

"How?" Webster asked baldly.

The earl spoke for some time, ending with the post book at The Temple of the Muses bookstore.

"I swear it shows ingenuity," Webster said at last as he wiped away the tears that had come from laughing so hard. "But just picturing you lurking about waiting to intercept their letters—ah, don't get me started again!"

"I did not *lurk*. I have never lurked. I merely waited until Andrew had left before I confiscated his letter."

"Have you seen Harry?" Webster asked next, his voice casual. His friend was not deceived.

"Of course I have. Several times. It was necessary to gain her cooperation."

"And she did cooperate? That's strange. I should have thought she'd be ecstatic at the match."

Morland frowned. "You could not be further from the mark. She told me any connection between her family and mine was repugnant."

"Surely she did not say repugnant."

"She did, indeed."

"Er, is she as beautiful as ever?"

"Yes."

"Just yes?"

"If you want to see for yourself you have only to accept all your invitations. I gather from her circumstances, Winthrop-Bates did not leave her beforehand with the world, and she hopes to marry her daughter off this Season. I am sure she will. The child is lovely. But she will not marry Andrew, of that I am determined."

Viscount Webster saw Harriet even sooner than he had expected, for later, strolling from Park Lane to Boodles in Pall Mall, he came upon her leaving a shop in Picadilly.

"My dear Harry," he exclaimed, sweeping his hat from his auburn hair. "How grand to see you!"

"Douglas, I mean, m'lord," Harriet managed to get out for she was flustered. No one had called her Harry for years; she had hoped never to hear that name again. "I am known as Harriet now, but perhaps, since I am a widow, it would be better for you to call me Mrs. Winthrop-Bates."

"No such thing," the viscount scoffed as he set his hat in place and took her arm. "Much too formal for two who played together as children."

"That was a long time ago," she said, biting her lip and looking down at the gloved hands that clutched her reticule.

"If Harry makes you uncomfortable, of course I shall not use it," the viscount said after a glance at her averted profile. "But tell me, where are you staying? And are

you attending any balls? It would be grand to dance with
you again."

She smiled at him now. "As it happens I will be at the
Nelson ball with my daughter tomorrow evening."

"I cannot believe you have a daughter old enough to
attend evening parties. I shall contrive to meet you there.
We have so much lost time to catch up on, don't we?"

They had stopped at the corner, and Harriet gently dis-
engaged her arm and beckoned to a hackney cab. "We
must part here. You will like my Lark. She is a wonderful girl."

As she went on her way alone, Harriet wondered
about Douglas Webster. She had first met him when
Marsh Pembroke brought him home from Eton for the
long holiday. Pembroke land adjoined her father's and
soon the three children were inseparable. But when Harriet's mother recovered from a prolonged illness that
summer, she was horrified to discover her daughter had
been running wild with their neighbor's son. No Pembroke had Mr. and Mrs. Fanshaw's approbation. While
he had been alive, Mr. Pembroke had been a dissolute
man, and it was whispered his son was growing up just
like him, unable to be controlled by his widowed mother.

Harriet had been furious to have her freedom cur-
tailed, but she soon found ways to join her friends without her mother's knowledge.

Harriet shook her head as if to clear it. Those days
were like a dream to her now; the fishing expeditions,
learning to punt and fire a gun, the elaborate tricks they
had played on each other. And then when Harriet was
seventeen, Douglas nineteen, and Marsh twenty, it had
ended. She told herself she would not think of that time
again and she began to wonder if she could afford another silk gown. Perhaps if she fashioned it herself?

The Nelson ball was a crowded affair, but Douglas
Webster had no trouble finding Harriet and taking her to
a nearby salon when she informed him she did not
dance.

"I never heard the like," he protested. "You were a wonderful dancer."

"I thank you, sir, but those days are far behind me. I am a widow now. What would all the dowagers say if they saw me prancing around the floor quite as if I were seventeen again?"

"You don't look much older than that. And why would you care what they think? Ah, forgive me. Of course you do. Any mother would who had a daughter to present.

"Why are you wearing that thing on your curls?" he added, pointing to her cap.

Harriet was reminded of the earl's comments about her cap and she blushed. "It is to show respect," she told him. "And to announce my situation. Never mind it. Tell me what you have been doing all this time. Did you ever visit the Americas as you wanted to?"

They conversed for some time before Lark came to find her mother. She was escorted by a beaming Sir Roger Beaton who seemed most reluctant to give up his prize.

The viscount inspected her carefully as they were introduced, but although he thought Lark a pretty girl, he agreed with his friend Marsh she was not as lovely as her mother.

"You are not dancing this set, Lark?" Harriet asked as her daughter settled down beside her and the viscount went to fetch a chair.

Lark waved her fan before her heated face. "No, I excused myself. It grows tiresome, dancing all the time."

Her mother did not remark this unusual statement, nor point out how only a few weeks ago her daughter had hated to leave a party until the very end.

"I'm sure there's many a young man who regrets that," the viscount said with a smile as he took his seat near them. "I knew your mother when she loved to dance."

"Oh, did you indeed, sir?" Lark asked, looking more

animated than before. "What was she like when she was my age?"

"Douglas!" Harriet said, quick to warn him.

"I'll not give away your secrets, Har—er, ma'am, I promise."

"But now you have as good as told me there is something that must be kept from me," Lark said demurely. "I wonder what that could be?"

"You will never find out," her mother said firmly. "Not that I ever did anything bad. I am afraid m'lord is teasing you."

"I? No such thing!" he exclaimed as he beckoned a footman to bring them refreshments.

Another couple joined them then and eventually Freddy Colchester claimed Lark for the supper set.

"You will permit me to take you in to supper?" Webster asked, bending over Harriet and taking her hand to help her rise.

"Thank you. If you would care for it," Harriet said. She was more than a little flustered. There had been a look in Douglas's eyes that made her wary, an intent, masculine, possessive look she knew from of old.

"Yes, I still love you," he said. "I never stopped loving you."

She put up a hand to deter him, but he would not be silenced now. "No, Harry, you will listen to me," he said, grasping her shoulders. "I never told you all those years ago. I knew it wouldn't do any good when you could see no one but Marsh. But at last I can speak. Marsh told me himself how you feel about him, so my way is clear. *Finally* clear.

"You don't have to say anything now. Just think about what I've said. And please, please think kindly of me. I have waited so long," he said. "Twenty-one years to be exact.

"Everything I have is yours, Harry. It has always been yours. I would give you anything in the world you want and count myself lucky to be able to do so."

"M'lord—Douglas—you honor me," she began. Her

throat was thick with tears for him, for she knew there was no way she could ever marry this dear, good friend. She did not think of him that way. She never had.

"I must tell you immediately I cannot marry you, for I would not have you waiting for an answer that will never come. It is nothing to do with you personally; it is just that I do not intend to marry again. That part of my life is over. And you must not hope to persuade me. That would be impossible. I am sorry. I have always loved you, you know."

"Yes, as your childhood companion, the brother you never had," he said bitterly as he finally released her. "That is not how I wanted you to feel about me."

"If we could order our feelings, how much simpler life would be, wouldn't it?" she said a little sadly, raising a finger to wipe away a tear.

"Here now, Harry, none of that! You know I cannot bear to see you cry. Why, I'll be howling myself in a minute and then what will those dowagers you worry about think? Come on, old girl, let's go to supper before all the lobster patties have been devoured. I won't say another word about this. We'll be the companions we always were. I promise.

"Tell me about your daughter. She is very like you and I can see she has a sense of humor . . ."

The two went back through the ballroom to the supper room. As they ate their repast, the viscount kept up a careless chatter that made Harriet chuckle occasionally in spite of the ache she felt for him.

As for Douglas Webster, no one could ever have known that the heart he had thought long mended was breaking again.

# *Six*

The Earl of Morland had not attended the Nelson ball, but he heard later from two different sources that Viscount Webster and the lovely young widow, Harriet Winthrop-Bates, had spent most of the evening together. His informants, two ladies each intent on becoming his next countess also told him the widow's daughter had been much sought after and there was a general consensus among the *ton* that the girl's betrothal before the Season's end to either Freddy Colchester or Sir Roger Beaton was as good as accomplished.

Satisfied that his plan to separate his son from the young lady in question had worked so successfully, he took the viscount to task only a few days later.

"I am aware the reason you have abandoned your friends and all your usual activities is because Miss Winthrop-Bates is lost to you now, but don't you think the time has come to put it behind you?" he began as the two sat over their port one evening after dinner.

The viscount shielded his face with his hand. "I cannot forget her. I will never forget her," he said, his voice choked with emotion.

The earl hid a sigh. There was no doubt the boy was troubled and he was not unsympathetic no matter how hard he might appear. Still he was finding Andrew's not quite silent suffering, wan looks, and moods of depression, a bit difficult to live with.

"I don't suppose it will help for me to tell you you will forget her one day, and in a much shorter time than you now think possible, but I assure you that is the case.

Come, admit that at not quite twenty years of age, you are too young to marry anyone."

"You married at twenty!" the viscount blurted out, his tortured eyes rebellious still.

"Which is exactly why I am so intent on keeping you from making the same mistake."

"Sir, you insult my mother!"

"Do me the favor, Andrew, of curbing this distressing bent you have for the dramatic. If your mother were here, she would be the first to agree our marriage was a mistake. I had neither the maturity nor wisdom to be responsible for another. Why, at the time I was barely able to accept responsibility for myself.

"And your mother was not my social equal. When I became the Earl of Morland, she found life very difficult. Surely you were aware of that, even as young as you were."

"I loved my mother! I honored you for putting aside worldly considerations and censure when you chose your wife," the viscount said, then ruined this noble sentiment by adding, "Not that any of this matters. I doubt I shall ever marry . . . now."

"So you think but you will change your mind. Look, Andrew, I won't insist you marry a duke's daughter, indeed, anyone at all." The earl paused and bit his tongue. On the tip of that tongue had been the phrase "until you grow up," but saying anything like that would only antagonize the boy.

"More port?" he asked instead, gesturing with the decanter. As his son shook his head, leaning back in his chair with his lower lip pushed out in a pout that made him look about eight, his father changed the subject. "What do you plan to do after the Season is over? Shall you return to Morland with me, or have you an eye to Brighton? If you do, I suggest you see about rooms immediately. I have it on good authority all the best ones on the Front have been snapped up already."

The viscount shrugged. "I have no idea what I'll do," he said, his tone of voice implying that for one suffering as he was, one place was as another in a world become gray and ugly and hopeless. His father controlled a strong urge to hit him.

"Perhaps you might find Morland as enthralling as you did last summer," he said instead. "Although may I suggest you stay away from the dairy?"

"Sir?" the viscount asked, his head whipping around in surprise.

The earl smiled grimly. "That milkmaid of yours. You were lucky you did not leave her with child. Surely you didn't think I was unaware of her, did you?"

"Well, I hoped you were," Byrn admitted.

His father waved an impatient hand. "Precious little escapes me, as you have every reason to remember."

His son nodded glumly. "There were times when I was young I could have sworn you had eyes in the back of your head," he said. "And more than one pair of ears."

"Infallibility—or at least the appearance of it—has always been one of my talents. Come now. It is more than time you started going about in society again. I see the mass of invitations you refuse, and your friends have been asking me about you." Seeing this only reinforced Andrew's decision to continue his self-imposed exile, the earl added, "Of course if you do not care that you are making a perfect cake of yourself and well on the way to becoming a laughingstock, there is nothing more to be said."

"What do you mean?" Byrn demanded.

"Only that everyone begins to suspect that not only did you and the young lady have a falling out, you got much the worst of it. *She* has not stopped going to parties and balls, you know. Indeed, rumor has it she is in a fair way of becoming betrothed to one of two young cubs. And since you remain in seclusion, what can the *ton* think but that she dismissed you and you are taking it hard? Even if it were true which I know it is not since it was I who forbade you to see her, I would still have you face the world with a smile, head held high. But to wear your heart on your sleeve for all the world to laugh at, no, no! There is nothing so foolish and funny as the dejected, discarded suitor."

He paused, and seeing the viscount's intent look, the fists he had clenched on the table, knew he had reached him. Pushing back his chair, he rose and said, "I'm off to White's. Would you care to join me?"

Byrn rose as well, throwing his napkin on the table. "Thank you, but no, sir. I believe I'll take a look-in at the Earl of Tremaine's soiree."

Marsh Pembroke hid a smile as they walked to the dining room doors, and wisely he said no more.

But strangely as he strolled along Park Lane later on the way to his club, he did not think of his son or the successful ploy he had just used to prod the boy from his lethargy. Instead he found himself thinking about Harriet Winthrop-Bates. Friend Douglas had been quick off the mark, he told himself as he nodded to a watchman who was saluting him. It seemed there had never been a time he had not known of the viscount's love for their childhood playmate, and he supposed he must wish him well now. Still, a part of him resented Webster's nipping in and capturing her so easily. Harry Fanshaw had always been his, not Douglas's. There had never been any question of that in any of their minds. But all that was long ago, he reminded himself. It is over now. His mouth formed a grim line and a beggar who was approaching him hoping for a coin, scuttled away from his black frown.

Long over and best forgotten, he told himself as he waited for a hansom to rattle by before he stepped from the curb. There is no more Harry. Now there is only the widowed Harriet Winthrop-Bates. Harry is dead.

Still, he thought as he entered White's and handed his hat, cane, and gloves to the waiting servant, I admit I do miss sparring with her. It had been so amusing watching her trying to control her temper no matter what outrageous things I said.

As he went into a card room where his friends were

waiting for him, he had to admit she had come away
with the honors for he had been unable to goad her into
losing either her temper or her composure. But of course
that was because he was dealing with the widowed Mrs.
Winthrop-Bates, not the Harry he remembered.

In the following days, Viscount Byrn was once again
seen in company for he went everywhere. He observed
Lark on more than one occasion, but generally it was
with the width of a room between them. He could not
tell if she had seen him as well—she gave no sign of it—
but he thought her very gay. And when he saw Freddy
Colchester and Sir Roger so often beside her, he had to
admit his father had been right.

Byrn could not know that Lark was always aware of
him whenever he was in a room with her, no matter how
crowded that room might be, she immediately became
her most vivacious. She was determined he would not
have the satisfaction of knowing how he had hurt her,
and she flirted over her fan with all the men near her
even though she felt her heart was breaking.

On one particular evening, Byrn spent the time chatting with friends, bowing to his elders, and smiling
gamely at all the prettiest girls while avoiding being anywhere in Lark's immediate vicinity. How devious
women are, he told himself as he pretended to listen to
the results of a boring wager two of his friends had
made, how cruel and shallow. I shall never be taken in
by one again.

Lark's gay laughter rippled out and he winced. Heart-
less jade! Impossible Jezebel! His father was right and
he would forget her. It was only a matter of time.

Still, it was strange that later that night he had a great
deal of trouble getting to sleep, and as for Lark, tucked
up in her tiny bedroom in the house just beyond the
more fashionable streets of Mayfair, she cried until her
pillow slip was soaked.

Both Lark and Byrn had been invited, along with a
throng of others, to a picnic fête to be given on the banks

of the Thames near Richmond at the home of the elderly Lady Carr. Lady Carr was famous for her gardens and her outdoor fêtes. Harriet Winthrop-Bates had also been invited, but she excused herself from attending. She knew Viscount Webster would be there and she was trying as hard as she could to avoid him. She could tell Douglas had not given up his pursuit of her. No, for although he might prate of companionship, that was not what he wanted. What he wanted was obvious with every word he spoke, every touch of his hand, every intimate glance. He had not given up his pursuit of her, and she was afraid in order to convince him, she would have to hurt him, something she was reluctant to do. Much better to avoid a day spent in his company in such beautiful, romantic surroundings.

She did not fear for Lark's reputation for Mrs. Colchester had offered to take her to the fête with her own daughters.

Harriet watched from the window that morning as Lark climbed into a spacious carriage to be greeted by the Colchester ladies. She saw Freddy Colchester had elected to ride alongside, and she did not wonder at it. There would be little opportunity to advance his suit under not only his mother's indulgent eye, but those of his younger sisters who, she was aware, would probably tease him unmercifully if he attempted anything of the sort.

Safely arrived at Lady Carr's, Lark spent some time wandering through the gardens on Freddy's arm. The roses were in full, riotous bloom and their scent was so insistent it made her dizzy. She had never seen such a selection of colors, each more beautiful than the next. As she parried all of Freddy's attempts at lovemaking by refusing to discuss anything but gardens, she shielded her face with her parasol. The sun was very strong and there wasn't a cloud in the sky.

When Freddy was called away by one of his sisters who had been stung by a bee, Lark continued her walk alone, thinking how restful it was to be by oneself.

Freddy was nice, and it certainly soothed her ego to be adored so fervently, but Freddy was not Drew. Then, as if her thoughts of him had conjured him up, Andrew Pembroke appeared before her at the juncture of two paths. Lark gasped and whirled, as if to escape any confrontation with him.

"There is no need for you to run away," she heard Drew say in strangled tones. "I shall leave immediately. Never let it be said a Pembroke was so insensitive he did not recognize another dismissal."

Poised to flee, Lark paused. What could he mean by that statement? What could he possibly mean?

She turned back and caught her breath, he was so close to her still. "Sir?" she said at her haughtiest. "I do not understand you."

"Oh, don't you though?" he replied, his blue eyes glowering at her in a way that reminded her so of his father she shivered.

"I suppose not answering my letters and never explaining why is not a dismissal of the most painful sort?"

Lark's green eyes widened, and in spite of the rage he felt, the urge he had to hurt her as badly as she had hurt him, Byrn could not help drinking in the sight of her sweet face, those rosy lips, and the wealth of honey colored curls he could see under her bonnet.

"But I *did* answer," she said at last, sounding ruffled. "It was *you* who stopped writing and not only that, took the letters I wrote to you away so I would be sure to know you didn't love me anymore. Let me pass, sir! You are despicable and I want nothing more to do with you, ever."

She tried to push past him, in a hurry lest the tears she feared she was about to shed spilled over and disgraced her, but he put out his hand and detained her.

"But I didn't take your letters, Lark," he said, his voice shaking with the urgency he felt to make her understand. "There were none there whenever I went to the post book."

The two stared at each other aghast. Dimly, Lark was

aware of the laughter of some of the guests in the background, the humming of the bees busy among the roses, even the faint strains of a guitar down near the river, but she could only look at Byrn, desperately searching his face trying to find out whether he was speaking the truth or not.

"They were not there?" she whispered. "But . . . but who . . . ?"

His face had darkened. "I imagine the answer to that is easily discovered. I cannot see your mother sneaking into Lackington's to steal our letters, but I can certainly picture my father doing so."

"Oh, no," Lark wailed. "To think he read all those words of love and then despair I wrote to you. I shall never ever be able to hold my head up again. What must he think of me but that I am an abandoned strumpet. Oh dear, oh dear!"

The viscount looked around and saw in the distance the red head of Freddy Colchester bobbing between two flowerbeds as he hurried to reclaim his prize, and he took Lark's arm and hustled her away. "Come on," he said as she clutched her bonnet to keep it from falling off, "Freddy's coming and we have too much to say to each other to bother with him."

"I should not go with you," Lark protested even as she skipped along beside him. "My mother has forbidden it, and so did your father and . . ."

"Do you think we have to obey them now after what they did to us?" he asked as they reached the shade of the woods. The path there twisted and turned and soon they were out of sight of the others at the party. He did not stop until they reached a rustic bench beside a small brook. There he pushed her down gently before he took his seat beside her. He was too close, Lark thought. So close it was even making her feel dizzier than the scent of the roses had.

"They must have planned this together, don't you think?" he said, and she forced herself to concentrate.

"I suppose so," she said at last, even now reluctant to

admit her mother had been so devious, so vile. "Fanny always knew when the earl came to call on her, and as I remember, he never did come again once the letters began to disappear."

She began to cry and had to take her handkerchief from her reticule to dry her eyes. "I cannot believe she would do such a thing," she said brokenly. "I thought she loved me. I thought that even though she did not approve our attachment she would never do anything that would hurt me. How wrong I was!"

Her tears turned to sobs and the viscount took her in his arms to hold her close. As she cried he whispered words of love; told her she would not need her mama anymore for she had him and he would take care of her always; said they would never be separated again.

At last her sobs ended on a little hiccup, and she buried her face in his cravat. In spite of his elation in their reunion, Byrn hoped his love was not making him look too unpresentable. There were, after all, all those other guests to be faced later. Taking his own handkerchief from his pocket, he grasped her chin with one hand while he dried her face with the other. Before she could dissolve on his chest in despair again, he bent and kissed her.

It was several breathless joy-filled minutes later before Lark leaned back in his arms and whispered, "Oh, darling, we must not."

To her surprise and chagrin he let her go at once. "You're right," he said, his voice firm. "We have too much to discuss and too many plans to make to waste time. Because I don't see how we are going to be able to keep in touch. We can't use The Temple of the Muses again, now m'father's found out about it. And I doubt we'll be able to see each other alone either, not in London."

He thought Lark looked ready to cry again at this information and he wished she would not. Her eyes were already swollen and red. To his relief she sniffed and sat up straight, her mouth set in a resolute line.

"Even if we can't see each other alone, we must never let them trick us again," she said. "We must remember how we love each other, and be firm in our resolve. But, Drew, what are we to do? We have to see each other sometime; tell each other our plans."

She looked at him expectantly and he wished he might unfold a grand scheme complete in every detail for her perusal. Alas, he had no such scheme in mind. As he pondered, he realized that although it was shady here in the woods he could still feel the summer heat.

"Where are you and your mother going after the Season ends?" he asked.

"Why, I have no idea. We only took the house until the end of July. But Mama has not said where we go next. Not home. We can't go home for we had to sell that to settle Papa's debts."

"I wonder if you could persuade her to follow Prinny to Brighton. Most of the fashionables will be there. And in the more relaxed seaside atmosphere, surely we would be able to arrange to meet."

Lark nodded, smiling now. "I shall certainly do my best. I know Mama has been worried about me. Perhaps I could pretend to be going into a decline and so need the sea air?"

"I've never been able to figure out just what a decline is," the viscount admitted. "It sounds like one must waste away until even a wisp of a breeze could bowl you over."

She laughed at him. "Yes, it is something like that. You just get paler and sadder and unable to eat and then you die."

Quickly he went down on one knee before her, wrapping his arms around her legs. "No, Lark, don't even jest about it!" he cried. "I could not bear to live in a world that did not have you in it!"

"Darling, of course I won't die," she reassured him tenderly although she could not help but be thrilled by this emotional reaction. "Come, I fear you have sadly crushed my gown. Get up, do. Suppose someone comes around the bend and sees us? Suppose Freddy finds us like this?"

He rose and helped her to her feet. As she shook out

her wrinkled skirts, he said, "Yes, we must return before we are missed. Tell me, does my cravat look all right?"

She studied it intently and made one or two adjustments to the folds of once crisp white linen. He in turn set her bonnet straight and fluffed up the ribbon that held it under her chin that had become so badly flattened in their embraces.

As they retraced their steps, he said, "If I have any news I shall contrive to get a note to you through your maid. I dare not send it to you directly."

"Oh no, for Mama reads everything that comes for me," she said. "You might also try to hand me notes at the events we both attend, and I shall do so as well. If you remember, that was successful before."

"I wish I could ask Freddy to help us, but I fear he would hardly be sympathetic to our cause," he muttered as they left the shadow of the woods and he saw his friend a short distance away.

The truth of this statement became clear when they met face to face and Mr. Colchester glowered at him. To ease the situation, Lark bade the viscount a cold goodbye, and taking her redheaded beau's arm, smiled at him as he took her away.

She passed the rest of the fête in a haze of happiness. Now that she knew Drew loved her still, Lark's senses seemed heightened. The roses smelled even more divine, the lovely day was more priceless, the food ambrosia, and the guests the most amusing, witty people to be found on earth. She was even able to coax Freddy from his sullens with her glowing smiles, although she wondered as she did so why she did not simply float away she felt so heady with joy.

# Seven

Lark was careful to ask Mrs. Colchester her plans for the summer during the return trip to town. That good lady told her the family intended to repair to their estate in Dorset. When Lark mentioned Brighton, Mrs. Colchester said she had no desire to emulate all those who thronged to the former fishing village in the Prince of Wales's wake. In fact, she compared such people to a flock of silly sheep. Lark smiled at this sally, but she was disappointed. She had hoped the fact Freddy would be in Brighton would be an added incentive to make her mother plan to go there too.

Safely home, she found the situation not only awkward but difficult beyond belief. She knew she must not act any differently; knew if she did it would arouse suspicion, but it took all her resolve to force herself to kiss her mother as was her custom whenever she returned after an absence of even an hour. You schemed with the earl, she accused her silently as she took a seat and waited for the appearance of the tea tray. You agreed with him that Drew and I should be separated. You even helped him. I think I hate you.

"Did you have a pleasant time at Lady Carr's party?" Harriet asked, looking up from her needlepoint with a smile.

"It was very festive," Lark said without the hint of an answering smile. She thought she saw some doubt in her mother's eyes and she rushed on, trying to sound her normal self. "It was such a magnificent day! I only pray I did not get a sunburn. The rose gardens were outstanding. You should have seen them, Mama. And the food was so lavish and so delicious."

"I have always thought food eaten in the fresh air the most tasty," her mother agreed. "Did you see Viscount Webster to talk to?"

"No, for he was not even there. I understand he sent his regrets at the last minute."

Lark saw her mother color up and lower her eyes to her sewing again and she wondered at it.

"Lady Mainwaring asked for you as did Mrs. Fitton. And Mrs. Colchester said to give you her regards," she added as Biggs came in and set the tray down before his mistress.

While Harriet prepared the tea, Lark wandered over to the window to pull the curtain aside so she could gaze out at the street. This was terrible, even harder than she had thought it would be. She wished she might go to her room but she knew if she asked to be excused, her mother would begin to suspect something was wrong. And it would not be difficult for her to discover Drew had been there, and they had spent some time together. The fête was sure to be talked about for days, and they were to attend a concert at the Duke of Severn's London establishment this very evening. Someone might even mention it to her mother then.

"Your tea is ready, Lark," she heard her mother say, and she returned to her seat again.

"Something seems to be troubling you, my dear," Harriet said as she stirred her tea. "Is it something we can talk about? Perhaps I can be of help."

I wish I never had to tell you anything ever again, Lark thought. Then she had an idea she considered a stroke of genius. "It is just that Viscount Byrn was there today. I could not avoid him. We—we spoke together," she said slowly, as if loathe to confess her behavior.

To her satisfaction, her mother showed her alarm. "You did? What did he say?"

Lark shrugged, her lips pressed together and her eyes

lowered. "Nothing very much. It was—it was painful for me. I was sorry it happened."

"Oh, my dear, I am sorry too," Harriet exclaimed, putting down her cup to go and put her arms around a strangely stiff daughter and hug her close. "But next time it will be easier, and the time after that, easier still. And soon the Season will be over and we will be leaving and you won't have to see him again."

"I daresay you are right," Lark replied as she pulled away from the suddenly hateful shelter of those arms and reached for a watercress sandwich she did not want in the slightest. She did not breathe easier until her mother was back on the other side of the table once more.

"I learned today a great many people are going to Brighton this summer," she said next, now her mother had inadvertently given her an opening. "How I wish we could go as well!"

Before Harriet could comment, she sighed deeply and went on, "I have been feeling so low lately. Perhaps the salt air would help return me to my former good spirits. And I quite long to see the ocean. Do say we may, Mama!"

Harriet frowned. She wished with all her heart she could indulge Lark in this for she could tell how much she wanted to go by an eager little note in her voice she had been unable to hide. But the truth was, she did not have the money. She had spent part of the day going over her bills and she had discovered their stay in London had been even more costly than she had expected. She knew she would have to exercise the strictest economy for the next several months lest she fall into debt. Reminded of the plans she had set in motion for the summer, she said, "I am afraid that will not be possible, Lark. It would take a lot of money, money we do not have. I have another location in mind, but I shall not tell you of it until it becomes a reality."

She saw Lark was pouting and looking dark and she was hard put to control a spurt of temper she felt. Didn't the girl realize how difficult all this was, how expensive to try and get her established comfortably? Why couldn't she understand? Help, even? Why did she always beg for another gown, or a new bonnet? Why did she constantly bemoan this mean little house and their lack of a proper butler?

But could it be Lark's behavior was her own fault? Perhaps she had not brought her up properly. Perhaps it was because she had been petted and indulged that made her so selfish and spoiled now.

She remembered then how all her troubles would be over when Lark was suitably betrothed, and she said, "But no more of that now. Tell me, did Mr. Colchester say anything to you today? It was such a distinguished attention you know, asking you to go to the fête with his mother and sisters."

"He said a million things," Lark told her. *But not the proposal you want to hear about, for I was careful to keep him from making that, Mama.*

"I did think . . . and gardens are such romantic spots," Harriet murmured ruefully. "But there are still a few weeks of the Season left. I do implore you, Lark, to forget the viscount and try to see other young gentlemen as possible husbands. You told me how much you liked Mr. Colchester, Sir Roger, too. Surely it would not be too difficult for you to learn to love one of them, would it?"

"Yes," Lark said baldly. Then, aware she had spoken abruptly and revealed too much, she added, "I am sorry, Mama. I am not myself this afternoon. Please excuse me. Perhaps I would feel better if I had a short rest."

"Yes, go and lie down, dear," her mother said with a lovely smile. "There is the concert at the Duke and Duchess of Severn's this evening, and you will want to look your best for that."

After only a brief smile, Lark beat a hasty retreat.

She left behind her a mother both confused and apprehensive. Harriet Winthrop-Bates had never seen her daughter quite this way in her life. As she poured herself another cup of tea she wondered if seeing the viscount, speaking to him for the first time since the exchange of their letters had stopped so abruptly, was the sole cause for such different behavior. Lark had been depressed and distant ever since she had come home this afternoon and most of the time she had avoided her mother's eye.

Was she hiding something? Had something more than just a hurried meeting, awkward and quickly terminated, happened today? But how was she herself to find out? She couldn't even ask Douglas if he had noticed anything for he had not attended the fête either.

She rubbed her forehead with the tips of her fingers. She could feel a headache coming on.

Her old friend was another problem she would have to deal with and she did not know how she was to do that. She knew he had canceled today because she was not going to be there. And she knew it was only a matter of time before he began pressing her again, pressing her to love him as she knew she was incapable of doing. She sighed. Poor Douglas, she thought. And poor me, she added, then wondered why she would think such a thing.

She got up and rang the bell. She didn't seem to have any appetite for tea either. Perhaps she would be wise to follow Lark's example and rest until it was time to dress for dinner and the concert.

Unlike many of the *ton* parties this Season, the one given by the Duke and Duchess of Severn was singular for several reasons. The musicians who entertained the guests were of the first quality, the champagne was excellent, and the other refreshments outstanding. But it was the absence of throngs of people that made the evening so unique. No one would ever say tonight had been a perfect squeeze. Harriet had once heard the duchess explain that Severn saw no virtue in crowding every room in his house with as many people as possible until even some of the gentlemen had to be carried outside to be revived from a faint. He preferred to invite only a few of the *ton* at a time. And surely it was a refreshing change to be able to move about freely without being elbowed, stepped on, or almost overcome by someone's sour breath, overpowering perfume, or body odor. Not all the *ton,* as Harriet knew very well and Lark had discovered, were fastidious in their personal habits.

Unfortunately this satisfying evening was marred for both ladies by the appearance of the Earl of Morland and his son, Viscount Byrn. Lark felt she had good cause to fear the earl's all-seeing, all-knowing severity, and Harriet could only lament that Lark was forced yet again to endure an evening in Byrn's company. She was further disconcerted when Douglas Webster joined her and stayed beside her until they were summoned to take their seats for the first part of the concert.

Harriet looked around. Lark had joined a group of younger people and she was happy to see Byrn was not one of their number. How pretty she looks in that primrose yellow crepe gown, she thought fondly. I must be sure to tell her so later.

"Shall we sit here, Harr, er, Harriet?" the viscount asked and she nodded.

Looking up she saw the Earl of Morland regarding her with a most sardonic curl to his lip. He bowed with a flourish and she felt herself coloring up and was relieved Webster had turned aside to greet a friend and so had missed the exchange.

At the first interval, she took the viscount's arm to stroll about. "The soprano was excellent, was she not?" she asked him as they moved to the hall. "Such a clear, true voice."

"And not a bit shrill, even on her highest notes," he agreed. "I think it must be one of the most unpleasant experiences in the world to have to listen to a bad performer. But madame was superb. Trust Severn to see to that."

"His duchess is lovely, isn't she? I understand she spent many years in America."

"Yes, in one of the southern states. I believe she only returned to England after the death of her mother. Of course, at the time, the United States was not the happiest location for anyone British."

"Ah, that terrible war," Harriet said.

"Well, my dears, are you enjoying the concert?" a deep drawling voice asked, and she turned to see the Earl of Morland standing behind them. He was not smiling and her heart gave that funny little skip again which she attributed to nervousness.

She sensed the viscount moving closer to her and knew by the gleam in the earl's eyes he had noticed it as well. Determined not to be disconcerted by him, she said coolly, "Yes, we were just remarking the excellence of Madame Renaldi."

"Do you know, I have been thinking how strange it is the three of us have been reunited here," Morland said. "Especially when you remember as I do what our activities were all those many years ago. And yet look at us now, proper adults all done up in our finery and murmuring polite nothings about the soprano."

"But as you say, m'lord, our previous acquaintance was long ago," Harriet was quick to remind him. And, her tone implied, best forgotten.

But Viscount Webster began to chuckle. "Remember the night we met to camp out in the cave like American Indians, and Harry tripped over a root on the way there and tumbled into that stream? Lord, I never saw such a cold, miserable creature in my entire life. And remember how she went for you, Marsh?"

Harriet had a sudden vision of herself shivering and dripping and unhappy because she felt she had ruined the adventure and it had taken so much planning to escape the house after everyone thought she was in bed. And she remembered as if it were yesterday how she had attacked Marsh when he dared to laugh at her. Had she really flailed at him with her fists, even been able to knock him down he was so surprised by her sudden rush?

"I see you recall the incident too, madam," Morland said smoothly.

"Yes, I do, but I regret it now. What a hoyden I was! Of course I was only thirteen and didn't know any better—"

"Yes, you did, but you were furious," he contradicted her. "Still, I can't say I blame you. It was rude of me to laugh at you when you were so frightened."

"I was not frightened," she retorted.

"Yes, you were. You thought you'd be found out because of those wet clothes. But if you recall, we built a fire at the mouth of the cave so you could get dry, and we did spend the night there."

"I swear sometimes I can still taste those potatoes and sausages we cooked over the fire," the viscount mused. "I say, Marsh, do you remember . . ."

Harriet stopped listening. In her mind's eye she could picture the two boys leaving her alone to get out of her wet things and wrap herself in an old horse blanket. And how later she had dried her hair by combing it with her fingers, even how she had looked up to see Marsh staring at her across the leaping flames of the fire. How when she had dressed at last the three had curled up under the blanket together, a boy on either side of her. She even remembered how she woke at dawn to find herself held close in Marsh's arms, his heartbeat steady and reassuring under her cheek. Douglas had been cuddled close to her back, spoon fashion, the three of them like young kittens surprised by sleep. And she could still see the look in Marsh's eyes when he woke and discovered her so close, how his arms had tightened for a moment before she flushed and pushed him away to jump up and run from the cave. And she knew now that was the time when everything began to change for them, with no going back; one of the moments that marked the end of childhood.

"This is a most improper conversation," she said as the two men chuckled over the viscount's anecdote. She wondered she could feel so sad as she accepted a glass of champagne from a footman's tray and turned aside to tell their host how much she was enjoying the concert.

She sensed the earl was watching her, but when she turned back, he was nowhere in sight.

The next morning in the early post, Harriet had a reply to a letter she had sent earlier, and she smiled in relief as she read it. Looking up she noticed Lark toying with a piece of toast and frowning. She braced herself. The news she was about to convey would not be happy news, not to someone who had wanted to go to Brighton that summer.

"I have had a letter from your Grandmother Fanshaw, Lark," she began. "She agrees we may come and stay with her for the summer."

Lark stared at her, aghast. "Stay with Grandmother? In Suffolk? No, no! I could not bear it!"

"Lark . . ." her mother said in a warning voice.

But her daughter was not to be deterred. "You know she does not approve of me, Mama. And you know how horrid she is, always whining and complaining and being sarcastic. And there's nothing to do there, nothing! I shall be bored to distraction!"

"I see you have been overindulged indeed to speak in such a shabby, saucy way of your grandmother," Harriet reprimanded her even as she kept a tight rein on her temper. "She is kindness itself to have us when she is at an age she prefers to live alone, managing things her own way. And if she had not extended the invitation we would have been hard-pressed for money.

"You will survive, Lark. There may be things you can do to help your grandmother, and there are walks and rides and excursions to enjoy. I hope a London Season has not made you so jaded you cannot see the simple pleasures to be had elsewhere.

"You may be excused. I am most displeased with you."

With a sob, Lark rose, threw down her napkin, and ran to the door. Harriet could hear her feet pounding up the stairs as she went to her room, and she shook her head.

Later that day, after she had abjectly apologized to her

mother, Lark went out to The Temple of the Muses, accompanied by the faithful Fanny. She knew there was little chance she would see Byrn there, but she felt she had to do something. In a short time she would be carried off to Suffolk—Suffolk!—and he would not know where to find her. As she walked along, her eyes searched both sides of the street, the passing carriages as well. She did not find him that afternoon or the next, or the next, and the note she carried held tight in her gloved hand had to be rewritten because it became so creased and soiled. She did not see him at any of the parties she and her mother attended either, and those parties were dwindling in number as more and more people left town.

Suddenly it occurred to her that although Drew could not write to her, there was no reason she could not write to him. She was sure the earl did not insist on reading his grown son's post, but just to be on the safe side, she pretended to be a male acquaintance of his.

"Byrn," her note began abruptly. "It was splendid to see you again, old chap, at Lady Carr's fête the other day. As for that Brighton scheme we discussed, alas, it is not to be. My mother insists I attend her at the ancestral acres in Suffolk this summer. Perhaps some other arrangement can be made to meet? I shall wait to hear from you. Yours, etc. L."

# Eight

If the time before they were to leave for Suffolk seemed to fly by to Lark, it dragged endlessly for her mother. Harriet was aware there was something wrong—something very wrong with Lark. It was not her outburst when she discovered where they were to spend the summer—Harriet told herself she might have expected that, given the shaky relationship between her mother and her daughter—it was more the complete change in her. Gone was the gay laughing girl so quick with a kiss or a fervent hug, and in her place had come this wary stiff formal creature who alternated between brooding silences and frantic prattle. She did not understand Lark now and that troubled her.

She was positive it had something to do with Viscount Byrn, and she began to count the remaining days before they were to leave. Surely when she had Lark safe out of town and his reach, things would improve. Surely Lark would not brood much longer. Still, she felt the need of some reassurance.

She had not seen the Earl of Morland since the Severn evening, although Douglas Webster was a constant visitor. But she did not feel that old companion was the man she wanted in this instance, and at last she overcame her slight reluctance and wrote to the earl, begging him to call on her on a matter of some importance.

He came that afternoon. Fortunately, Lark had left the house as was her wont most days now, and Harriet was able to receive him in the sitting room without fearing interruption.

As he came in, she rose from her knees where she had been packing some small personal possessions in a crate.

"I see you are preparing to leave London, madam," the earl said as he went to pour them both some wine.

"Yes, we go the end of next week," she told him.

"And where might you be going?" he persisted.

"I intend to spend the summer in Suffolk with my mother, m'lord," she said, staring at him as if daring him to make some comment.

But the earl seemed to have no interest in her destination. Instead, as he handed her a glass and took his seat, he said, "What is this important matter you wished to discuss with me, madam?"

Harriet looked into her glass as if it could tell her the right way to begin. "It is Lark," she said, frowning now. "She is so different." She went on then to tell him about her daughter and the changes she had noticed in her lately.

"And she has begun to go out so often," she ended. "When I question her, she often names Lackington's as her destination. Do you think she and your son could be corresponding again?"

He thought for a moment before he spoke. "Even if they are, I doubt they would use the same location. It is true Andrew is silly, but he is not simple. If they have discovered they were found out, they would be sure to devise some other means of communicating. But how could they have found out?"

"Lark admitted she had met the viscount at Lady Carr's fête. She said it was an unpleasant experience and she regretted it, but isn't it possible they could have spent enough time in conversation for it all to come out?"

"I was not aware they had been able to meet," he said coldly and she stiffened. He had sounded accusing, as if it had been her negligence that had allowed the meeting, and it was a few moments before she could speak again.

"Now that I think of it, that afternoon when she returned was the first time I noticed how Lark had changed. She was so stiff and unforthcoming and she excused herself almost immediately."

Harriet put her glass down and rose to pace the tiny sitting room. She wrung her hands as she said, almost as if to herself, "If she discovered how you took their letters, and connects me to the deed as well she might, that would explain why she is so cold to me now. No doubt she feels I have betrayed her, and—"

"Yes, yes, and you are a terrible mother and it is all your fault, and she will never forgive you. Cut line, madam! You did what any responsible guardian would have done. You must not forget it is not you or I who is in error here, it is our rebellious children. We gave them an order and they chose to disobey us. I am beginning to wonder what punishment is severe enough for Andrew. A spell in the Morland dungeons, do you think?"

Harriet was not tempted to smile although she felt somewhat better for his rallying words. As she took her seat again, she thought to say, "How has your son seemed to you since Lady Carr's party? Has his personality undergone a change, too?"

"If anything he has become more cheerful. And thank the Lord for that. The moodiness and half-choked sentences abruptly cut off that I was treated to when first the letters went missing; the despairing looks, the doleful sighs—unbelievable. It was all I could do to keep my temper in check. You do remember my temper, don't you, madam?"

When she did not answer but only observed him gravely, he went on, "But now I would have to say he is his old self again. He was even whistling as he ran down the stairs this morning."

The earl paused and his expression darkened. "Because he and your daughter have renewed their pledge to each other? Because they have been seeing each other or have made plans to do so? Is it possible Andrew has been so undutiful as to disregard my direct order he was not to see Miss Winthrop-Bates again?"

He looked so angry Harriet would have been afraid if

she had not known him so well. "And did any direct orders given to you when you were his age keep you from doing just what you wanted?" she asked. "He is your son, m'lord."

He touched two fingers to his forehead in mock salute. "A point well taken," he said wryly.

He went to the fireplace then as had become his custom, to lean on the mantel above it. "Would it be possible for you to leave town any sooner, madam? Perhaps in a few days or so?"

Harriet shook her head. "I cannot. There is too much to do, and I have planned a small party here to thank my husband's great-aunt for her kindness to us this Season. She is elderly. It would upset her if I changed the date."

"I see. Then I shall see to it Andrew leaves, and by tomorrow morning, too."

"How are you to do that?" she asked as he straightened up preparatory to taking his leave.

His look spoke volumes and she blushed.

"Of course we must remember all this may be just idle conjecture. Your daughter may only be feeling depressed because the Season is over and she is forced to rusticate. And Andrew may well have forgotten her in the arms of some pretty little opera singer."

"But you don't believe that, do you?" she demanded as he went to the door.

He turned there, one hand on the knob. "No, I do not," he said. Harriet thought he sounded disgusted—impatient. "This situation has been ludicrous from its inception," he went on. "So much so, nothing that happens could surprise me. And I have no doubt the gods are having a hearty laugh at our expense.

"A pleasant stay in Suffolk, madam. I won't ask you to remember me to your dear mother. Once more I bid you good-bye."


"Darling, sweetest Lark! How marvelous it is to hold you in my arms again," Byrn said in a husky voice when at last he could bear to take his lips from hers.

The two were in the little copse in Hyde Park they had used before. The leaves were thick and full grown now and they were safe from any prying eyes.

"Drew, my love," she murmured, her eyes closed and a faint smile playing over her lips. But when he would have kissed her again, she put her hands on his chest and pushed.

"No, no, we must not, not now. Come, tell me what we are to do. To think I am to be imprisoned at my grandmother's house for months, with no chance to see you or even write to you. I shall die, Drew, I know I shall die!"

To her surprise he began to smile and she ruffled up. What could be the matter with him? It was hardly a laughing matter.

"No, sweetings, you won't die because you *will* see me. Have you forgotten my father and your mother grew up right next door to each other in Suffolk? The old Pembroke place is still standing, although I don't believe my father has been there for years. But there's no reason I can't go and stay."

"But what good will that do?" she all but wailed. "It will soon be common knowledge you are in the neighborhood. My mother is bound to hear."

"No, she won't for I'll make no stir. There's no one there now but an elderly couple who serve as caretakers. I shall arrive after dark like a thief and live secluded. We can meet every day—well, every fine day that is. All you have to do is establish a routine where you go out riding in the afternoons at a special time. Shall we say two? Ride along the boundary line between the two properties. I'll find you, never doubt it."

"Yes, that might work if you are careful," she said slowly. "But I do fear you will become weary after only a short time. I mean, all those hours cooped up inside are hardly a fair exchange for an hour or so with me."

To Lark's regret, Byrn did not immediately clasp her tight again and assure her that only a *minute* in her company would more than compensate for his isolation. In-

stead he agreed it was sure to be a dead bore but he
would manage, and she wondered men could be so
dense and unromantic, even the dearest of them.

The important matter of their future meetings being
settled, they spent the remainder of their time together
exchanging fervent kisses, but Lark broke away from
him when his hand closed over her breast.

"Drew!" she said, horrified.

The viscount reproached himself. He should have remembered Lark was an innocent who had never known a
man's passion. But it was getting harder and harder to
control himself when he had her in his arms.

"Forgive me, my darling," he panted, making no
move to capture her again lest she feel his arousal. "You
are so tempting I forgot myself."

"I had better go now," she said, eyeing him suspiciously. As they left the copse a few minutes later after
Byrn had checked to make sure the coast was clear, Lark
had to admit she had been feeling rather wanton herself,
and she was confused. She knew such sensations were
only appropriate for married ladies. Perhaps having
Drew come to Suffolk was not such a good idea after
all? Perhaps all those hot summer afternoons spent alone
might prove too much for him? And her? But if she did
not dismount surely they would be able to manage, she
told herself.

As she rejoined Fanny and left the park, she wondered
what it would be like when he made love to her. When
she recalled how long a time must pass before he was
twenty-one and she could find out, she almost groaned
aloud. How much better it would have been if he were,
say, twenty-five to her seventeen. There would be no one
to stop him from courting her then, no one to say nay
when they became betrothed.

Fanny called her attention to a stunning hat in the
shop window they were passing. It had a brim that swept
down one side and up on the other where it was adorned
with a handsome plume. In her admiration of it, Lark
was able to forget her disturbing thoughts.

At a reception the following evening, she learned Byrn had already left London and she wondered he had been so quick when he knew she would not travel to Suffolk for over a week.

Freddy Colchester was the one who told her. He always seemed to be at her side these days, and he called often with flowers or candy or a book he thought she might enjoy. At parties, he hovered about her, glowering at all the other men who would have approached her. If Lark had not been so involved with Andrew Pembroke, she would have found his devotion touching. He had even managed to discourage Sir Roger Beaton by some method she could only guess at. So it came as no great surprise when one afternoon a day or so later, Biggs ushered him into the sitting room of the homely little house both Winthrop-Bates ladies would be delighted to leave.

His mistress was out driving with Douglas Webster, but Biggs had no qualms about leaving the two young people together, with the sitting room door ajar, of course. He knew the form. And he knew Mrs. Winthrop-Bates was hoping Mr. Colchester would come up to scratch before they had to leave town. Biggs knew all about the Colchesters. No title but well connected and everywhere received. A tidy fortune as well from woolen mills, coal mines, and astute investments. All most suitable, he told himself with a sniff as he stationed himself a short distance from the door and strained to hear more than just the murmur of voices he could make out now. If only Miss didn't toss away her chances because of that there viscount Fanny had told him about, he thought.

But of course that was exactly what Lark tried to do. Seizing his chance now they were alone, Freddy had gone down on one knee before her, and clasping her hands had told her of his love so fervently she had felt humbled.

She liked Freddy very much. If only—but no, it was not to be. She would be true to her first love.

When the lady he was imploring neither blushed nor smiled, Freddy renewed his efforts.

"You would never want, indeed, I can promise you a luxurious life, dear Lark," he said. "And if right now you cannot feel the passion for me I do for you, I shall not regard it. I am sure we will deal famously together and in time you will come to love me. Say you will try, dear, dear Lark. Give me some hope!"

"Mr. Colchester, I—"

"Freddy, please."

"Very well, Freddy. I am fond of you, indeed I am. But I cannot promise I will ever love you. You see, there is . . ."

To her surprise, Freddy rose quickly, sat down on the sofa beside her again, and covered her lips with his hand.

"No, you don't," he said firmly. Lark suddenly remembered that redheaded people were said to be very stubborn. "You don't love Byrn, you only think you do. It's—what's that word—yes, infatuation. Besides, he's a mere boy."

Thus spake the graybeard three years the viscount's senior. Lark squirmed a little and he released her, but she was not allowed to speak for he hurried on, telling her all about his home in Dorset, his relatives, his mother's real regard for her.

"And of course m'sisters think you a paragon, they admire you so," he ended.

"Don't say anything now. I see I spoke too soon. I only ask you to think of me over the summer months and remember me. I shall write to you. I would be so pleased if you replied. Then, come autumn, well, we shall see."

Lark tried to smile but she felt it was a poor effort, and she was relieved when Freddy took himself off a few minutes later.

She would have been stunned if she had known her mother was also receiving a proposal, and one delivered rather more deftly.

"You will notice, dear Harry, the clip we are traveling," Viscount Webster said with a warm sideways glance. "That is because I don't want you leaping from the phaeton while I tell you what is on my mind. Yes, yes, I see from your face you would so much rather I didn't, but the opportunity is too tempting and I was never much of a one to abide by the rules. Even, dearest Harry, your rules if they run counter to my purposes. Besides, you are about to leave town, and I must make haste.

"You see, I find I cannot be just your companion. The urge to be your lover is much too strong.

"I want you, Harry. I want you as I have never wanted anything else in my life. I have always loved you, but these weeks in London with you, watching you, admiring you, being near you, have only made me love you more."

Then, like Freddy Colchester, he said, "I know you do not feel that way about me. It doesn't matter. I love you quite enough for the two of us."

"What can I say?" Harriet asked, clenching her hands in their neat kid gloves tightly together. "I am honored, indeed, Douglas; you deserve better than me. But I can't accept, I can't. I think all the capacity for married love was drained from me over the years I spent as James's wife. I can give you friendship and I hope you know you will always have that, but I cannot give you—anyone— love."

"He must have been a bastard," he said softly, looking straight ahead now, his mouth set firmly.

"No, no, he was everything that was kind, indeed, I was not worthy of him. But to my eternal shame I did not mourn his death. I felt alive again then, freed from the cage I had spent so many years in. Please, I don't care to speak of that time anymore. I am sorry, Douglas. It just can't be."

He halted the team in the quiet country lane west of London where he had driven her. Transferring the reins to one hand, he raised hers in the other and kissed them.

"I would not distress you, Harry. Don't worry," he

said in a husky voice. "I wish I might be the man to change your mind about love and passion and marriage, but if it is not to be I shall survive somehow. Come now, you look like you are about to cry again."

He released her to wipe a tear from her cheek. "Don't weep over something we can do nothing about, Harry," he told her. "Instead, let me thank you for the dream of you I've cherished. I think it has kept me warm these twenty years and more."

"Oh, Douglas," she wailed, tears flowing freely now.

He pulled out his handkerchief and mopped her face before he put his arm around her and hugged her close just as a loaded cart lumbered around the bend and came toward them. As the farmer and his young son peered at them, Viscount Webster released Harriet and set his team in motion again.

# Nine

Five days later, Harriet Winthrop-Bates and her daughter left for Suffolk. They were both tired from packing and handling all the myriad details that had to be taken care of before they were free to leave. And, if truth were to be told, they were tired as well from the vast spectrum of emotions they had individually been treated to this Season in town. But it is over at last, Harriet thought as she peered from the window on her side of the hired carriage at the gray London streets they were traveling this dull, humid day. The servants had been dismissed, the house closed and the keys returned to the agent, and all their accounts settled. Even the rather tedious party for Miss King had passed almost without incident, although Harriet had been startled to hear her great-aunt say in the loud voice of the hard-of-hearing as she was about to take her leave, "Do get some rest in the country, niece. You look worn to a thread. As for that daughter of yours, I shall continue to hope she does not grow up silly."

Harriet had not dared ask the old lady what she meant, not when Lark was scarlet with embarrassment, and the other guests, some of Miss King's particular friends, did their best to pretend they had not heard.

She looked across the seat to where Lark sat huddled in her place, one hand clutching the strap to steady herself and her pretty mouth drooping.

Yes, she could see Lark was tired and sad. But she was young. She would be her old self in a week. Harriet was afraid it would take much longer for her to regain her good spirits. Thinking of her mother and the house

that awaited her, those spirits sank even further until she
forced herself to sit up straight and comment on the
passing scenery. Only Fanny, seated facing back, answered her remarks.

By the time they reached Tuddersham, the nearest village to the Fanshaw estate late the following afternoon,
Harriet began to look about eagerly. She had not been
home for some time, and she could see there had been
changes. The village had acquired a bustling inn and
there were more cottages than she remembered. But the
old gray church was just the same, and so was the black-
smith's shop, and she smiled when she saw the ducks
paddling in the pond on the green. How many genera-
tions of ducks had there been in that pond since she was
a child? she wondered.

Lark was glad her mother and Fanny had so much to
say. Their conversation hid her own silence. But she
couldn't help it, she told herself. Every mile they had
traveled caused her to feel more depressed. For even
now she could not help but wonder if her scheme and
Andrew's to meet here would ever come to anything.
What if he had not been able to come at all? What if he
had had second thoughts? What if his father had forbidden him to leave Derbyshire? That would be just the
kind of thing he would be apt to do, he was so severe, so
prone to frown, so—so *disapproving*. That word reminded her of her Grandmother Fanshaw and she grimaced.

She did not know for sure of course, but she would be
willing to wager that that woman, far from doting on her
only grandchild, had disapproved of her from the cradle.
Her mother had told her she had been a colicky baby.
Her grandmother, who considered any noise most ill-
bred, must have loathed the screaming miserable infant
she had been. And things had not improved as she grew
older, for during the infrequent times they spent together,
Mrs. Fanshaw had been quick to tell her she was pert,
clamorous, entirely too vivacious for a proper young
lady of quality, and the sin of all sins, *froward*.

Yet here she was, trapped here for heaven knows how long. Months, anyway. Had anyone in the world ever been more miserable than she? she wondered as the carriage turned into the gates and the Fanshaw establishment bulked large and dark against the dull gray Suffolk sky. The landscape surrounding it was flat and uninteresting to Lark's critical eye.

"I will expect you to try very hard not only to subjugate your will to your grandmother's but to be pleasant as well," her mother said in a soft but firm voice as Fanny jumped down before the groom could adjust the steps.

"I shall do my best, Mama," Lark told her. She even tried a smile, and when she saw her mother's face light up in return, she felt a pang of guilt. At least she did until she remembered the part her mother had surely played with the earl, retrieving her letters and Andrew's. Still, she thought as she stepped down and stretched discreetly, it was uncomfortable hating Mama. They had been such good friends and companions. Falling in love meant a lot of things changed; she wondered she had never suspected that before. For by gaining a lover you were forced to put away childish things and look at people in different ways—make hard choices. Of course, she told herself as she followed her mother up the steps, Andrew was worth anything, anything at all. No sacrifice could be too great, no former attachments too sacred, to be put aside for him. She would remember that.

Head up and full of resolution, Lark Mary Winthrop-Bates advanced to the drawing room to greet her grandmother.

The first thing that lady said was "So, you are here." This less than effusive welcome was followed by a long, deep sigh.

"Mama, how good to see you again," Harriet said serenely as she went to give her mother a kiss. Lark followed her example without being prodded to do so. As her lips touched the plump check, her grandmother's familiar smell almost overwhelmed her. Waves of lavender, rice powder, cinnamon and clove drops, dust, and something she thought could only be age enveloped her and she was delighted to step back.

"You have grown," the lady said, eyeing her granddaughter with a scowl. "I trust you have also learned how to conduct yourself with propriety. I'll have no undisciplined romps in my house."

"But Lark is a young lady now, Mother," Harriet said as she took a seat nearby and gestured to her daughter to follow her example. "You know she has just completed her first Season."

"And is the capital still standing?" Mrs. Fanshaw inquired.

*I hate you,* Lark thought. *You are a disagreeable nasty old lady and I hate you.*

"I suppose you will want tea," their hostess said next. "You may ring for it, Harriet. In fact I expect you to oversee the housekeeping entirely while you are here. My health has deteriorated sadly over these past months and it is the least you can do."

"I shall be glad to help any way I can," her daughter said as she went and rang the bell. "Lark will do all she can as well, won't you, dear?"

"Certainly, Mama," Lark said, speaking so softly her grandmother had to cup a hand to her ear.

"What did she say?" she demanded.

"She said she would be glad to help, too," Harriet told her as she took her seat again. She could see the drawing room needed a good turnout. It was dusty and there was a stale smell to it as if it had not been aired since the previous autumn. And the brass on the firedogs and fender was dull, the silver vase that held the everlasting her mother was so fond of, tarnished.

"I am sorry to hear your health has not been good. You did not write and tell me of it," she said next.

Before Mrs. Fanshaw could elaborate, the footman appeared and Harriet ordered tea. She remembered Jenkins from her childhood. He was elderly now and much frailer looking than his mistress, who in spite of ill health still sported large jowls that flowed into the broad column of her neck and shook in unison when she was annoyed.

As Jenkins bowed and went away, Harriet reminded herself she must look into the state of the servants. If the footman was any indication, most of them should be pensioned off. Of course her mother would argue that; pensions cost money. Harriet knew she would prefer to work the servants till they died. No wonder the house was so neglected looking, so forlorn.

"I did not write because I barely had the strength," Eudora Fanshaw informed her, and hastily, Harriet reminded herself to pay attention.

"The doctor has been of no assistance. Indeed, since your dear father was taken from me, Doctor Dodd has been almost rude to me. Sometimes when I summon him, he does not come for hours. And then he has no excuse except to say he had to attend a farmer who had had an accident with a scythe, or a child who had tumbled into the fire. How dare he?"

Harriet made no attempt to point out how much more urgent such injuries were compared to her mother's vague symptoms for she knew it would do no good at all. Neither did she try to change the subject, for nothing irritated her mother more than someone trying to coax her from her complaints. So she sat quietly and listened, occasionally murmuring, "I am so sorry," or "how unfortunate," as she silently thanked Lark for holding her tongue.

It did not take Harriet very many days to discover how serious her mother had been when she put her in charge of the household. All decisions were left to her discretion. This would have suited Harriet very well, except nothing she did escaped her mother's scrutiny and criticism. She had ordered the orchard pruned? The trees had always thrived without pruning. As for painting the outbuildings, surely that was an unnecessary luxury. The drawing room draperies were to be replaced? Couldn't that useless child be set to mending the current ones? It was not good for her to be idle and besides, they were only thirty years old. As for having Cook serve beef twice in one week, she rarely ate flesh. It did not agree with her. Nor did seedcakes or brussels sprouts or herring or any number of other food that appeared on the table. And she did wish Harriet would stop opening the windows. Did she want her mother to die of a chill?

Harriet managed to hold her temper and she tried to ensure Lark was nowhere about when her mother took her to task. Her daughter had inherited her temper, but what could be controlled at thirty-seven was likely to explode in a firestorm at seventeen, and woe to them both if it did.

She was glad Lark was behaving, however. She fell to with a will helping around the house and if she sometimes looked disgusted by the fusty old place, at least she kept it to herself. She only ran away in the afternoons to go riding, and Harriet was glad she did for she always looked so much better when she came back.

Of course there had been a serious problem in the beginning, Lark claiming she could not possibly ride the swaybacked old slug that was one of the few horses in her grandmother's stable. There was another even poorer saddle horse as well, an ancient pair to pull the equally ancient Fanshaw carriage and a fat donkey which Harriet grew accustomed to having hitched to the dogcart whenever she wished to consult with the Fanshaw farmers. Faced with riding the slug or not riding at all, Lark had swallowed her scruples, although she was hardly happy about it.

As she drove about the estate, Harriet sometimes found herself thinking of Marsh Pembroke and Douglas Webster and the adventures they had shared as children here. She told herself she only did so because she was lonely. Her mother was no companion; she never had been, and Lark was still inclined to be somewhat distant. Harriet put her behavior down to her unwillingness to spend these months in the country, which she was no doubt still blaming her mother for arranging.

One afternoon Harriet even went so far as to tie the donkey to a branch and to wander into the woods to see if she could find the cave where she and her two friends had played at red Indians one chilly autumn night. As she pushed her way through brambles and past slender young trees racing toward the light, she told herself that of course the woods had changed in twenty years. Now she would not have known where she was, yet there had been a time she knew every bend in the path, every wild berry bush, every badger's den.

At last she stumbled upon the stream quite by accident and she stared at it as if trying to will that night to return. The stream flowed placidly by, chuckling only over a pile of rocks that dammed its way, before it disappeared around a bend. Following it upstream, Harriet came to the cave at last.

Or the remains of it, she thought sadly. The two heavy tree limbs Marsh and Douglas had rigged up over the entrance to shield it had decayed and fallen in on it, and new growth had sprouted in the rich debris those limbs had left behind. She could barely see the entrance to the cave. It looked small to her, even smaller than when she had come here to say good-bye when she was eighteen and about to become the bride of James Winthrop-Bates. She remembered how she had cried then, cried as if she would never stop. But no amount of tears could erase the hateful words Marsh had hurled at her when she had told him of her betrothal, and no tears she could shed could change the decision her parents had made for her future.

Harriet sat down on a fallen log near the cave. In the background she could still hear the quiet murmur of the stream, and somewhere a little distance away, the scolding of an angry squirrel. Suddenly she heard a girl's laughter and she turned toward the sound, wondering at it. Had that been Lark? But what would her daughter be doing here deep in the woods?

"Lark, is that you?" she called as she rose to her feet.

It seemed to her the woods stilled instantly. Even the

squirrel ceased to scold. And no one answered her call. No one at all.

She waited, holding her breath and feeling nervous suddenly for no reason she could fathom. Obviously it had not been Lark after all. Perhaps some servant girl came here on her afternoon off to meet her young man. Harriet remembered there was a good-sized pond downstream. But today, finding they were not alone as they had thought, they were making off as fast as they could. Even now she could hear the faint sounds of two people beating a hasty retreat and she smiled, sorry she had invaded their trysting place. She wondered who they were. All her mother's servants were old except the little scullery maid, and at nine she was hardly of an age for dalliance. And the only other house nearby was the old Pembroke place. Her mother had taken great satisfaction in telling her no one lived there now but two elderly caretakers.

Harriet shrugged as she began to make her way back to the road. It could have been two youngsters from the village, she supposed. Country folk were used to long walks. Still, she thought as she untangled her skirt from a persistent bramble, she would ask Lark about it this evening when they were alone after she had put her mother to bed.

Lark professed ignorance of the laughter, saying she had been riding in quite the opposite direction.

"Whatever were you doing in the wood, Mama?" she asked, never looking up from the needlepoint she was stitching by the light of a pair of working candles.

Harriet told herself it was ridiculous to feel self-conscious. "I played in those woods when I was a child," she said. "There was a cave there I went to find. Alas, it has fallen in now, so I might have saved myself these bramble scratches."

"I can't imagine you as a child," Lark said, her eyes still lowered. "It must have been lonely for you here, with no brothers or sisters, nor anyone your age nearby."

Then she paused and said, "But perhaps you knew the

Earl of Morland, Mama? I mean when he was just a boy and a mere Pembroke?"

"Yes, I knew him; Viscount Webster as well," Harriet admitted.

"Were you friends? Did you all play together?" Lark asked, her needle stilled. She stared at her mother now.

"Well, yes, for a while," Harriet confessed. "But of course as we grew up, we grew apart. But enough of my past. All that was long ago before I met your father."

"My, my! It sounds to me you must have been the kind of hoyden Grandmother deplores," Lark said pertly, darting a glance at her mother to see if her daring was being badly received. "I wonder she did not take you to task, hating such females as fervently as she does."

"She did take me to task. Many times," Harriet said dryly, and then to her daughter's relief, she changed the subject. Still, it was a long time later before Lark's heartbeat steadied to normal.

# Ten

When Viscount Byrn had returned to Morland House after seeing Lark in Hyde Park, he had discovered his father waiting for him in the library.

"You wished to see me, sir?" he asked courteously as he came in and shut the door.

From behind his massive desk, his father eyed him coldly. "Not particularly. And I believe I shall survive not seeing you for some time to come. No, don't sit down. You're not going to be here long and you have much to do."

"Sir?" Byrn asked, straightening up and looking confused.

"You will be on your way to Morland no later than ten tomorrow morning," the earl told him. "Do you have any quarrel with that, Andrew?"

"Why, er, no, not at all," his son said, trying to sound casual. "Is there something amiss at the Park you want me to take care of for you, sir?" he added.

The earl snorted. "That's hardly likely," he said as he picked up some papers before him and shuffled them into alignment. Then fixing his son with a baleful eye, he said, "I merely want you out of London and thus out of trouble. You need not look so nervous. I'm not about to question you. I have an excellent idea what you've been up to and I intend to see it does not happen again. You are excused. Pack only what you need for the journey. Your man can follow with the rest of your belongings and your phaeton later."

"Certainly, sir," Byrn said, beating a hasty retreat.

As he went leisurely up the stairs whistling so the butler and the footmen would not suspect he had just been ordered to the country like a naughty little boy, he wondered how his father had discovered he and Lark were together again. And when he thought how close he had come to miss seeing her and making plans for the summer, he was horrified. Of course he still had to get his father's permission to leave Morland. How was he to do that? Where could he say he was going?

He thought he managed it very neatly, for the following morning early as he was eating breakfast with the earl and still wondering what to do, a letter arrived from one of his friends.

"I say, sir, here's Jerome Haviland asking me to be one of a party he's got up to climb in the Lake District this August," he said, trying to sound enthusiastic. "I should like it above all things! Reggie Calder told me all about his experiences there last summer and what a splendid time he had. I have longed to see for myself ever since. Er, would you object if I joined the group? They leave from London in a few days but they will have to pass through Derbyshire on the way, and I could join them there."

His father held out his hand and Byrn gave the letter to him. He held his breath as the earl read it and tossed it back.

"I see no harm in the scheme," he said at last. "It might even direct your mind to something other than the opposite sex."

"Sir?" Byrn asked, his brows knitted as if in confusion.

The earl gave a careless wave and disappeared again behind the morning newspapers.

Elated now, Byrn finished his breakfast, bade his father a civil if hasty good-bye, mounted his high-spirited gelding, and headed north out of London. He thought hard as he did so. He supposed he would have to go to Morland Park for a few days at least, but that didn't matter. He had forgotten when Lark had said she was to go to Suffolk, but surely not for a week or so. Then after his man arrived with the rest of his clothes, he would have him put together a wardrobe suitable for both a month's climbing and staying concealed at Pembroke House seeing his darling Lark. The morning was still fresh and his spirits rose as he left the capital with its noise, dirt, and confusion behind. Surely that letter from Haviland had to be a sign the gods were smiling on him and Lark at last.

He did not arrive in Suffolk for almost two weeks. It had taken time to get to Morland, collect his clothes and rig, and head south again. But at last he drove up the overgrown drive of his father's childhood home late one evening, trailing the gelding behind.

This is something like, he told himself as he peered ahead, searching for a light in the dark house. Why, it was better than the most exciting adventure he had ever read, and surely better than climbing around some northern hills. And somewhere nearby was his Lark. He hoped she had not been here for long, riding out every day and wondering where he was.

He drove around the back of the house and was relieved to see a faint light in what he assumed were the kitchens. He put the phaeton on one side of the stables, and led the team and his gelding inside. There was no one there and only one old plow horse who eyed the high-bred newcomers with a yellow eye. Hurrying now, Byrn rubbed the horses down, watered them, and filled their mangers with feed before he picked up his bags and crossed the yard to the house. Tomorrow he'd get the caretaker to put the phaeton in a shed. He wouldn't be needing it for quite a while and he didn't want anyone to spot it.

To say the elderly caretakers, a Mr. and Mrs. Crosby, were surprised to see him would be to understate the situation to an extreme. Mrs. Crosby almost fainted with shock when he entered the kitchen, and when she was informed she was to have the honor of cooking, cleaning, and laundering for the young Pembroke, she could only open and close her mouth soundlessly.

"No one is to know I am here, do you understand?" Byrn asked, trying to sound as stern as his father. "I cannot explain why, but it is very important. You must not reveal my presence to a living soul."

"Eh?" Mr. Crosby asked bending closer and cupping his ear.

" 'E says no one's ter know 'e's 'ere, Father," his wife screamed in his ear. Byrn prayed there were no close neighbors. If there were, he was undone.

"Oh, aye," the old man said with a smile that revealed he had lost more teeth over the years than he had retained. "But wot if yer Da comes arsking fer ye? Wot then?" he asked.

"The earl will not come here. There is no chance of that," Byrn told him.

He sat down a little later to a hastily prepared meal of beef broth, bread, cheese, and home brewed ale, and he hoped the good woman would put on a better spread in the future. After he ate he chose a bedroom that overlooked the drive, and went out to stroll up and down inspecting what he could see of the property in the near darkness, leaving the two servants to prepare his room.

He was feeling very proud of himself for the ingenuity he had shown, but he admitted he also felt uneasy when he remembered how he had misled his father. He had never done such a thing in his life, and somehow it did not sit well in his mind. But then he recalled how the earl had stolen his letters and Lark's as well, how he had probably had a good laugh over the tender sentiments written in them, and he felt vindicated. Such infamy more than excused his disobedience and the lies he had told about the climbing trip, he reminded himself as he went back inside. In fact, one might even say all this was Morland's fault. For if he had not meddled, if he had not disapproved of Lark as the future countess, none of this would have happened. Feeling righteous now, Byrn undressed, climbed into bed, and closed his eyes to dream of his meeting with Lark on the morrow.

It was just as well he had appointed the afternoon for the meeting, for with no one to wake him, he slept well into the morning. Dressing, he came down to a house that frankly horrified him. He had not been able to see much of it in candlelight the previous evening, but in the clear bright sunlight its lack of amenities was all too apparent. There was little furniture and what there was was covered with dust sheets. The small rooms smelled musty and there were water stains on most of the ceilings and around the windows. The woodwork and walls were dirty and the rugs were a disgrace. Used to the studied elegance of his father's other estates, he could hardly reconcile himself to his surroundings. If Lark had not been so close, he would have left the place immediately.

Swallowing, he told Mrs. Crosby she need not bother to clean the house. Instead she was merely to make the library habitable, and a small room where he could eat his meals. She bit her lip but she dropped him a curtsy and went away mumbling under her breath. Byrn decided he had better ignore her although he was sure she wouldn't have dared to mumble if his father had given her an order.

He went out after breakfast as much to escape the place as to investigate. He found Mr. Crosby hoeing some vegetables in the garden. Not wanting to shout at him, he only waved and moved on to the stables. It seemed an endless time before he could saddle his horse. He had asked Mrs. Crosby where the Fanshaw property was, and armed with her directions, he rode out to meet Lark.

They had a wonderful reunion, Lark quite forgetting her resolve never to dismount she was so glad to see him at last. Byrn tied the horses to a branch and they sat down under an oak tree to exchange news. Lark was impressed at the clever way Byrn had misled his father, and when he asked rather diffidently if she thought he had

done wrong, was quick to say it had not been his fault.
And, she had added seriously, she was misleading her
mother, too, wasn't she? That was equally bad.

Byrn could not agree, and for a few minutes they had
a spirited argument about whether lying to your father or
your mother was more sinful.

"Well, never mind," Lark said at last when it appeared
Byrn was about to try and convince her for the third
time. He sounded sometimes like a schoolmaster, she
thought. Perhaps he would outgrow it?

"I've been here for four days and I was getting so
worried," she went on. "It is just horrid at my grandmother's house. You would not believe how miserable I
have been."

Byrn interrupted to give her a detailed picture of the
hovel he was reduced to, and she had to admit it did
sound terrible.

"Still," she said when he had finished describing Pembroke House and its elderly servants, "you don't have
the likes of my grandmother to deal with. She calls me
'that child' and she is constantly giving me orders or
commenting on my clothes, my hair, and my manners.
Why, just this morning she said I need not think I was
going to eat her out of house and home just because I
took another muffin."

"Is she poor, then?" he asked idly, twisting one of her
curls around his finger.

Lark snorted. "Don't you believe it. She is well-to-do
and I think she is the most selfish, horrid woman. If you
weren't here, I don't think I could stand being with her
for all the months Mama says we must stay."

"Well, she probably won't live much longer and then
you'll be free of her. And she's sure to leave all her
money to your mother and then she can be comfortable."

Lark plucked up a handful of grass and threw it at
him. "You wretch," she said. "Don't you realize if she
dies we won't be able to marry for I will be in mourning
for an entire year?"

"Then we must hope she either does so this summer

since I'm still only nineteen, or has the decency to hang
about till I reach my majority," he said, lying back to
stretch out comfortably on the grass.

Lark eyed his long, masculine frame—those broad
shoulders, his slim waist and muscled thighs, and she
felt a tide of warmth somewhere deep inside. Quickly
turning away from him, she began to chew a long piece
of grass.

"Where did you get that ghastly mount, darling?" he
asked next and she glanced over to where the horses
were tethered. Byrn's high-bred gelding made her horse
look more pathetic than ever.

"It is one of my grandmother's two riding horses. And
would you believe it is the better of the two at that?"

He laughed. "Ask her to buy you another one," he
said carelessly. "She cannot want you to make a specta-
cle of yourself on such an animal."

"She wouldn't do it," Lark replied, wondering if Byrn
really listened to anything she said. "It would cost
money, and besides, she does not approve of young
ladies who ride. She thinks a sedate walk in the shrub-
bery and around the garden all the exercise I need. That
way, I am at her beck and call, you see."

"Know what, Lark?" Byrn propped himself up on one
elbow. "I think the old lady's got to you. Bet she knows
it, too, and it's amusing her no end. You ought to learn to
ignore her. Yes, that's what you must do."

Lark felt vaguely angry. What did Drew know of her
situation? It was all so easy for him to give advice, tell
her what she should and shouldn't do. But he did not
have to live with a nasty old woman and listen to her
whine and complain until he thought he would go mad.
Lark told herself that sometimes her love was entirely
too pontifical. He even reminded her of a pompous
bishop she had heard speak in church one time. All seeing, all knowing, all . . . all wonderful.

He reached up then and pulled her down beside him to
hold her close, and in a moment Lark had forgotten all
the distressing tendencies he exhibited occasionally, in

the passion of his kiss. But she did not completely sur-
render. In the back of her mind, she kept telling herself
she must take care. They were alone, far from prying
eyes, and it would be so easy to give in to the sensations
that surged through her body. Then the cat would be
among the pigeons for sure. No, even though she knew
they were going to marry, they had to wait. She was not
some bar wench after all. She was Lark Mary Winthrop-
Bates, she told herself as she pulled loose and sat up to
do up her hair.

"I must go, Drew," she said, squinting up at the sun to
judge how late it was. "I dare not risk being late and
having to answer questions."

"But you just got here," he complained. His voice was
husky and his face flushed, and she was sure she had
stopped him in the nick of time.

"I will meet you right here tomorrow," she promised.
"Perhaps we could go exploring then. I have not dared to
go into the woods alone lest I get lost, but it must be
cooler there. Maybe we can find a stream, even a pond."

He brightened as he rose to help her to the saddle before he untied her sorry mount. And all the way home he
pictured the two of them swimming naked in the pond,
making love on its grassy banks. Life, he told himself as
he took a deep breath of the soft country air, was good.
No, more than good. It was excellent.

Of course his vision came to nothing, for right after
they found the pond and he dared her to swim and she
laughed at the suggestion, they heard her mother call her.
She sounded so near that for a moment they stood
frozen, staring at each other appalled. Then without exchanging a word, they bolted.

They were both panting hard when they reached the
horses and perhaps that was why they still did not say
anything as they mounted and cantered off in opposite
directions. At least Byrn cantered. Lark could not urge
her horse to anything but a sedate trot as she rode to the
other side of her grandmother's land.

The next day Byrn was delighted to hear Mrs.

Winthrop-Bates had no idea he was anywhere in the neighborhood, but he could have screamed with frustration when he arrived back at the old Pembroke place and discovered someone had come to visit.

"Who is this?" Byrn asked Mrs. Crosby as he inspected the stranger leaning against a fence. He hoped they did not notice the quiver of alarm he himself heard all too clearly in his voice.

"Why, it's me nephew, sir," Mrs. Crosby said. "Henry Aikens he be, my sister Mabel's boy. He's come ter see how we be gettin' on. Henry, this be—"

"No!" Byrn said loudly. Then he coughed behind his hand and mumbled to her, "Remember, no one's to know I'm here."

"Yus, but he's seen ye, ain't he?" she asked.

Aikens inspected Byrn from head to toe, but he did not say anything. The viscount had the happy thought he might be simple, or even dumb. How fortuitous that would be! But such a grand solution to his problem was dashed when the yokel came away from the fence and said he guessed he'd be on his way. As he climbed up to the farm cart he was driving, he asked his aunt if he could fetch her anything from the village, and Byrn's blood ran cold. Should he try to bribe the fellow to keep his presence secret? he wondered. Or would doing so make him suspect there was something amiss here, something he would comment about to everyone he met? While he was debating all the pros and cons, Aiken clucked to his horse and left the yard.

Byrn cursed under his breath. He would just have to pray for the best. It was out of his hands.

The next three days were wet and he knew he had no chance of seeing Lark. Left to his own devices in the ugly house, he was despondent. He had never felt so grim, he told himself as he stared moodily at the raindrops tracking their crooked courses down one of the library windows. How tiresome it was with no one to talk to. He couldn't even write letters, for he could tell no one where he was. He was not conscious of any irony.

He had seldom put pen to paper in the past and had not, until now, thought it a pleasant occupation. But since he was desperate, he was willing to consider it an option.

Byrn had always disliked quiet and immobility. He was happiest in a raucous crowd bent on action, the more athletic the better.

He had no taste for reading either, but now, driven to it, he looked over the library shelves with growing distaste. The Pembrokes seemed addicted to slim books of poetry and fat tomes of local history. There were no novels, no books on sport. He tried the poetry but it made him yawn, and soon he found himself turning over the mildewed pages of a tome about Derbyshire in the early 1500s. He thought it deadly stuff.

Beside his isolation, he had other reasons to be unhappy. His bed was uncomfortable and Mrs. Crosby seemed to have no more idea how to do a gentleman's laundry than her husband had about polishing one's boots. And the food had been terrible. When he had complained, Mrs. Crosby told him she couldn't afford "fancy eats." He had been forced to give her quite a bit of money lest he starve.

When the sun shone again, he felt like a man released from imprisonment. But Lark did not come to the oak tree that afternoon although he waited about for her for hours.

To his great relief she was there the next day, although she said she could not stay. "My mother and I went to Wickham Market yesterday," she explained. "I could not say I didn't want to go after I've been complaining how bored I was here. And today I've promised to help cut out the new draperies. We bought the material yesterday. I must say I did not think we would be able to do so well in a little market town, but the stuff is handsome. A soft gold brocade. Now if only we could replace some of that dated, fusty furniture. But of course my grandmother says . . ."

Byrn wondered Lark could go on and on, and about such a tedious subject as well. Didn't she realize how he had been suffering, alone and cooped up in that dreadful old house those three rainy days? Didn't she care? What were brocade draperies to him, a man forced to resort to a dry history of ancient times in order to save his sanity? Surely she had never used to be so unfeeling.

And, he thought as he started back to his prison only a few minutes later, Lark had changed in other ways, too. She did not seem to welcome his kisses as much as she once had, and she was quick to stop him if he tried to go further. He told himself he must have this out with her on the morrow.

If it didn't rain.

# Eleven

The next afternoon he waited until she squirmed out of his arms, scolding him as she did so, before he asked her point blank if she were having second thoughts about their love. Her eyes opened wide in astonishment.

"Of course I am not, dearest," she said. "Whatever can you mean?"

He saw she was backing away from him and he said, "See, there you go again, putting space between us. And you don't seem to want to kiss me anymore and when I hold you and fondle you, you push me away. That's not the Lark I fell in love with."

"But don't you see, I have to do that," she tried to explain. "The two of us are alone for hours every afternoon, and it is too tempting. I'm afraid, truly, of what might happen."

"But we are going to be married," he argued. "What difference does it make if we are lovers now or later?"

"We are not going to be married for over a year," she said, the practical side of her coming to the fore. "And after all, Drew, I'm not some little bit o' muslin."

"And what would you know about such things?" he asked, intrigued.

"Not much, of course, but I know the way a man treats one of them is very different from the way he treats his future wife." She took a deep breath. "You say I seem different to you. Well, you are different, too. Now you are only concerned with your own desires. You don't seem to care anything about me."

"How can you say such an awful thing?" he demanded. "I do so care for you. I adore you completely. If anything I love you more than I did in London. But, Lark, it is very hard. You don't understand, don't know how maddening it is for a man to be close to a woman he loves, yet never be able to possess her."

"Well! I am frustrated too, but I manage to control myself."

"Who asked you to? Besides, it's not the same thing at all," he said hotly, then blushed. "I mean, er, I don't see why you are being such a prig. If you truly loved me, you wouldn't think twice about making love because—"

He stopped in mid-sentence as she glared at him then turned and marched to her horse, untying it and struggling into the saddle while he hovered behind her. He was afraid to say anything or help her, she looked so furious. Just before she rode away, she said in an icy voice, "And I suppose it would be just wonderful if I found myself with child, wouldn't it? I never realized what a selfish, horrid person you were, and I am sorry now I ever met you."

She rode off at that irritating trot, but perhaps the elderly horse's gait was just as well for she was crying so hard she could not see where she was going.

Lark spent the next two days working on the new draperies. She was very quiet, so quiet her mother looked at her in alarm and her grandmother found herself without a single thing to complain about, a state of affairs she found annoying rather than pleasing. And if Lark cried herself to sleep at night, no one knew of it but her maid, for Fanny was still her only confidante.

Lark went out riding the following afternoon at her mother's urging. She told herself she would not go anywhere near the oak tree, but somehow she found herself there, and when she saw the way Byrn's face lit up when he saw her, how he ran to her, she was reassured.

Not that I forgive him, she told herself as he lifted her from the saddle straight into his arms and held her close to him, her feet dangling a good six inches above the ground while he kissed her and told her he couldn't live without her—he was so sorry—he would never, ever do anything again to displease her as long as he lived, and other, even more impossible promises to keep. Lark forgot she did not intend to forgive him, and when he vowed he would not try to make love to her until they were indeed man and wife, she felt a sudden elation at the amount of power she had over this tall, godlike young man.

"I am so glad," she said, holding his face between her hands. "But I have been so unhappy, Drew. I never thought we could ever quarrel, yet that is just what we have done. It is sad, isn't it, that two so deep in love could say such things to each other, raise their voices and their fists, stamp their feet?"

Byrn could not remember doing anything of the kind, but mindful of the thin ice he was probably still skating on, he only smiled and agreed.

As they sat down together under the tree they had come to think of as their own, Lark added, "I wonder if it might not be a good thing if we were to part for a time. It has been wonderful having you so near, but as we have discovered, dangerous. Perhaps you should go back to town, or to Morland . . ."

"But I can't do that," he said, taking her hands and holding them tightly. "I'm supposed to be on a hiking and climbing trip in the Lake District, remember? I can't go home till sometime in mid-September."

"Oh, I forgot that. But it is worrisome, isn't it, to always have to be concerned we might be found out? Sometimes I am sure my mother must suspect something, she looks at me so strangely. But it is probably just my nerves. Isn't it odd that what was at one time such an exciting adventure has become a burden."

He hurried to reassure her but when they parted and he turned his horse's head for Pembroke, he thought about what she had said. Yes, he admitted it was tedious spending all this time here while only being able to be with her for a hour or so on fine days. In fact he had never been so bored. Not with her company, of course, he made haste to tell himself, no, no! It was just he missed his friends, all his usual activities—and, dare he say it—his freedom.

When he reached his destination he was horrified to see the curate had come to call. Summoning up every ounce of courage he possessed, he joined the man as he prepared to climb back into his gig. Fortunately he saw that Mrs. Crosby remained by the kitchen door, and he knew he didn't have to worry about her deaf husband overhearing anything.

"Good afternoon, sir," he said with a bow. "You must be the local curate. Allow me to introduce myself. I am—I am Jerome Haviland."

"Indeed?" the curate asked, his gray brows high. "That is not what Mrs. Crosby told me. You are sure you are not a Pembroke, son of the Earl of Morland?"

Byrn forced himself to chuckle. "No, I am not, sir, although I did tell her I was Morland's son. The earl thought it best, for he didn't want the old pair to know he was thinking of selling this place. That's why I'm here, you know, to look it over. Time enough to upset the old dears if I decide to purchase it."

"Indeed," the curate said again. "I wish you good fortune then, Mr. Haviland. And good day to you, sir."

Byrn watched him drive away, secretly congratulating himself on his masterful handling of the situation. Still, he thought as he strode to the door and prepared to give Mrs. Crosby a scold for disobeying his orders yet again, he had not liked the speculative look in curate's eye just before he drove away. Surely the man had believed him, hadn't he?

Later, he told himself it didn't matter what the curate thought. To his knowledge no one from the area ever communicated with his father. And his father thought he was with his friends scaling the hills in the Lake District. I'm just getting edgy, Byrn told himself. It's those nerves Lark mentioned. All was well. All would continue to be well.

This mood of optimism disappeared rapidly a week

later. Byrn had decided to ride home from his meeting with Lark by the road. It would not only be a change for him, it would give his horse some needed exercise. Devil was getting out of sorts with no hard gallops to settle him down. But as Byrn rode hard around a bend in the road, he spied a gentleman approaching from the opposite direction. The man was still a good distance away but there was something familiar about him that convinced Byrn it would be better to avoid a meeting. Desperately he looked around and was fortunate enough to see a narrow lane a little way ahead. Checking only slightly, he turned into it, thanking heaven Devil was so surefooted. He did not stop until they were a mile from the road. Then he paused and had to wait for his heart to stop pounding before he was able to listen for any sounds of pursuit. To his relief there were none and he continued on his way, swearing he would never be so careless again.

Viscount Webster was almost sure he had seen Morland's son in the distance as he rode to the Fanshaw property, but once arrived there, he made no mention of it for Harriet seemed so glad to see him, it drove every other thought from his head.

"And how is it you are here in Suffolk, Douglas?" she asked as she poured him a glass of wine.

"I am on my way back to Derbyshire," he explained.

"I was not aware Suffolk was on the route there."

"Of course it isn't, but it's not so far I could not come and see how you are getting on. But, Lord, how the memories well up, now that I am here."

"Have you been to Pembroke House?" she asked, smoothing her embroidery.

"No, I'm putting up at the inn at Tuddersham. I don't think I'll even stop by. It is bound to be different."

"I think you are wise," she told him before she revealed how she herself had gone to search for the cave.

"And it is no more?" he asked when she had finished.

"No. What is left seemed so small and shallow to me.

Yet once I thought it a marvelous place, so secure and dry and safe."

"I suspect we embroider our memories much as you are doing to that piece of hooped cloth you hold," he told her.

He rose to his feet as Harriet's mother bustled in full of curiosity about this unusual caller.

"So you are Viscount Webster," Mrs. Fanshaw said after introductions had been made. "A friend of my late son-in-law?"

Webster caught Harriet's eye. "No, I cannot say I knew Mr. Winthrop-Bates, ma'am. I met your daughter this spring in London."

By the time the viscount rose to take his leave, Mrs. Fanshaw was in possession of all the facts she most wanted to know. He had never married and so had no children, he owned several hundred acres of farmland in Derbyshire as well as a house in London, and the lady surmised by the quality of his clothes, he was a gentleman of means. Still, when he went away promising to return on the morrow, she told Harriet she could not like him.

"I agree he seems a pleasant man but I have to wonder what he wants," she said, staring at her daughter as if she suspected her guilty of luring the gentleman to her side. "I do hope you are not thinking of marrying again, Harriet. There is something repugnant about a widow embracing a new husband, don't you agree? Besides, I have been thinking you might make your home here from now on. To do so is surely your duty, and it would be a comfort to me in my old age. And that girl of yours will be marrying one of these days, and you will be alone. Most suitable!"

Harriet tried not to shudder. Her mother had discovered she made a handy slave, and like one, her services were free. But she had no intention of living with the lady again so she only smiled and said she had no interest in the viscount as a husband and didn't her mother think the new draperies a vast improvement?

The following afternoon when they met, Lark was disturbed to see the frown Byrn wore and how his voice shook as he told her of the unfortunate things that had happened that he had kept from her so far.

"First there was Mrs. Crosby's nephew, and I've never known a country person who didn't gibble-gabble about every new thing, did you? And after him came that curate. I doubt he believed I was who I told him I was. And now there's m'father's old friend, Viscount Webster. Could anything be worse?"

"But he can't have said anything to my mother," Lark reassured him. "She didn't question me about you, and surely she would have done so if he had mentioned he saw you. I'll wager you were too far away for him to identify."

"That could be," Byrn said, looking more cheerful. Then he frowned again. "But he saw Devil clearly."

When Lark merely looked confused, he added, "My horse. I bought him at Tattersall's only a week before I left town. Cost me a pretty penny, he did, too. He's one of Ridgely's mounts and everyone in town knows him by sight and knows I purchased him, too. What cursed luck!

"Has Webster left the neighborhood?" he asked next.

"Mother says he is staying at the inn for now."

"Damn! That means he'll be out and about and he may well decide to visit Pembroke House. He stayed there often you know with my father when they were boys."

He got to his feet to pace up and down under the elm. Lark watched him, frowning in concern herself now.

"You see the danger we are in, love?" he asked, coming to a halt before her. He hunkered down and added, "The very great danger that we will be found out and separated? It can be only a matter of time. And I do not think my father will be at all forbearing. He is sure to exact some dreadful punishment for my disobedience to him."

Lark was very pale. "What are we to do, Drew? What *can* we do?"

He thought for a moment. "There's nothing for it but to run away together," he said finally. As she gasped, he added, "Yes, we must go to Scotland and marry over the anvil. There is no other course."

"But I couldn't do that," Lark whispered. "Why, only the most depraved girls do such a thing, and then they are ruined. Do you want to ruin me, Drew?"

"Of course I don't. I intend to make you my viscountess, and in time, the Countess of Morland. How can that ruin you?"

"I can't do it," Lark repeated. Byrn wished she would stop shaking her head. "I simply cannot do such an outrageous thing."

"You don't love me enough then," he said in a bitter voice. "I am willing to risk all for you without considering the consequences. But I see your love for me is weaker stuff."

"That's not fair," Lark cried. "You know I love you to distraction, but *this* . . . no, no! There must be some other way, there must. Perhaps it might be better if we were to confess and take our punishment; wait to marry till you come of age."

Byrn had a vision of his father's furious face, the icy words that would engulf him in a cascade of sarcasm; the punishment she spoke of so carelessly blighting his life for a long time to come. Confessing would be easy enough for *her.* What could her mother do to her to punish her? Keep her from attending a party or two?

"I know how it will be," he said. "My father has property in the West Indies. He will send me there and make sure I don't return. We will never see each other again."

"No, he would not be so cruel!" Lark cried out, tears coming to her eyes. "You are his heir and I believe the Indies are a dangerous place of fever and slave uprisings and terrible storms that wreak havoc on anything in their path. And there is the ocean passage there as well, fraught with peril. No, my love, no!"

"He would not care for any of that," Byrn told her. The picture she painted both repelled and fascinated him. To be sure it was as dangerous as she said, but it did sound exciting, too. He could see himself fighting the wind and waves in a ferocious storm, giving orders to the crew now the captain had been washed overboard. Recalled to Suffolk by a little hand tugging on his sleeve, he said, "I'll be lucky if he doesn't horsewhip me. I disobeyed him; he'll not stand for that."

Lark threw himself at him and hugged him tight as he tumbled backward on the soft grass. She was crying in earnest now, and Byrn felt a large lump in his throat as he put his arms around her in turn and kissed the top of her head.

"I suppose there's nothing to do but confess and throw myself on his mercy," he said.

Lark leaned back in his arms to consider him where he lay beneath her. Even frowning, he was so handsome, she thought. If they had to wait, would he remain true to her? He had already proved how impetuous he was. Might he not fall in love with some more willing, less conventional girl if she let him out of her sight? A year and a third was a long time. And he was a young man, eager and virile and yes, terribly appealing.

"I've changed my mind," she said and his hands tightened on her back. "You are right, Drew. We cannot be separated. I could not bear it. We must run away. To Scotland."

"Do you mean it, darling?" he asked, his face lighting up and a glow warming his blue eyes. "Really?"

She nodded, suddenly too frightened of what she had agreed to do, to speak.

"Come on, now, sit up," he said, his voice urgent as he rolled her off him. "We have a great many plans to make. It must be tonight. I dare wait no longer. You must escape the house unseen and make your way to the road by ten o'clock. I'll be there waiting in the phaeton. There's a moon. We should be able to make good time.

"Now, Lark, bring only essentials and no finery. We

must travel as lightly as we can for speed is of the utmost importance. They are sure to come after us, you know, and we must put as much space between us and them as we can. Do you understand?"

She nodded again, caught up now in the scene he sketched. And if Byrn had allowed his mind to wander to his heroism on the high seas, so too did his love as she pictured the two of them dashing through the dark night being pursued by a furious Earl of Morland, his cape billowing out behind him as he galloped closer and closer. She could see the silver chased pistol he brandished, imagine the huge hound racing before, hot on the scent. And like Byrn, she shivered with a mixture of delight and horror and anticipation.

# Twelve

Harriet was at breakfast the following morning when the upstairs maid knocked and asked to speak to her. She nodded, and when she saw the neatly folded and sealed paper the maid was holding out, she was quick to dismiss the footman.

"Yes, Jane?" she said as he closed the door behind him.

"I found this on Miss Winthrop-Bates's bed, ma'am," the maid said. As Harriet took the note in suddenly reluctant fingers, she added, "She's not in her room nor has her bed been slept in. And her maid is missing as well."

Harriet looked at the clock. It was only ten. Her mother would not come down for another hour at least. As she opened the note, she tried to say casually, "Yes, I am well aware of it. Lark has gone to visit friends in Ipswich for a few days. In order not to upset her grandmother, they were to pick her up very early this morning at the gate. Thank you. That will be all."

She waited until the maid had gone away before she read the note Lark had left for her. Had she managed to quell the servants' gossip, she wondered, or only fanned it with her supposedly artless admission? She could not tell.

She was frowning when she finished the note. Lark sounded almost incoherent in her distress, and she had crossed her lines, quite forgetting there was no need to do so since the note was not to be posted. But Harriet could read enough to know Lark had run away with Viscount Byrn who had, all this time, been sequestered in Pembroke House where he was able to see her daughter every fine afternoon. The two had taken fright at Viscount Webster's appearance, and decided to make a dash for it. To Gretna, Harriet thought, horrified. Gretna! Lark would be ruined whether they made it there or not, her reputation irrevocably destroyed.

As the breakfast room door opened, Harriet looked up, quite unable to wipe the anguish she felt from her face.

"Yes, yes, you want to announce me as is customary, but I assure you Mrs. Winthrop-Bates and I do not stand on ceremony," the Earl of Morland said as he shut the door in the elderly footman's distressed face.

Morland took a seat beside her at the table. "I can see from your expression, and the way you are clutching that paper, madam, that you have been apprised of our children's latest start, hmm? Just so. What did she say?"

"What are you doing here?" Harriet whispered although she admitted she had never been so glad to see anyone in her entire life.

"I hope helping you recover your errant daughter, madam. Tell me, have you ever considered a convent? Preferably one deep in the country, miles from anywhere?"

She ignored his sarcasm. "She writes that Byrn has been at Pembroke House ever since we arrived here, and that they have been meeting every fine afternoon. But now that Douglas is come, they have decided they have no recourse but to flee—"

"To Scotland, of course. Well, at least Andrew plans to make an honest woman of her now he's seduced her."

"There is no proof she has been seduced," Harriet was quick to say, trying to keep her voice calm.

"I would not refuse a cup of coffee, madam, if you were to offer one," he said, ignoring her remark. "The caretaker's wife at Pembroke House is an abominable cook. Your daughter's charms must be outstanding. I can think of no other reason Andrew was able to remain so long else."

Harriet took a deep breath. Her first reaction, to rip up at him, was quickly discarded. There was a fine white line around his mouth and his dark brows were knit in a ferocious frown. He was angry and he was upset and she did not care to aggravate the situation further.

"We cannot be sure there has been anything but those meetings and a few stolen kisses," she said, and when he looked ready to argue the point, she held up her hand. "Allow me to pour you that coffee, m'lord. Then perhaps we might begin to talk about what can be done, instead of speculating about what might have happened."

For a moment he continued to glare at her and she felt the little pulse in her throat begin to pound until he leaned back and laughed in genuine amusement. Harriet had not heard that full-throated laugh for more than twenty years; now it pulled at her and made her want to weep.

"When did you last see your daughter, madam?" he asked as she handed him his cup.

"Last evening. She claimed she was feeling tired and wanted to go to bed early. She went up soon after my mother did."

"How did she behave? Was she different in any way?"

"Now that I understand why, yes, she was. She hugged me for a long time and her kiss was the warmest I have had from her in weeks. You see, she never did return to her former easy manner after she discovered my part in the confiscation of the love letters."

The earl made a disgusted sound deep in his throat. "She needs to be spanked," he said.

"Well, there is nothing for it but to go after them, no matter how tiresome that will be. I suggest you have your maid pack a portmanteau of bare necessities. I have my phaeton outside. Andrew has a good team, and he has the advantage of several hours on us, but I believe we can catch them up if not today or tomorrow, soon after that. They must stop to eat and sleep sooner or later."

Harriet stared at him. "You want me to go off with you just like that?"

"Just like that. I need you to convince the child she has been very wrong and must return to you. Your appearance will lend the expedition a prosaic, normal appearance. Besides, I cannot believe you would prefer *me* to deal with the chit. I could not guarantee to keep my hands from her.

"You may leave Andrew to me. His punishment is going to be severe." The earl took a sip of coffee before he added, "Spare me any tearful, womanly arguments about how their love for each other excuses a great deal. I grant you they *may* be in love, but nothing—nothing!—can excuse the fact my son not only disobeyed me, he lied to me."

He looked so grim and so disillusioned, she rose quickly. "I shall be ready as soon as I can, m'lord. Please wait for me outside. My mother will be coming down soon and she is not well."

"And the knowledge a Pembroke is within her doors might cause her to have a fit? It is tempting, but no, it would only delay us. I'll wait for you in the drive. Hurry, madam. Minutes count."

In her room, Harriet rummaged through the chest and wardrobe for shifts, petticoats, and hose. Now let me see, she thought, pausing for a moment with a fresh nightrobe in her arms. What else will I need? A pelisse and bonnet and a warm shawl, for Scotland can be cold any time of the year, and perhaps we will not come up with them in a day or so, or even a week, no matter what Morland says. And I'll need a pair of sturdy shoes, my slippers, and toothbrush and comb—one or two plain gowns . . .

"My child, what is the meaning of this?" her mother demanded sharply as she threw the door open and swept inside still clad in her dressing gown. Behind her, the upstairs maid peered over her shoulder, only retreating when Harriet glared at her.

"Come in and sit down, Mama," she said as she went and closed the door in the maid's avid face. "I am glad you were awake so I did not have to leave you a note. Lark left early this morning to visit friends in Ipswich, and I am to join them there for a few days, I am sorry I did not tell you sooner, but it was only recently all our plans were confirmed."

"Yes, yes, and the moon is made of green cheese, and there are fairies in the garden," her mother cried, her heavy jowls waggling with her indignation. "Who is that man outside? What is he doing here? And why are you going off with him like any brass-faced wench? And if you think I am about to believe such a story as you have told me, especially when it involves that hoyden of a daughter of yours, you are mistaken, miss!"

"You may believe it or not, Mama, but I cannot stay. The earl is waiting to escort me, so you may be easy. Do not fret. I shall return before you know it," Harriet said, packing the clothes she had selected and fastening the straps of her portmanteau.

"What earl?" her mother demanded, arms folded across her ample bosom.

"The Earl of Morland, Mama, which you already know since Jane no doubt questioned Jenkins before she came to relay the news to you. I wonder you can have such a gossip and sneak in the house. If it were up to me, I'd send her packing today."

Mrs. Fanshaw collapsed on the bed, clutching one of the corner posts for support. "Morland," she said in a fading voice. "He who was Marsh Pembroke. No, no, it must not be! You know how your sainted father felt about the Pembrokes, how determined he was not to have anything to do with them. How he insisted you never see young Pembroke again. And yet now— *now!*—you are about to stain his memory by jauntering about with the man? I shall die of shame, and my death will be laid to your door, daughter."

"You won't die, Mama," Harriet said briskly as she pinned her bonnet on and put her pelisse over her arm. "Please calm yourself. I shall be back in a few days. And it would be wise for you to remember I am not a giddy young miss Lark's age. I am thirty-seven and a respectable widow. No one can look askance at any traveling companion I choose."

She bent and kissed her mother. As she picked up her bag and went to the door, Eudora Fanshaw said in a weak voice, "If you marry him, I swear I shall never speak to you again, Harriet."

Her daughter turned, one hand on the doorknob. "You may be easy, Mama. I have no intention of marrying the Earl of Morland, and he, I can assure you, has no designs on me. Far from it."

On this note she was gone, pushing past the upstairs maid who was plying a feather duster nearby and pretending disinterest. Harriet ignored her and the piteous moans issuing from her room as well as she ran down the stairs.

The earl handed her portmanteau to his groom who stowed it in the boot as Harriet took her seat. They were gone in less than a minute, trotting down the drive. Harriet could almost feel the eyes on her back like knives, and she was glad when the phaeton rounded a bend and reached the road. To her surprise, the earl halted the team.

"Off you go, Harris," he said over his shoulder to the groom who was clinging to the perch. "I won't need you anymore. Remain at Pembroke House till I return. Oh," he added as the groom jumped down and saluted, "eat at the Tuddersham inn. I'll pay the tab when I return."

As he clucked to the team, Harriet remarked, "I did wonder about him and his weight since we are to travel fast, m'lord. Why did you even bother to bring him this morning?"

"To lend you consequence, of course. Did your mother cut up stiff about this traveling?"

"You must know she did," Harriet said, staring

straight ahead at the road that wound away before them. She was uncomfortable this close to him on the narrow seat, but she knew if she attempted to edge away, he would have some acerbic comment to make.

Suddenly she remembered something and she said, "I forgot to mention it, but Lark took her maid with her. At least the girl was not in the house this morning, and I cannot imagine where else she would be."

He turned slightly to look at her, disbelief in his eyes. "Her maid? What was she thinking of?"

"I suppose, she thought as you did, m'lord, Fanny would lend her consequence."

"I'll wager Andrew got rid of the maid in short order. He did not even attempt to trail his riding horse lest it slow them. Instead he entrusted it to the tender mercies of old Crosby. When I learned that, I knew how desperate he was. He dotes on that horse."

"Obviously, he dotes on Lark more. Tell me, when did you arrive?"

"I came early this morning. I was forced to delay in Sudbury till late afternoon yesterday for some needed repairs to the rig. I decided to spend the night at the inn there. If I had not, there would have been no need for this mad chase. The Crosbys said Andrew drove away at nine-thirty last evening."

"Do you think he was planning to travel through the night then?" Harriet asked.

He seemed about to make some comment but when she turned and gazed up at him, he only said, "I imagine he'd try and put as many miles as possible between them and any pursuers. He has no idea, of course, that we are so close behind. No, for he believes the only one chasing them can be Webster. And I imagine he thought it would take you quite a while to summon him and decide what to do. Surely he does not know I was anywhere close by."

"If he did, no doubt he'd be attempting to swim the North Sea by now," she remarked.

He did not reply for a long time and she wondered if

she had offended him. "That is very possible," he said at
last. "He knows me for a hard taskmaster. His mother
died when he was nine, and although she coddled him, I
have not done so since. I wanted him to grow to be a
strong man, a son I would be proud of."

As he shook his head, his mouth compressed, she
reached out and touched his arm for a fleeting moment.
"And I am sure you will be one day, m'lord," she said,
her voice soft. "You will not hold this fall from grace
against him forever."

"You are so forgiving, madam?" he asked, incredulous. "When it is your daughter's name that will be be-
smirched?"

"I hold Lark just as responsible as the viscount for
what has happened," Harriet said evenly. "Perhaps even
more so. You said once she was ten years older than
your son in many ways, and although I did not understand what you meant at the time, I do now. She could
have handled this situation better, but she did not do so.
And I do not forget she lied to me just as Byrn lied to
you. I could weep, remembering that. Lark and I have
been like sisters. Never would I have supposed she
would deliberately mislead me. But still, as disappointed
as knowing she did makes me, I will still forgive her in
the end. She is my daughter, my only child. I suspect
you will find it in your heart to forgive Byrn as well.
Eventually."

They were approaching a village and he did not reply
as he slowed the team and maneuvered past carts and
drays, evaded pedestrians, even a squawking hen crossing the road. She wondered if the business of weaving
their way through the village had not been a welcome relief to him, for it prevented him from having to comment
on her remarks.

Once clear, they raced on through the golden September morning. It was a lovely day, the sun warm but not
oppressive. If she had not been on a chase, Harriet
would have enjoyed herself. The earl asked occasionally
if she would care to stop, but she always urged him to go

on. At last, in the bustling market town of Bury St. Edmunds, he pulled into the yard of the largest inn. As an ostler came running to take charge of the team, Morland said, "I know. You want to press on. but I am famished and the team is tired. I would prefer not to change them for job horses any sooner than I have to. So we will rest here and eat, and still make Newmarket, possibly even Soham, by dark. And I want to inquire at the local inns. Our runaways may have been seen earlier."

"Surely they wouldn't be noticed in such a populous town," Harriet protested as he lifted her down. "Wouldn't it be time better spent to inquire in villages? People there seldom miss anything new or out of the ordinary."

As he released her and she nodded her thanks, he said, "We shall do that too, never fear. But we are traveling the most direct route north and the one over the best roads. I expect Andrew has found that out as well." He looked grim as he added, "And I hardly think a very young, very frightened couple in an expensive phaeton, possibly with a maid sitting gooseberry between them would go unnoticed, even here."

He took her arm and led her to the inn where he made arrangements for a private room and ordered a hearty meal for his return. "Get some rest," he ordered as he prepared to leave her. "And don't fret. We are making excellent time."

Harriet tried to do as she was told, but after using the close stool and washing her hands and face, she could not make herself rest on the comfortable sofa the room boasted. Instead she paced up and down, going often to the window to stare out at the busy inn yard and the main street beyond. It was strange, she thought. She had not felt so uneasy when she had been moving at such a rapid clip, but now she was getting edgy and nervous. Was that because she was no longer in motion, drawing closer to Lark with every mile? she wondered.

# Thirteen

It seemed an age before Morland came back although Harriet knew in all fairness, he had not been gone that long. Some inn servants followed him into the room to set the table and place several steaming dishes on it. He did not speak until they had been dismissed.

"They were seen at one of the smaller hostelries at dawn," he told her as she took the seat he indicated. "They stayed only to rest the team and eat, then they were off again."

He began to carve a standing rib roast, putting a slice on her plate and several on his own. "Serve us some of those veal collops if you would be so good, madam, and some salad as well. May I help you to a piece of game pie?"

Harriet was not at all hungry, but she knew if she did not eat, it would annoy him. And there was no telling when she would have the chance again.

"How did they behave?" she asked as she served the salad.

"Andrew told the innkeeper he was escorting his stepsister to their uncle's home in Leicester. A fatal illness he said, and he prayed they would be in time. Your daughter clutched a handkerchief to hide her face and sobbed almost continually. The host said it would break your heart to hear her. You did not mention she was an accomplished actress, madam."

"She does tend to the dramatic, yes," Harriet admitted, wishing it were not so. She could just imagine how Lark had thrown herself into the role of grieving niece, and she wished she had her here right now so she could shake her—hard.

"So is Andrew full of flights and fancies," Morland remarked, stabbing his beef with much more force than necessary. "Lord, would it be too much to ask that *one* of them have a modicum of common sense?"

They ate quietly for a while, then as he buttered a roll, he said, "I almost forgot to tell you. There was no maid with them. What did I say?"

"Well, that proves your son is not as witless as you claimed, m'lord. I wonder what they did with poor Fanny. We certainly did not see her forlorn by the side of the road."

"I don't believe I ever said Byrn was witless. I only said he was an idiot. There is a vast difference," he told her. Harriet could feel the corners of her mouth turning up and she ducked her head lest he see she was about to laugh and take her to task for it.

A rap on the door was followed by the entrance of a dusty, tired-looking Viscount Webster. His face did not brighten when he saw his two old friends at the table together.

"Why, Douglas," Harriet said, rising and going to welcome him, "did you follow us then? You have had a ride of it."

"How did you hear?" Morland asked. Before Webster could answer, he went on, "I suppose you are about to sit down and eat my food again. Was there ever such a cadger. You should be ashamed of yourself."

"I admit I'm hungry. I'll rejoin you presently after I have a wash. And as for cadging your food, Marsh, you could not finish the half by yourself. I merely hope to keep you from wasting it."

When he returned a few minutes later, he looked much refreshed and a great deal less dusty. As he settled down at the table and Harriet began to serve him, he said, "I called on you this morning, Harr—Harriet, as I said I would. Your mother was laboring under a heavy cloud of ill use, and she told me perhaps more than she

intended. I rode to Pembroke House next and persuaded
your groom to tell me your direction, Marsh.

"I gather that Lark has run off, and with Byrn to boot.
What a farce!"

"You may well say so," Morland said morosely as he
stared down into his mug of ale. "How lucky you are
they are not your responsibility."

"Have you had any news of them?" Webster asked as
he tucked into a plate heaped high. As he ate he listened
intently to what they had to say.

"I take it we may assume they are making for
Gretna?" he asked finally.

"Yes, we are sure that's so," Harriet contributed. "Besides going in that direction, there is nowhere else they
could be married except in Scotland."

The viscount reached out and took her hand in both of
his. "You will not find them today, you know," he said
kindly. "I'm sorry, my dear, but that is not possible, not
with the head start they've had."

"I know that," she said, gently withdrawing her hand
and being careful not to look the earl's way.

"I'll come along. I might be able to help," he said
next. "And since I'm on horseback, I can ride other
routes, ask questions more easily."

"You are so good," Harriet said, swallowing her tears
of gratitude for this dear old friend's ready assistance. "I
could not ask, but I am glad you volunteered."

"You could not have expected any different! Don't
you remember how we always helped each other when
we were younger, you and Marsh and I?

"Where are you making for tonight, Marsh?" he
asked, still smiling fondly at Harriet.

"Newmarket, possibly Soham if we make good time."

"May I make a suggestion? It seems to me it would be
better to have a plan, perhaps a route established before
we charge off, willy-nilly. There must be a shop in this
town that sells maps. Let me go out and see if I can find
one."

"Oh, no, there is no time for maps," Harriet protested. "We must be off again as soon as possible."

The earl looked from one to the other. He was frowning now. "Yes, it is true haste is important, but in this instance I believe Douglas is right. It will save time in the long run, and with a plan we may be able to outwit them, even get ahead of them so we can intercept them."

Harriet longed to argue the point, but it was obvious she was outnumbered. And just as when they had been children, she would have to abide by majority rule.

"You will hurry, won't you, Douglas?" she begged as he took a last swallow of ale and wiped his mouth on his napkin.

"I'll be as fast as I can," he promised.

She went to the window and watched him as he left the inn a few minutes later. When he turned left at the gates without any hesitation, she knew he had questioned the innkeeper about a likely shop.

"You are very fond of Douglas, aren't you?" Morland asked from behind her where he still sat at the table cracking nuts. Harriet turned, a question in her eyes. His voice had been quiet—speculative—no more.

"Of course," she said, meeting his glance for a fleeting second. "He is a good man, and a dear one. I do not think it would be possible for anyone to dislike him, do you?"

"No. Are you going to marry him, now you're free to do so?"

"I—I can't imagine why you ask, or why I should answer that," she told him, wishing she were not so flustered.

Morland shrugged, his eyes intent on the walnut he held. As his long fingers cracked it, he said, "I suppose I ask because I am his friend. He has waited for you such a long time, loved you in fact since we were children together. But you knew that, didn't you? And I, well, I've known of his love since then too. I used to be sorry for him, but there's no need now. You are a widow. You can marry any man you please. I only hope you will not hurt him again."

Harriet turned back to the window. There didn't seem to be anything she could say in response. Yes, Douglas had waited for her, and she knew how he loved her. She also knew she could not marry him, but she had no intention of telling Morland that. It was none of his business, and she was under no obligation to satisfy his idle curiosity.

The viscount came back some thirty minutes later. He had a large parcel containing changes of linen since he had come without his bags, and a pair of rolled up maps he said were the cartographers' latest offerings. They covered all of England and Scotland from Land's End to John o' Groats.

To Harriet's relief, the earl did not intend to study them now. "Let us be off," he said. "We'll have plenty of time to formulate a plan tonight at whatever inn enjoys our custom. We are wasting daylight now."

He saw the viscount was about to protest, and he clapped him on the shoulder. "Come now, sir, they must head to Newmarket. Where else can they go? Directly north leads only to The Wash, going west gains them nothing, and south is out of the question. They will continue on this route for now heading north until they are able to turn directly northwest to Scotland, probably in the neighborhood of Market Deeping. It is then we must begin the game of wits."

"Very well, I'll bow to your judgment," the viscount said. As the earl murmured "good of you," Harriet made haste to say, "Shall we see you on the road, sir?"

"I believe I'll try a few byroads. Be sure and order me a room at whatever inn you choose, Marsh. I may well take longer to arrive, but I don't want to leave any stone unturned."

"Have it your own way," Morland said carelessly as he pulled on his driving gloves and settled his top hat on his head. "Shall we, madam?" he asked, holding out his arm.

They caught no glimpse of the runaways the rest of that afternoon, and the few times Morland stopped to inquire, they could get no information about whether they had come this way or not. It was as if they had disappeared after leaving Bury St. Edmunds. Harriet began to worry the two had gone off by another route and the earl had been outsmarted after all.

"Don't frown so. You'll get wrinkles," he said after a sideways glance at her.

"At my age I expect them any day," she said although she tried to smooth her worried expression.

He made a disgusted noise. "Of all the silly remarks I've ever heard you make, that one ranks right up there with the silliest. You are far from old, madam, and wrinkles are well in the future for you. And don't say I can't possibly know that, for I remember your birthday clearly. You will not be thirty-eight until next April seventeenth."

"Fancy you remembering that," Harriet marveled, then looked away when she realized she remembered the date of his birthday, too.

"I was just wondering why we haven't had a word of them since we left Bury St. Edmunds," she said, changing the subject. "I find that very worrisome indeed."

"Contrary to what you may believe, country people do not stand about leaning on stiles with a straw in their mouth watching who passes. They lead very busy lives. It is unreasonable to expect a clear trail, you know, like the crumbs left in the wood in that children's fairy tale. And the crumbs disappeared anyway."

He paused for a moment, and when he spoke again his voice was curiously gentle. "And you must not be disappointed if we do not catch them up soon. In spite of what I said earlier, we may very well have a long, hard search ahead of us."

"I know that. I am prepared for it."

"And even if they have spent day and night together, it does not mean your daughter is ruined, madam. For who is to know? Who to tell? You would not and I am sure you may trust both Douglas's and my discretion. As for Andrew, well, he is going to have a great many other things to think about almost immediately, once I get my hands on him."

"You are too kind. Thank you," she managed to say.

"The only way your daughter could possibly be ruined is if we are not in time to prevent the marriage," he went on. "They are both of them too young to know their own minds, and neither has enough experience or sophistication to make a good choice."

"That is so. But perhaps if they were to continue faithful . . ."

"I would be astounded if that happened. Andrew falls in and out of love with great regularity. Last summer it was one of the dairymaids at Morland, that autumn, his don's daughter at Oxford. Yet at Christmas he rather fancied a second cousin."

"Good heavens, how volatile he is!" Harriet exclaimed, appalled. "I did not know. I supposed his to be a firm commitment, a true love—"

"Like mine?" he interrupted in a harsh voice. "In this case, madam, I am afraid it is not at all 'like father, like son.'"

For a long moment Harriet concentrated on the road ahead. There was no way she could ignore what he had said; she must reply. Still she hesitated until she was sure of her composure.

"M'lord—Morland—can we not forget what happened all those years ago? The past is gone. We can do nothing about it, neither change it nor erase it. But now we are thrown together because of our children and the situation may continue for some time to come. Surely it would be better if we thought no more of the past while we are together. Please?"

The only sound was the horses' hooves as they cantered along. For a moment she thought he did not mean to answer, but at last he said in an even voice, "You are right. I was at fault for mentioning it. Forgive the lapse if you can."

She was so startled she could only nod. Marsh Pembroke had never been one to beg another's pardon. Harriet could only remember two or three instances when he had done so, and each time he had sounded as if the words were choking him.

Thinking wildly of some new subject she might employ, she said, "I have been meaning to ask you to keep a strict account of any moneys spent on the journey so I might reimburse you for my share. I do not have much with me, but I will instruct my banker to send you a draft as soon as we return."

"You will do no such thing," he said sternly. "The expenses are trifling and it is, after all, my son's fault you are put to the bother in the first place. I will take care of the cost—no, no, madam! We will not argue it, if you please."

It was full dark when they reached Soham at last, for the earl insisted on pressing on. Not, Harriet thought as she prepared to get down, that she had been at all loathe to do so. And they had made excellent time, too. Surely the gap between them and the young people ahead had been narrowed after this day's work, for Lark and the viscount had had no sleep for twenty-four hours. They must have stopped early to rest. She put the picture she saw of them in each other's arms firmly away. There was no sense in dwelling on it, for there was nothing she could do.

She had noticed earlier how the earl commanded instant attention and saw he was to do so here as well. It was not that he raised his voice, or made his rank known; still the ostler came running for the team and the innkeeper was quick to bow and send his minions scurrying to ready three rooms and his best private parlor.

"Bring two bottles of burgundy to the parlor, and a tea tray for the lady," Morland ordered. "And when the man we are expecting arrives, bring him to us immediately."

Harriet excused herself to freshen up, and he went to the parlor alone. A servant had just started the fire, and now he bowed himself away. Morland went to stand before it to stare down into the flames just beginning to lick at the logs. He could tell from the smell, it was applewood.

Why, *why* had he said what he had today? he wondered. He had not intended to, indeed, referring to that time so long past had been the farthest thing from his mind. Yet something he had no control over had caused him to blurt it out, reveal the deep hurt that still festered. Could anything be more unfortunate?

He had meant to continue aloof, to make no reference to that time they had known each other. He was not just Marsh Pembroke now, a questionable lad from a questionable family, completely unacceptable as either a husband or a son-in-law. No, he was the Earl of Morland. He need not bend to any man. Or woman, he added silently. Still, just being with her all day so close beside him on the narrow seat, had brought back all kinds of memories. He hoped he could lock those memories away again. The lady who was Mrs. Winthrop-Bates was right. The past was gone. It could not be redeemed. Surely it was best forgot.

Harriet found him there. "No sign of Douglas yet, m'lord?" she asked as she came in and took a seat at the table.

He shook his head, still intent on the fire. She wondered why she suddenly felt so uncomfortable.

Fortunately the innkeeper interrupted, coming in with the burgundy and two glasses. Behind him came his wife bearing a heavily laden tray. Harriet was glad to have something to do, as she set about making the tea. "Could I interest you in a sandwich, m'lord?" she asked. "Perhaps a muffin? They look delicious."

He came and took a seat across from her. As he poured himself a glass of wine, he said, "Perhaps later. Now I must attend to business."

Unrolling one of the maps Douglas had bought, he spread it out on the table, anchoring it with the wine bottles. Harriet came to look at it beside him.

"Here is Soham," he said, pointing to the spot on the map. "Tomorrow we must make our way here, to Ely and Chatteris. From there, hmm, to Peterborough and thence on to Grantham. That looks the quickest way with the best roads. Of course Andrew may try another route, possibly through Sleaford to Lincoln. It is a very good thing we have Douglas with us to help us search—"

"I am delighted to be so appreciated," the viscount said as he came in and threw himself into a chair. "Whew, I'm tired. You must forgive me in all my dirt, Harry."

"Did you discover any trace of them?" she asked eagerly.

He shook his head. "Nary a sign, and I can tell from your glum expression you had no luck either. Well, it's early days yet, my friends, early days."

He took a hearty swallow of the wine the earl had poured for him and sighed in contentment. "Ah, that's more like it! I felt as if I was swallowing dust the last ten miles."

Stretching luxuriously, he smiled at Harriet and the earl as they bent over the map again.

"How like the good old times this is," he said. Not noticing how both his companions looked up, their expressions identically wary, he added, "The three of us deep in an adventure, I mean. Lord, doesn't it make you feel twenty years younger? I do!"

# Fourteen

The romantic elopement Byrn envisioned did not begin smoothly. He was half an hour early to their rendezvous, she half an hour late. Then he discovered she had brought most of her clothes in a large portmanteau and two bandboxes, and she wanted her maid to come with them.

"But, darling," he protested, "don't you remember how I said we must travel light? And there's no room for your maid."

"She is coming," Lark told him. "You cannot imagine I would be so lost to convention as to travel without Fanny!"

Taking her hands in his, he gripped them hard. "Listen, Lark," he began, only to feel her stiffen. He went on more moderately, "Darling, have you forgotten we are to be married in a few days? You don't need Fanny or anyone to chaperone you."

She nodded, but she still looked troubled and he said as he urged her to the phaeton, "We must make haste. Every moment we waste chatting here is a moment lost to us, and one gained by our pursuers. Come!"

"But I can't leave her here to take all the blame! She must come with us at least as far as the next town. And you must give her enough money so she can take a coach home to her family in Ipswich," Lark insisted.

Byrn accepted the inevitable. It was extremely crowded on the perch, and he was not able to spring the team as he had hoped. And it was impossible to talk to

Lark with the maid listening to every word. He admitted he was getting very tired of Fanny.

They left her at the inn in Framsden, but not before a few sharp words had been exchanged, for Lark demanded he engage a room for her, too.

When they set out again at last, he felt positively unencumbered, and when dawn came he was encouraged by the amount of miles he calculated they had traveled.

He pulled up at a small hostelry a short time later. Lark protested it was far too mean and he said he did it to confound their followers. He had discovered Lark had a real dread of his father by now, and whenever she showed signs of balking, he was quick to mention him.

During the night's drive they had discussed who they were going to pretend to be, for they were both sure they might just as well have had GRETNA painted in red on their foreheads, it was so obvious they were eloping. Because of the difference in their hair, they decided it would be better if Lark pretended to be Byrn's stepsister. As for why they were traveling at such an early hour, they concocted the tale of the unfortunate uncle in Leicester on his deathbed.

This story was duly told and embellished by Lark's acting ability, and when they started off after a hearty breakfast and a short rest, Byrn asked her if she often sobbed that way.

She smiled at him, but it was not the glowing smile he knew and he could tell she was nervous. "Not often, only when I am upset about something," she confided. "Oh, dear, why does what we are doing seem so much worse in the daylight?"

"I was just thinking that myself," he admitted. "I suppose it is because we are more exposed and people are sure to see us and relay the information to those who follow. I wish I had a map. I'd like to be able to avoid the tolls."

"Won't that take longer?" she asked, looking over her shoulder for what he was sure was the twentieth time in the last half hour.

"Yes, but it will be much safer and, er, better."

"I don't understand," she argued. "Shouldn't we be making a dash for it? Changing the team as often as we have to?"

Byrn swallowed. "We can't. It would cost a great deal of money, money I confess I do not have. We have to rely on this team, and rest them often."

Lark stared at him. "But what about inns, and meals, and other things? And how are we to get home after? Surely you could send an express to your banker, couldn't you?"

He did not dare look at her as he said, "But I don't have a banker. My father gives me an allowance. I'm afraid I've spent most of this quarter's already." She was ominously silent, and he went on more quickly now, "Well, there was Devil, you remember. He cost me a pretty penny! And I had some debts to take care of, and—"

"You mean to tell me we will be dependent on your *father* after we marry?" she asked, horrified.

"But you must have known that, darling. I'm only nineteen. But I'm sure he can be brought to see I must have a bigger allowance when I'm a married man. For one thing I'll need to rent you lodgings at Oxford, and—"

"Do not say another word. I simply could not bear it," she interrupted, sounding as if she were suffocating.

Byrn opened his mouth, then closed it. At the next crossroads he headed east, hoping to confound any pursuers. The sun was well up now. Surely Lark had been missed, he thought, and the hue and cry begun. He glanced at her and saw she was still frowning, and he sighed to himself.

At noontime he stopped at a roadside inn Lark proclaimed little better than a hedge tavern. He purchased some bread, cheese, cider, and a couple of savory pork pies fresh out of the oven there.

As they drove on, Byrn looked for a likely spot to stop and eat. As he did so, it occurred to him they might do very well if they ate simple fare outdoors every day. And perhaps he could convince Lark to sleep in some deserted barn? If he could find one, that is. That would be grand until it rained, he remembered. Well, he would just have to cross that bridge when he came to it. Still, he wondered this wonderful adventure and the joy of having Lark beside him, not only today, but for all the days to come, could somehow have turned a little sour. Even, dare he admit it, disappointing?

A mile or so farther on, they came to a small empty field bordered by a wood. A brook ran along one side of it and he pulled over.

"I'm going to rest the horses here, Lark," he said as he jumped down and went to their heads. As he busied himself getting them out of the traces, he added, "We could use a rest, too. Lord, I'm tired! I know you must be, too."

As he led the horses to the brook to water them, Lark climbed down from the phaeton. She was stiff and sore, and, yes, as tired as he had said. It would be wonderful to stretch out in the shade and close her eyes. Not that she would be able to sleep, she told herself. Not when she was so upset by the things he had told her.

Still, as he came back to her, a discontented frown marring his handsome young face, she resolved to do better. She was wrong to reproach him for things he could not control. She might have guessed his horrid father would keep him in leading strings financially. But with all the optimism of youth she was sure they would be able to overcome not only that problem, but all the others they would face.

So when Byrn gathered up the packages of food and the stone bottle of cider, she smiled at him and walked close beside him to the spot he chose near the brook.

"This is nice, isn't it?" she asked after they had devoured the picnic. Byrn looked a little startled, and she smiled and added, "I mean, it is a lovely day and we are together. And I'm sure everything will turn out all right for us, aren't you?"

He kissed her eagerly and she kissed him back. Eventually they remembered the cider he had put in the brook to cool. They had to take turns drinking from the mouth of the bottle and Lark spilled some on her gown, but she only laughed. And when Byrn, encouraged by her behavior, mentioned sleeping in a barn, she declared it would be an adventure they would never forget.

"I'll buy some supplies in the next town," he said as he stretched out on the grass and sighed. "Oh, Lark, you have made me so happy!"

But he spoke only to the breeze for she had fallen asleep. For a moment he stared down at her, admiring her soft complexion, that lovely honey-colored hair, and the way her breasts rose and fell with her quiet breathing.

He looked around. The team was contentedly munching grass and there was nobody in sight on the road in either direction. Surely it wouldn't do any harm to have a little nap, he told himself. Just for a few minutes, of course, he promised himself as his eyes closed.

He woke to find Lark shaking him hard, and he was startled at how low in the sky the sun was.

"How could we sleep the afternoon away?" Lark demanded as she shook out her skirts. "Do get up, Drew. Why, even now your father may be getting closer and closer."

He rose hastily and hurried to get the team. "Bring the cider bottle and what is left of the food, Lark," he called over his shoulder.

A few minutes later they were off. The stop had been rash and unplanned, but the rest had done both them and the team good. At the next crossroads, Byrn studied the signpost before he turned west.

He noticed Lark looking over her shoulder again and again, and he said, "There's no need to do that. My father is safely in London, or at worse, Morland, and that is many miles from here. It is your mother and Viscount Webster we have to worry about."

But even though Lark nodded, she admitted she was

loathe to relinquish her vision of the furious earl, his billowing cape and baying hound—that silver-chased pistol he brandished as he thundered down the road in pursuit.

"Do you have a pistol with you, Drew?" she asked, reminded of a thought she had had earlier.

"No," he said. "Why do you ask?"

"I was thinking it might be a very good thing if we had one as a safeguard," she explained. "There are so many bad people about, and neither of us looks at all formidable."

"You need fear nothing when you are under *my* protection," Byrn proclaimed, putting his chin up and looking steadfast.

Lark admitted he struck a noble pose, still she could not help but say slowly, "I suppose."

The doubt in her voice was hardly complimentary, but before Byrn could tax her with it, she laughed and clapped her hands.

"I just had the most marvelous idea, Drew," she said, turning toward him, her eyes shining. "Why don't we sell the team and phaeton and purchase two saddle horses instead? Then you could buy me some breeches and a loose shirt and vest, even a smock, and some sort of large straw country hat I could bundle my hair up under? That way we could ride to the border, and no one would think to mention two young men on horseback when questioned about a man and a maid with a phaeton and pair. Oh, do say we may! It would beyond anything great."

Byrn was taken aback by the suggestion, for under his air of bravado he was very conventional. "Certainly not," he said sternly. "The very idea! And what, pray, are we to do when we reach Gretna? If you think I want to wed someone who looks like a rude hayseed of a boy, you are much mistaken. My word!"

"How stuffy you are," Lark accused him. "Of course I would bring a gown with me in the saddlebag for the ceremony itself. And we could leave the rest of our clothes safe at some respectable inn for our return. Why can't you see what a wonderful plan it is? We would not only make faster time riding cross-country, we would have plenty of money to spend from selling the phaeton. Besides, think what an exciting tale it would make to tell our children."

"I could never confess such a thing to innocent children," he muttered. "It would make us appear depraved."

Lark sighed. She had not realized how proper Drew was. And after all, she had burned all her bridges. She would be ruined if this marriage did not follow hard on the heels of their elopement, ruined beyond redemption if they were caught and separated. Surely a little eccentric behavior was excusable in such a case.

She wondered why Drew had even considered eloping when his attitude now was so weak and conventional. In later years would he become more so, hedging her about and insisting on the strictest propriety? And if he did, would she be able to bear it? For she knew even if she was not the hoyden her Grandmother Fanshaw named her, she had no great opinion of decorum and studied manners.

"Besides, you could hardly ride sidesaddle," she heard Byrn say, and realized he had been speaking for some time. "That would give the game away at once. And if we were discovered, you wouldn't like to be caught in men's breeches. No, no, it is not to be considered!"

Lark slid back to her side of the perch. "I daresay you are right, even though I learned to ride astride as a child," she said.

He heard the disappointment in her voice and he was quick to say, "I do admire you for your courage, you know, my brave girl. But we'll prevail without such a sacrifice, just you wait and see. I shall take care of all."

# Fifteen

At that very moment, the Earl of Morland said to his traveling companion as they were drawing away from the village of Little Ponton, "I don't believe I mentioned the new identities our tiresome children have assumed, did I, madam?"

When Harriet said he had not, he smiled a little grimly. "Andrew has become Sebastian Bassincourt. A *Mister* Bassincourt. One wonders he did not opt for a dukedom, but there you are. His, er, stepsister is Miss Isadora Bassincourt."

"Isadora?" Harriet echoed. "I wonder where she got the idea for that name? There are no Isadoras in the family nor among her friends."

Morland snorted. "I imagine she thought it just the thing to go with that pretentious family name. Bassincourt, my Lord!"

He sounded so disgusted, Harriet had to smile. "Isadora and Sebastian Bassincourt," she said almost to herself and then she began to laugh.

It was not the laugh the Earl of Morland remembered from years ago. No, for that one had been free and girlish. Still, her merriment now was reassuring. He knew how difficult all this must be for her, yet still she had tried to ease the situation for them both, and now had even found the courage to laugh at it.

"Isadora Bassincourt," she repeated when she could speak again. "No doubt her middle name is Elisha or some such thing."

"I myself would prefer Gloriana," he contributed. "Isadora Gloriana has such a ring to it, don't you agree?"

They considered other names, each more pompous than the last, until Harriet had to stop and wipe the tears from her eyes, she had laughed so hard.

Once in control of herself again, she said, "You know, you never did tell me how you happened to appear in the breakfast room at Fanshaw either. It was as if I had conjured you up in my dire need like a genie."

"Nothing so marvelous, madam," he said dryly as he concentrated on giving a lumbering overloaded hay wagon the go-by. "The local curate at Tuddersham, a Mr. Howard Wilson, took the trouble to write to me. He had called at Pembroke House and the caretaker's wife told him Andrew was staying there. But when Andrew rode into the yard as the man was leaving, he introduced himself as Jerome Haviland. You will note how far a cry that is from Bassincourt."

"I am sure that name must be laid to Lark's overactive imagination," Harriet said.

"Mr. Haviland is a friend of Andrew's," the earl went on. "He is on a climbing expedition in the Lake District, an expedition Andrew told me he intended to join.

"The curate said he found this Mr. Haviland's explanation suspect. I quite agreed. According to the letter, the so-called Mr. Haviland had assumed the identity of my son so as not to upset Mr. and Mrs. Crosby, the elderly caretakers. Mr. Wilson said that although he begged my pardon, he did not see why I should take the trouble to be so kind, even if I were, as the young man had assured him, thinking of selling the property. Such kindness, you see, did not, er, conform with what he knew of my character. Dear me. I wonder if I should be offended?

"I still remember the last lines of his letter. 'And I found it singular, m'lord, that a boy of no more than eighteen or nineteen summers would be purchasing property. I assume he must be your son indeed. I pray I have not overstepped my bounds in writing to you.' Etcetera."

"What a mad to-do," Harriet remarked. "How did Viscount Byrn hope to get away with such subterfuge, I wonder?"

"I imagine it was the best he could come up with at the time. And you know, I find I admire his inventiveness. He shows more bottom than I thought he possessed. Of course, hearing of the situation was what brought me to Suffolk immediately, for I remembered you saying you were to spend the rest of the summer with your daughter at your mother's estate. Alas, that I was one day late in arriving."

"You could not have known," Harriet said. "If Douglas had not come, I daresay you would have found your son still in residence."

"Yes, friend Douglas set all in motion quite inadvertently. I wonder how he is faring today, riding so far west of us? I question his route, but there is always a slim possibility."

One of the horses stumbled and he concentrated on it until it steadied. "We must change the team in Peterborough," he said, frowning now. "They have held up remarkably well, but they are tired and will need more than a short stop to recover. I am sorry. Job horses can be unreliable. You may be sure I shall choose the best available. And there is one advantage to them."

"What is that, m'lord?" Harriet asked. She had ridden behind any number of job horses in her lifetime and knew very well all the problems involved. Sometimes unevenly matched, they did not work well in tandem; sometimes they disliked each other and refused; and sometimes they were identically worn and slow. What advantage could there be?

"It would not do for us to get so far ahead of our tiresome Mr. and Miss Bassincourt we run the risk of missing them entirely," the earl explained.

"But even if we reach Gretna before them, and must

wait for them, we can still prevent the marriage," Harriet argued.

"If they come to Gretna at all," he said. "It is closest, of course, but nearby are Canonbie and Rowanburn, all the border towns to the east as far as the North Sea."

Harriet looked worried. "I had not considered that," she said slowly. "I guess I just assumed Gretna to be their destination."

"It probably will be. I think by now Andrew is getting concerned about the time all this is taking."

She looked a question and he went on, "He must know, you understand, I will soon be apprised of the situation and hot in pursuit.

"There is another factor that is sure to weigh with him. He is none too plump in the pocket at the moment, and the longer the journey, the more he runs the risk of running out of blunt."

"But how dreadful!" Harriet exclaimed, picturing her daughter not only hungry, but reduced to staying at the cheapest, dirtiest accommodations in rundown taverns. "Surely it was very ill advised of him to even suggest this elopement if he could not manage it in comfort."

"Do you think he wasted a second considering that?" the earl scoffed. "Of course, he didn't. He only thought of his passion for your daughter and, dare I say it, my inevitable fury when I discovered what he had gone and done."

He paused for a moment, then added almost pensively, "And I imagine he hoped something would occur that would help him. He is often optimistic when there is no reason to be. I can only pray that along with his many other faults, he will outgrow it."

"How can you be certain his purse is slim, m'lord?" Harriet asked, hoping he was wrong for Lark's sake.

"Well, by the middle of June he had to ask for an advance on his quarterly allowance due July first. The Season had become rather more expensive than he had anticipated. Then he acquired that costly saddle horse of Ridgely's, and I am sure he had the usual debts from wagers and cards to settle as well. Of course, his expenses have been negligible while he was rusticating hidden in Suffolk, but still . . . And his next quarter's allowance is not to be paid until the first of October. Yes, I suspect he is in quite a bind right about now."

His mouth twisted wryly. "I wonder if he has considered how awkward it will be to have to come to me later, hat in hand, after the blatant disobedience and disrespect he has shown me. Hmmph! That has not crossed his mind yet, I imagine."

"But he must know you would not cut him off without a penny simply because he married a girl of whom you do not approve," Harriet was quick to point out. She fell silent as soon as she realized what she had said.

"It is more than that, madam. Much more. He lied to me, remember."

They were silent for a while and Harriet closed her eyes to rest them. She was tired. Last evening they had spent considerable time planning today's route and where they would all meet later. Grantham had been chosen and she knew from signposts she had seen, it was still a distance away. And it had already been a long day. Awakened at dawn, she had barely had time to dress and bolt a hasty breakfast before they had been on their way.

"You are well, madam?" she heard him ask, and she nodded.

"I am sorry there will be no time for a rest in Peterborough. You may drink some coffee, however, and wash away the road dust while the team is being changed."

"Thank you," she said with real gratitude. She wished she might tell him he need not worry about her, but somehow she could not.

As they drove on, on an increasingly congested road the nearer they came to Peterborough, Harriet pondered how the earl had changed since their first meeting this past spring. Then he had been haughty and formal and brusque. Now, although he was scarcely free and easy, at

least he was kinder. It must have been difficult for him
to come to her as he had, and admit his son was in love
with her daughter. Very difficult, for of course she was
sure he had never wanted to see her again for the rest of
his life. He had said as much all those years ago, and she
had to believe he still held to that course.

She wondered what would happen when this mad fiasco was over and their children were either returned
to them single, or were married in truth. Would he re-
vert to his formal, haughty manner? But how could he,
after all they had been through together, all that still
lay ahead to be faced? Somehow she was sure he
would be successful in separating his son from Lark.
He was not only a mature man, he was an intelligent
one. His son, by Morland's own admission, was full of
fancies and wild notions, and although he had dis-
played some cleverness—witness the post book, and
seeing Lark right under her mother's nose,—he was no
match for his sire. Harriet only prayed Lark would
come out of the adventure with some shred of reputation left to her.

In this she was wholly dependent on the earl and Douglas Webster. She did not doubt the viscount, and now
she found she trusted Morland as well. He had said he
would keep it all quiet and she believed him.

In Peterborough, at the Swan and Bear inn, the earl
arranged for refreshments and a private room for her before he went off to the stables to inspect the job horses
and make arrangements for the care of his own high-
bred cattle. He had elected not to have them led on to
Derbyshire, for he would be coming this way again to
see Mrs. Winthrop-Bates and hopefully, her spinster
daughter, safe home.

There was nowhere near the selection of teams Morland had hoped for, but eventually he chose a pair of
strengthy-looking beasts the ostler said were good for
ten miles an hour over a long stretch.

Sipping the mug of ale the innkeeper brought out to

him in the yard, the earl stood and watched as the new team was hitched up.

"Oh, my God!" Byrn exclaimed as he drove by and spotted his father there.

"What is it?" Lark demanded, wondering at his agitation as he turned down a narrow alley.

"My father," he said, looking over his shoulder much as Lark was wont to do. "He is here in Peterborough! I saw him in the yard of that inn. I was about to turn in there, too, so I could do the shopping, and I saw him just in time. Can you imagine what it would have been like if we had come right up to him? I pray he did not see us. If he did, we are undone."

Lark paled. "How did he get here so quickly?" she asked. "It is not possible!"

"I have no idea," Byrn muttered as he wove his way along the alley. "Hey, you, out of the way!" he called to a man walking unsteadily from the nearest grog shop.

As the man lurched to one side, Byrn went past.

"I was sure he must still be in town, or at Morland," Byrn said, almost as if he were talking to himself. "There is no way he could have come here so quickly, even if your mother summoned him immediately. He must be on his way to Pembroke House and I escaped just in time. But he never goes there. Has he found out about us? How lucky I saw him. Whew!"

"I don't see anything to crow about," Lark told him as they left the alley for a wider thoroughfare. "What are we to do? Is it possible to avoid him? There are so few routes north. Oh dear, I am afraid for—"

"Be quiet! I must think," Byrn interrupted. Lark was so startled at his brusque order, she obeyed.

"He has no friends in this neighborhood that I know of," Byrn mumbled to himself. "There are those second cousins or whatever somewhere in Leicestershire, but he wouldn't be going to see *them*. We never see them. I must assume he is after us, although I suppose it's possible he's still in the dark and just wandering around. . . ."

"Kindly stop saying such ridiculous things," Lark scolded, stung into speech by such stupid reasoning. "Your father is not at all the type to jaunter casually about the countryside."

"There is that," Byrn admitted.

"Did you see my mother? Viscount Webster?"

"Not that I remember, but I cannot be perfectly sure. You see, I only caught a fleeting glimpse of him, and I turned away quickly lest he notice me."

"It is almost six. He might be staying at that inn and planning an early start tomorrow."

"If only I could be sure he is traveling north. Suppose he knows nothing yet?"

"To be on the safe side, I think we must assume he is searching for us," Lark told him. "It is possible he learned you were at Pembroke House somehow. If he went there, he would know we were both missing. But how can we escape him? Where can we go?"

"First we must get away from here as fast as we can. Then I intend to go directly west before heading north again. I suspect my father will keep to the post roads. They are in the best condition, and he can make better speed. And he is only human after all. We may well escape, for he cannot be everywhere at once."

"No, but how does it help us if he reaches Gretna before us? He has only to wait for us to drive up to catch us. Of course we could go somewhere else to be married, or we could wait him out somewhere. I assume he will not care to linger in Gretna indefinitely. Oh, I forgot. There is that matter of our straitened finances, isn't there?"

Byrn did not answer. It seemed to him Lark was only bent on bringing up problems they might have to face, instead of looking on the bright side of things. If there was one, he thought glumly. Hopefully they could reach the village of Oundle before the shops closed. He still had to purchase those supplies for he was more determined than ever to sleep out whenever they could. And it was not just to save money, either. No, for now he knew how close his father was, he did not dare stay openly in any inn or tavern. Mr. Sebastian Bassincourt and his stepsister Isadora would not confound a man of his father's intellect, not for a minute they wouldn't. He sighed. Could he get Lark to abandon those aliases? Surely plain Mr. Smith and Miss Jane Smith would be less noticeable?

As he drove west, the Earl of Morland was helping Mrs. Winthrop-Bates to her seat in the phaeton and turning north after he left the yard of the inn.

"I wonder where they are now?" Harriet mused, looking about her at the busy streets of Peterborough they were passing through.

"I imagine much closer than we think. To tell the truth, I am surprised we have seen no trace of them."

"Perhaps Douglas will have good news for us," Harriet said. She sighed and he looked at her intently for a second.

"That was a heartfelt sigh, madam," he said. "You are not getting discouraged, I hope."

"No, not exactly. But sometimes it does seem as if they have vanished completely. I wish we had had time to ask for them at the local inns in Peterborough. There might have been someone who remembered them."

"Ah, yes, for who could ever forget the handsome Mr. Bassincourt and his lovely but lachrymose stepsister, Isadora?

"But come, you must not fret. When we get to Market Deeping I'll investigate. And we will not leave quite so early tomorrow, so you may enjoy a good night's rest."

Before Harriet could comment, he became preoccupied with setting the new team to a canter to see what they could do.

# Sixteen

Unfortunately, when Viscount Webster arrived at the inn in Grantham at last, he had no good news to report.

"It's as if they've disappeared from the earth," he complained as the three old friends sat on at the table after dinner, the men drinking port and Harriet studying the map.

"What roads could they be taking?" he demanded of the earl. "You traveled the most direct route, and I ranged widely to the west of that, and there was nothing."

"I can swear they did not pass through Market Deeping for I inquired at every inn and tavern—a number of shops as well," Morland told him.

"How are we to search tomorrow?" Harriet asked the earl. It did not occur to her that both she and the viscount looked to him for their lead, just as they had done when they had been children.

He came and stood behind her to study the map she held. For a moment, he did not speak. Then he leaned over her shoulder and pointed to a spot on the map. "There is Chesterfield. Morland Park lies only a few miles away. I propose we go there to rethink our tactics, as it were."

"But that would delay us and we must not waste time," Harriet protested. "And surely young Byrn would not risk going anywhere near Morland! He cannot be sure you are not there."

"That is true," the earl said as he took his seat again. "More port, Douglas?" he asked as he filled his own glass. When the viscount shook his head, he went on, "Although I imagine he is regretting the fact he cannot. He could get a new team there, money, clothes—everything he needs to travel in comfort. But although he cannot avail himself of Morland's comforts, we can. And we will not be wasting time either, madam. I have men there I can send out searching in every conceivable direction. They will find Byrn and your daughter quicker than ever the three of us could."

"I shall not like the waiting," Harriet remarked.

"We will not merely wait. We will travel on ourselves to Gretna. My men will serve as safeguards our tiresome children do not outwit us by going to some other border village for the wedding service."

"I see," Harriet said and fell silent, frowning slightly as she drew patterns on the white tablecloth with the tip of her knife.

"I shall be able to put you behind my own horses again as well," the earl went on. "I do assure you, madam, the cattle in my stables will give you a more comfortable ride than those worthless animals we employed this afternoon."

"It would be hard for them to do worse," she said, smiling at him as she remembered the awkward team he had wrestled with all the way from Peterborough.

"We leave tomorrow at ten," he decreed, and Harriet rose to say her good nights and leave them.

As the door closed behind her, the earl turned to his friend. "You are very quiet all of a sudden, Douglas," he said. "Is there something amiss?"

"So, you are taking Harry to Morland, are you?" the viscount asked in a composed voice. He did not meet the earl's eye as he went on, "But you could send a message to your agent there, couldn't you? Let him handle the business of setting the men to search? Why go to Morland yourself?"

"Why, I suppose because it is so close and there is the matter of the horses. Once there, I can arrange to have one team sent ahead to wait for us, and change the teams to spare them. But you have some problem with that destination?"

Webster shrugged. "Perhaps I do. But it is not one I intend to discuss."

"I do not understand you, sir."

The viscount gazed at him steadily now, his long pleasant face an enigma. "No, you don't, Marsh," he said. "But take my word for it, you will."

He rose and stretched. "Lord, but I'm stiff. I suppose if we were twenty again I wouldn't feel all this riding so badly. I'm off to bed. I'll ride east tomorrow since you and Harry are going west. And I don't believe I'll make for Morland at all. I'll go north by way of Doncaster and York. We'll meet at Gretna if our paths don't cross on the road before then."

As he went to the door, he said, "Good luck to you." He chuckled softly as if secretly amused by something and added, "In the hunt, that is. I plan an early start. Say good-bye to Harry for me, there's a good fellow. Tell her I shall not fail her if it is at all possible. And tell her I will be waiting for her at Gretna."

He was gone before the earl could comment. Morland frowned as he sat on alone in the private parlor. It was not like Douglas to be cryptic. He had always been so open and easily read from boyhood. And why shouldn't he go to Morland? It was his seat, wasn't it? And he would feel so much better setting his plans in motion personally, rather than relying on written messages. That way there could be no mistakes.

He yawned, wondering what Harriet would think of Morland Park. It was a noble place, begun in the fourteenth century and still full of old-fashioned nooks and crannies and conceits. He had not liked to change it as some of his contemporaries were doing to their family places. No, for to him Morland was perfect. He remembered now how awed he had felt when he first set foot on the grounds and saw it in the distance, its northwest tower rising up above the battlements, the narrow windows in gray-stoned walls overlooking the gently rolling landscape set about with stone fences that wandered in every direction for miles, and the flocks of sheep that looked like so many fluffy moving balls of wool from a distance. But of course he had been awed, awed and humbled, for he had never thought to come into the title. His uncle and three healthy cousins had been before him. It was only by the wildest turn of fate he had become earl. He hoped he had been a good steward. Morland deserved no less. It was unfortunate Andrew was an only son. He was the last of the Pembrokes in the direct line. Remembering the boy's mother, he grimaced. Poor Annie. She had hated being a countess although she had tried her best to be a good one. Alas, it had been to no avail. He shouldn't have married her, and he wouldn't have, except . . .

He pushed back his chair and as he rose, he swallowed the last of the port. No, he would not think of that again. He had made himself a promise years ago, and for the most part, he had been able to keep it. It was only having the still beautiful, still desirable Harriet Winthrop-Bates seated beside him for hours on end that had weakened his resolve. But now, in just a few more days or so, they would catch their runaways and after he had escorted the two ladies back to Suffolk, he would not have to see Mrs. Winthrop-Bates again. Ever. And then, perhaps, he could get on with his life.

He had decided to send Andrew to the West Indies for an extended period of time. There were few if any English girls on St. Kitts as far as he knew, and he would instruct his agent there to keep the boy so busy working on the plantation he would not have time to fall in love with yet another unsuitable female. And perhaps when Andrew was twenty-four or five, he would allow him to return to England. Perhaps.

Harriet was surprised and dismayed for no reason she could name to discover Viscount Webster had left early without saying good-bye. But of course they would meet again in Gretna, she told herself as the earl lifted her to her seat in the phaeton.

It was a gray day that threatened rain. Harriet eyed the dark clouds massing to the northeast and hoped they could avoid a soaking. And remembering Lark, she prayed she was safe and well and would be able to stay dry, too. Where could that unprincipled young man have taken her? she wondered for at least the hundredth time. How were they managing? Was he taking good care of her only daughter? And what, *what* was she to say to Lark when they came face-to-face at last? How to punish her?

She had worried about this a great deal. It was true Lark had been wrong to run away to elope—very wrong. Harriet knew the viscount had to have been most persuasive; obviously the major fault was his. Lark would not think of such a drastic move on her own initiative. Never. But although Byrn was a rascal, Lark was in love with him. Surely that excused a great deal of her behavior, did it not? How could she punish the child for *loving* someone? It was a problem she had yet to resolve.

She refused to consider the possibility they had become lovers by now. No, that could not be. Lark would make him wait till the ring was on her finger. She was not so brazen, so *froward* (no matter what her grandmother might think), to do anything else. At least her mother prayed that was the case.

The new team Morland had had harnessed to the phaeton was an improvement over yesterday's, and the drive was pleasant. The earl stopped any number of times to inquire of a farmer in his field, a housewife in her garden, or at an inn—anywhere there was a crossroad where the two runaways might have been seen. The answer was always the same. No rigs bearing a young couple had passed that way. Only once did a yokel nod at the earl's question, but after only a minute or two, Morland dismissed him. When Harriet asked why, he told her in disgust that the man had been so anxious to please and be rewarded, he would have sworn he had seen the runaways even if he had been told they both had purple hair.

They arrived at Morland Park by midafternoon. The estate was impressive even on an overcast day. Rain began to fall as they went up the long drive past fields of grazing sheep and some woods, to rumble finally over a humpbacked bridge that spanned a wide stream. The gray-stoned mansion came into view moments later. It was set on a slight rise and it was unusual because it was not surrounded by sculpture gardens, shrubberies and fountains, or fronted by a sheet of ornamental water. Instead, the fields continued almost to its walls, although Harriet could see the ditch that was called a ha-ha that kept the sheep from grazing too close.

As the earl pulled up before the front, a footman ran down the steps holding a large black umbrella. Others followed to attend to the baggage. Morland exchanged a few words with them. Harriet was surprised how easy master and servant were with each other.

Once inside, she could see the mansion was very old, medieval in fact, and that little had been done to modernize it. Still, it was a pleasant place once you were past the intimidating entrance chamber, all soaring ceiling and dark woodwork, with suits of armor and old battle flags set against the stone walls.

The earl took her to a salon that was just as old, but it had some comfortable furniture and a good fire burning in the hearth, and the draperies and upholstered pieces glowed with soft greens and golds.

"Forgive me if I leave you to your own devices, madam," Morland said. "I want to assemble my men and explain what must be done. A room is being readied for you and I will order a tea tray. Please ask my housekeeper for anything you need."

"M'lord," Harriet began, and when he paused and waited, his startling blue eyes intent on her face, she felt a little flustered. "I was only going to say there is no need to make a fuss. I am quite content."

She saw a gleam in his eyes and unconsciously, she

braced herself. "Fuss, madam?" he asked politely. "But I am not aware of any 'fuss.' I do assure you the things I mentioned would be done for any guest at the Park."

As he bowed and left her, she felt as if in this, as in so many other contests between them, she had been bested by a master.

The housekeeper came with the footman bearing the tea tray, and after introducing herself as Mrs. Kerr, stayed to recommend one delicacy after another.

"I am that sorry we did not have word of your coming, Mrs. Winthrop-Bates," she said at last. "Then your room would have been ready for you. But perhaps, after tea, you would care for a tour of the mansion? It is unusual. Or would you prefer to rest? The earl thought that might be best. Dinner is not served until seven at Morland Park."

"I should be delighted to have a tour for I am not the least bit tired," Harriet informed her. She had liked Mrs. Kerr on sight. An older woman, stout and immaculate in her black gown and lace collar and cuffs, she had a merry look about her, and from the wrinkles etched on her face, Harriet could see she was more apt to smile than frown.

"Won't you join me for a cup of tea?" she asked. "That way you can tell me something of the Park before we start."

"Now where shall I begin?" Mrs. Kerr said after a sip of tea. "Did you know the Park dates from 1350?"

"As old as that?" Harriet asked, astounded.

"Oh, yes, that is when it was begun, although the building continued periodically for some time. You will see many Flemish tapestries from the sixteenth and seventeenth centuries on the walls, and the oak paneling is outstanding. There is also a magnificent Long Gallery with tall leaded glass windows on three sides. It is often filled with light, although today it will not show to advantage."

She smiled and tipped her head to one side to regard her guest. "There is a legend that at one time in the fif-

teenth century, a daughter of the house, an Alyce Ver-
lain, fled from that room to elope with the lover her father had refused to consider as her husband. The young
man's name was Pembroke and that is how Morland
passed from the Verlains to the Pembrokes, for her father, Sir Harold, had no male issue."

Harriet made a noncommittal murmur as she refilled
her cup. This part of the story of the Park was coming
too close to real life to make her comfortable.

"Mrs. Winthrop-Bates," the housekeeper said as she
put down her cup. "I do not mean to speak out of turn,
but I have been here for a very long time, longer than the
earl himself. I was here when his son was born, and I
watched Drew grow up. All the servants know Drew ran
off with your daughter. I know how hard this must be for
you. You have my sympathy. I just wanted to tell you
Viscount Byrn is surely the best young man in the world
so you may be easy on that head. Of course, what he has
done is wrong."

She shook her head and compressed her lips. "Yes,
there is no denying it is wrong, but he is such a high-
spirited boy. And if he loves your daughter, she will be a
lucky woman, indeed she will. I tell you this in the hope
it might comfort you."

"Thank you. You paint a different picture of the viscount than his father does," Harriet said tartly.

Mrs. Kerr smiled. "Ah, the dear man," she said
fondly. "As if he wasn't that proud of his son. But he
will hide it. You know how men are. And I can tell you
there is no finer master than the earl. He is good and fair,
concerned for everyone's well-being. It was a shame his
countess wasn't . . . ah, but I forget myself. I will say
though she didn't deserve him.

"But I see you have finished. Shall we commence the
tour?" she added as she rose and smoothed her gown.

Harriet was delighted to agree. She hoped there would
be no more references to this paragon of a nobleman she
did not know.

To her relief, Mrs. Kerr said little of either the hope of

the house or his father. Instead she kept up a running commentary as she showed Harriet the drawing rooms, the library, the salons, the famous Long Gallery, and even the Chapel. The walls there were covered with murals, the only light coming from small diamond-mullioned windows set high in arches against the walls. In the nave was a white marble effigy of a young girl. Mrs. Kerr whispered she was an Arabella Pembroke who had died in childhood in 1556. The chapel was simple, but somehow there was an air of lingering reverence to it that Harriet had not found in other more ornate churches.

As the housekeeper took her to her room at last, Harriet admitted she was impressed by Morland Park. But when she was alone, she wondered about the earl Mrs. Kerr had described. He was a Marsh Pembroke she did not know. But of course he must have changed, she told herself. You have not seen him for twenty years, and only consider how you yourself have been altered by time.

She noticed her bags had been unpacked and there was a comforting fire burning in the grate to take away the chill. The rain still beat against the windows but Harriet did not notice or worry about Lark. Instead, she continued to think about the lord of all this magnificence. How had the Marsh she had known adjusted to the place and his new standing? It must have been very difficult for him for she knew he had come into the title almost as soon as he had married when he was only twenty. A year older than his son was now. Was he remembering the disastrous marriage Mrs. Kerr had implied he had made when he had told her of his distaste for any union between his son and her daughter? Surely not! Lark was a gentlewoman, and his wife had been nobody. A farmer's daughter she had heard. Or a barmaid. Something of the sort at any rate.

She went to the windows then and found herself looking down into a center courtyard garden. Here were all the flowers she had missed when they drove up, beds and beds of them; roses and larkspur and phlox. Flowering vines clung to the old stone walls and in the center of the garden, set off by a large section of lawn, was a square pool. There was a bench beside it under a fruit tree. It looked like it would be a delightful spot on a sunny day.

Just before seven, refreshed by a bath and attired in a newly pressed gown, Harriet went down to join the earl. His steward escorted her to a small salon.

The earl was not there and Harriet amused herself by inspecting the portraits of long dead Pembrokes that hung on the walls. Not a one of them looked like Marsh, she noticed.

When he came in, he apologized, but as he took her in to dinner, he told her all was now in train. "The men leave at first light," he said as he seated her to his right at the massive dining room table. "I suggest we wait for better weather."

He raised a finger and the butler advanced to lay a napkin in his master's lap. A footman performed the same office for Harriet. There was no further conversation until the wines had been approved and the soup served.

"I hope it will be fine tomorrow then," Harriet remarked staring into her bowl as if she had never seen such a thing before.

"Drink your soup, madam," the earl ordered. "It is excellent and a far cry from the meals we have endured these past few days."

Hastily, Harriet obeyed. "Morland is truly unique, m'lord," she said. "I have never been in a home so old yet so well kept. It is magnificent."

"Yes, it is a wonderful old place," he agreed. As the butler removed the soup bowls, he added, "But aren't you interested in where my men are to begin their search?"

Harriet stared at him, then looked up to where a footman was setting a clean plate before her.

"There is no need for reticence, madam," Morland told her. "All the servants know what Byrn has done and

who you are. You see, I have never believed in keeping
anything from the other members of the household. They
are Morland, too, and they are concerned. It is only nat-
ural they would be, don't you think?"

"Why, why, yes," Harriet agreed although she was
startled. It seemed an odd conceit. She hoped the young
footman helping her to a piece of Dover sole would not
suddenly remark on the elopement, for if he did she
would not know how to respond.

But the servants gave no indication they heard a single
word of the conversation, and at last Harriet relaxed
enough to comment and make suggestions. To her surprise, she enjoyed their meal together and it was only
later when she prepared to leave the earl to his port that
she realized she had not even thought of Douglas Webster, nor wondered how he was faring on his lonely
quest.

# Seventeen

Instead of allowing Harriet to retire solitary to one of the formal salons, Morland took her to a room she was sure must be his own personal retreat. There were a great many books there but she knew it was not the library for she had seen that impressive room on her tour of the house. No, this room was small and simple. It had a couple of comfortable chairs, a desk littered with papers, a few select landscapes in oil, and a pair of hunting dogs that were sprawled in front of the fireplace. They rose, tails wagging when Morland came in, but they did not bark or jump up on him, and after he had patted them both, they settled down immediately at his quiet order.

"Will you join me in a glass of port, madam?" he asked.

Harriet nodded. For some reason she was nervous and she could not imagine why. She had been in the earl's company almost exclusively for three days now and although she had been self-conscious at times, she had not felt the malaise that affected her now. Was it because she was here with him at Morland, his magnificent personal kingdom? A place where he was undeniably lord and master? Or was it because here he was so different from the young Marsh Pembroke who had called a neglected estate home?

She bent to pat the dog nearest her feet to recover her poise and she did not look up until she sensed the earl before her with her glass of port.

"Is it still raining?" she asked for want of anything else to say.

"Lightly. We may well be able to drive on tomorrow. But even if we cannot, you may be easy, madam. My men will find our runaways, and when they do, they will bring them here."

"You are so sure of that?" Harriet asked. "But why would your son obey a servant?"

"Because he is my son and he knows well any servant from Morland is my emissary. He will not question their authority."

"I wonder if you can be right in this instance," she argued. At his dark look, she added, "There is Lark to consider. Might she not convince him to disregard any of your orders? After all, she is aware you do not want her to marry Byrn. I am sure she also knows only too well that if she does not marry him now, she is ruined indeed. And remember, he did abandon his favorite horse for her sake. I think it would be wise to assume she has, er, powers of persuasion a mere father cannot hope to challenge."

He did not speak for a moment but merely looked into the flames rising from the wood burning steadily in the hearth. "Yes, of course she must have such powers," he agreed. "For only consider how she seduced Andrew."

Angered, Harriet said quickly, "No, you have that backwards, m'lord! If there was any seduction practiced, it must be laid to your son's door."

To her surprise, he did not argue with her. Instead he shrugged. "We are not likely to learn the truth of who is most at fault until we catch them up. Since that is the case, may I suggest we do not waste time assigning blame? Except to agree they are both of them willful, shortsighted, and maddening?"

Well, he has certainly changed, Harriet thought. Twenty years ago had he ever been so conciliatory? Not Marsh Pembroke! No, then he would have waded into the fray with un unholy light in his blue eyes as he argued, cajoled, mocked her reasoning, determined to force her to agree with his assessment of the situation.

As Harriet looked around the pleasant room, a line

drawing of the head of a young girl in profile caught her eye. She went to lean on his desk to study it.

"I see you have a Copley," she remarked. "I am not familiar with his work, but how impressive it is. Just a few pencil strokes and he has brought her to life."

"Yes. It's one of his earlier sketches, no doubt one of a series drawn as preparation for an oil portrait. I found it in a little shop in London and a bargain it was, too. He never did achieve the fame here he had in the States."

Harriet turned again to study the drawing and as she came back to her seat, she wondered why he looked so preoccupied suddenly.

"Do you have the map handy we have been using in our search, m'lord?" she asked.

"Of course," he said as he went to rummage through the papers on his desk. "Ah, here it is. May I ask why you want to see it, madam?"

She thought his voice as cold and stiff as it had been when he had first come to see her in town, but she ignored it to say, "Didn't you tell me Byrn was supposed to have gone on a climbing expedition in the Lake District this August and September?"

When he nodded, she went on, "Then perhaps the reason we never found any trace of him and Lark after Bury St. Edmunds was because he headed in that direction immediately, hoping to meet his friends there."

"But of course. He could borrow the money he needed from them," Morland said, leaning forward. "How clever of you to think of it, madam, and how stupid of me not to. And that location is only a day's travel from Gretna, almost on the way. It will be easy for us to go there and search for them."

As he bent over the map, Harriet joined him. "See there, the town of Kendall," he said pointing to it. "It can be reached easily from here by turnpike. And from Kendall we travel west. There is a problem though. There are sixteen lakes and innumerable peaks in that part of England, and do you know, I don't recall which village young Haviland named as a base. Was it Ambleside? Conniston? I imagine most youngsters would want to climb the Old Man of Conniston, but there are many others."

He looked at her then but Harriet knew he was not seeing her. "But would Andrew take the time to search for them?" he mused. "Surely any delay makes the game more dangerous for him. And he cannot know for sure where his friends are. The Lake District is a large, wild area and the passes can be treacherous in wet weather."

Harriet said nothing for he seemed to have forgotten her completely.

"Still," he went on, "I can but try. I might be lucky enough to come upon them by chance. But I don't think it wise to waste much time there. No. I'll have a word with Goodwell; tell him to alert the men going in that direction to Andrew's possible interest in it."

He rang the bell and Harriet said, "If you will excuse me, m'lord? I find I am tired and I would go to bed without waiting for the tea tray."

He whirled to stare at her and she saw a flush on his lean cheekbones. "Your pardon, madam," he said, bowing a little. "I have not been very polite, have I, ignoring you as I did? I must beg you to excuse a certain absent-minded state I succumb to occasionally."

Harriet smiled as she curtsied. "There is no need to apologize, sir. Any state that restores my daughter to me would not only be forgiven but welcome. I give you a good night."

Mr. Goodwell, the earl's agent, was summoned and duly informed of the new plans, and he hurried away to tell the searchers. After he left, Morland folded the map carefully and put it aside to turn and study the line drawing he had kept for so many years next to his desk. To think he had not even realized he had been admiring her profile all this time, he thought, shaking his head in wonder he had been so unperceptive. Why, tonight, when he had looked up and seen her studying it, it had been as if John Copley's sitter had suddenly appeared, glowing with life and color. And he must have been drawn to it because it looked so much like he remembered her. He grimaced. And he had been so sure he had put her behind him and locked the door on all his memories. What a fool he was!

And that of course was why he had brought her to Morland, so he could show her how high he had risen, the almost feudal empire he commanded. He had liked having her in his house, sitting near him at the table, then here in his private retreat. Even now he was enjoying the feeling he had knowing she was going to bed in that sumptuous room above him. At the time he had given the order to the unperturbable Mrs. Kerr, he had thought he did it only to impress her. He knew better now. He had done it because he wanted her there. Not the poor ignorant country girl he had attempted to install in her place to help him forget her, but his own Harry.

But what did all this newfound knowledge do for him? Nothing had changed. Nothing at all. It was too late for them. And Harriet Winthrop-Bates was not for him now any more than she had ever been.

Contrary to her mother's hopes, Lark had not been able to stay dry that day. The viscount's phaeton had a very inadequate hood, and moisture seeped in and around it until she was thoroughly damp. And the frequent stops to rest the horses, the hours of jolting she had to endure after a night spent in the open did nothing for her disposition or her peace of mind.

Leaving Peterborough, and hopefully, the earl far behind, they had traveled in tense silence to Oundle where Byrn was fortunate enough to find a shop still open. He bought two blankets, a cup, and a knife, and then, thinking the old lady who waited on him was looking at him suspiciously, he had bolted from the village quite forgetting he had not bought anything for their supper.

Several miles from the village, he had found a deserted shed a little distance from the road, and relieved, had pulled over for the night. As he watered and hobbled the horses, Lark inspected their quarters with a disdain-

ful eye. The shed smelled peculiar to her, and the straw
in it was old and musty. And there was very little bread
and cheese left for supper. By the time she was wrapped
in her blanket, trying to avoid all contact with the straw,
any romance that might have been associated with an
elopement was long gone. She spent a wretched night,
too. Not only was the straw lumpy and the dirt floor
hard, there were mysterious rustlings all around her
which she prayed were mice; she was afraid of rats. And
as she lay there sleepless, she discovered yet another
fault in her lover—Drew snored. And no matter how he
insisted the following morning he had never snored in
his life, she knew what she had heard. It had kept her
awake all night hadn't it? How could she be mistaken?

Climbing to her seat in the phaeton after some hot
words of accusation and denial, Lark wondered how she
was to bear it the rest of her life. At least she did until
she remembered married people often had separate bedchambers. She did not wonder at it, she thought as she
bundled her untidy hair up under her bonnet and tried to
ignore how her stomach was rumbling with hunger.

Byrn was as hungry as she was, and he stopped in the
village of Slawson an hour later to buy provisions. He
was aware neither he nor Lark were very presentable, although he had done his best to brush the straw from his
clothes and straighten his limp cravat. But he had not
tried to shave in the cold water of the brook he had discovered, and he thought Lark looked just as slovenly and
unkempt. He had to wonder what girls were ever taught.
Of course he didn't expect them to have any education
or practical knowledge, but was it too much to ask they
at least be instructed on how to take care of themselves
instead of having to depend on a maid?

Later, feeling better after a quick meal of sausage,
more cheese, and some muffins, they continued on their
way. But late that afternoon, when by Byrn's calcula-
tions they still had a way to go, it had begun to rain.
Lark commenced complaining at the same time. She was
cold, she ached, she was getting wet, she wanted a hot

cup of tea, and on and on and on! Finally, lest he rip up
at her, Byrn promised they would spend the night at an
inn. That quieted her and she subsided on her side of the
perch to fall into a brooding melancholy.

The inn Byrn chose was on the outskirts of a small
village a few miles south of Stoke-on-Trent. It was a
rundown place but he didn't care for that, intent as he
was on saving money. He could tell Lark thought it
dreadfully shabby by the way she sniffed as he lifted her
down, but he ignored her. He seemed to have heard a
great deal of sniffing today and he was tired of it. He
was doing his best, wasn't he? At least she might show
some appreciation.

He asked for two private bedchambers and a private
parlor as well, and ordered the suspicious innkeeper to
send up some hot water immediately. And once again he
related the tale of the dying uncle who at this telling had
removed to Preston and whose fault it was they had set
off so precipitately they had not had time to make themselves presentable.

His host merely shrugged and bellowed an order to his
buxom daughter.

An hour later, washed, changed, combed, and shaved,
he and Lark sat down to a meal of stew, biscuits, and ale.
It was not very good, but it was hearty and filling and
they devoured it. The innkeeper's daughter served them,
and Lark noticed how she smiled at Drew, even brushed
against him when she gave him his plate and bent over
so he could not help but see down the front of her gown.

When at last he dismissed her, Lark decided she
would say nothing about it. They had more than enough
to worry about and the maid meant nothing. Besides,
Drew was so handsome now he was cleaned up, she
could hardly blame the girl.

For a while they sat at the table talking about their
journey and wondering where the earl might be. Byrn
was sure they had outwitted him, and although he did
not mention it to Lark, he was relieved he had somehow
managed to travel so close to Morland and yet escape

detection. It had been his foremost concern, since for part of the day he had been only twenty miles south of where he was well known. But fate had smiled on him and he was beginning to think they might well win through. Looking across the table at a blushing Lark, he felt again his love for her. Of course it was difficult for her, a gently bred girl. He must be more patient with her, and he would be, he promised himself.

They parted at her door with a tender kiss, and Lark's cheeks flamed when he reminded her that in only a few more nights, they would not have to do so ever again.

Her bed was not very comfortable, but compared to musty straw and a dirt floor, it seemed heavenly to Lark and she was soon asleep.

She woke at dawn and for a while snuggled under the covers to consider her situation. She told herself she still loved Drew, but there was no denying there had been times since they had run away, when she would have given anything to be safely back with her mother in Suffolk. But even if such a thing were possible, she could not consider it. She had, effectively, eliminated all the possible ways of retreat. Now she must marry. It was a sobering thought.

At last, hearing voices in the yard beneath her window and heavy footsteps thundering down the stairs, she rose and rang for water. The buxom maid brought her a pitcher. She seemed inclined to linger and chat, but Lark dismissed her abruptly. Finally dressed and with her portmanteau repacked, Lark had nothing to do but wait for Drew to come for her. She considered going down to the private room they had shared the evening before, but she remembered just in time Drew had told her they could not afford to engage it for breakfast.

Still Drew did not come and she grew impatient. Surely she had been waiting for over an hour, she told herself. She would have to go to him.

As she left her room, she realized she had no idea where his room was located and she stared appalled at all the doors that opened onto the hall.

It was then she heard a muffled snore and she recognized it immediately. Going to his door, she knocked hard. Nothing happened. Indeed, and to her indignation, the snoring did not even check. She looked up and down the dingy hall, wondering what she was to do. She knew she could not linger here. Heaven only knew what unsavory types might be staying in such a ghastly place, and she did not care to run the risk of having to converse with one of them. Taking a deep breath she tried the doorknob. To her relief, it turned easily and she slipped inside.

The curtains were still drawn across the windows, but in the light that came through the rips and worn spots in them, she could see Drew stretched out on his back in bed, his dark curls disarranged and the beginnings of another beard already shadowing his jawline. And he was snoring: great rolling rumbling snores that seemed to Lark to threaten to break the windows, they were so resonant.

Annoyed, she went to the bed. Hadn't Drew said more than once last night they must make an early start? Hadn't he insisted they had to cover many miles today? Yet he lay in bed still, fast asleep, while she had been waiting about for him, dressed and packed and ready.

"Drew," she said, bending close to his ear. "Wake up, Drew!"

The snores stopped abruptly in a gargle, but before she could congratulate herself, they commenced again even louder.

Grabbing his shoulders, she shook him as hard as she could. "Wake up, I said," she ordered, afraid to shout lest someone hear her. "Oh, do wake up!"

He gave no response except to free himself and roll on his side away from her. As she considered what else she could do, Lark heard a knock at the door. Startled, she looked around for some place to hide. She realized she couldn't get under the bed in time even if she wished to get dust all over her clothes, and there was no screen around the chamber pot and basin. There was however a large chest against the wall and she fled to it, crouching down close to the side farthest from the door.

As that door opened slowly, she was sure she must be seen, but the buxom maid who entered had eyes only for the gentleman snoring away in the bed.

"Aye, lad, that's a mighty snore ye got," she giggled as she edged closer. "Can it be ye got sump'n else jest as mighty?"

Lark dared to peek around the chest. To her horror and indignation, she saw the maid shuffle out of her slippers, drop her gown, pull her shift over her head, and climb into the bed as naked as the day she had been born. Well! Lark thought. Well, I never!

"Come on now, laddie," she heard her say, and unable not to look now, she saw the maid stroking Drew, cuddling close to his back as she did so. And, Lark noticed, his snores had stopped. "It won't cost ye sixpence, it won't neither, ducky, 'cause I took a fancy ter ye, I did. Come on then, wake up, do."

Suddenly Drew rolled over and put his arms around the girl to pull her close. "Mmm, darling," he mumbled. "Darling Lark."

For the eavesdropper, this was the last straw. To even think her intended could imagine she would do such a thing as creep into his bed was horrible enough. But to call that great lump of a girl with those huge breasts and broad hips by her name when she had always prided herself on her dainty figure was more than she could bear in silence.

Standing up, she marched up to the bed, grabbed the covers, and pulled, hard. As the cold air rushed over him, Byrn awoke to find his arms around an unknown female and his betrothed standing over them with fire in her eyes. For one moment he was sure he was having a terrible dream; it was worse when he realized he was not.

"Get up!" Lark hissed at the maid. "And get out of here, you—you hussy!"

"Jasus an' 'is saints!" the maid exclaimed, her mouth hanging open in shock.

Lark refused to look at Drew. She had seen enough to know he was wearing a shirt, for which she told herself she was extremely grateful.

"Yer his sister, ain't ye?" the maid asked, recovering her presence of mind but still not moving. "Wot's it ter ye who 'e tumbles then?"

"I—said—get—out—of—that—bed!" Lark ordered from between gritted teeth. When the maid still made no move to obey, she strode to the hearth and picked up the poker. Brandishing it, she approached the bed again.

When she saw the poker, the maid pushed an apparently paralyzed viscount away and climbed out of bed. As she threw on her shift and gown, she mumbled under her breath. Lark did not take her eyes from her until she shuffled to the door, her slippers half off and half on.

Once safely there, the maid turned back to the bed. "Sorry about that, my fine lad," she said with a wink at Drew. "Bet we could o' had a time o' it, if that skinny bit o' a sister o' yers hadn't barged in like she did. Ha! Prolly fancies ye herself, she does."

"Get out!" Lark screamed, beyond caring who heard her now as she raced for the door, poker raised. The maid whisked herself around it and slammed it shut. There was nothing to be heard then but the sound of her footsteps clattering down the stairs.

# *Eighteen*

Lark's hand was shaking as she leaned the poker against the wall. Without turning around, she said, "I am ready to leave. I'll wait for you in the yard."

"Lark, don't go," Byrn said, and she heard the bed creak as he prepared to climb out of it. "Please, darling. You can't think I wanted that girl! Let's talk this over. . . ."

She waited to hear no more. Head held high, she left the room quickly, slamming the door behind her just as the maid had done. She felt like crying, but she knew she could not do that. Instead, she forced herself to think only of what must be done before they could leave this terrible establishment behind. She must of course fetch her portmanteau, take it to the yard, and order the ostler to hitch up the team. As she struggled down the steep stairs with her bag, she prayed Byrn would hurry. She had no desire to see the maid again, to have to watch her sly smiles.

Again it seemed an endless time before Byrn appeared in the doorway. He had his own bag in one hand and he was munching a large sweet roll with the other. Lark stiffened. She knew very well how he had come by *that*! Not waiting for him to help her, she scrambled to the perch and sat there staring straight ahead as he tipped the ostler and climbed up beside her.

*Don't you say a word to me, not a single word, you horrid man,* she thought as he maneuvered the team through the gates and headed northwest again. Then she wondered why she was so disappointed when he did not.

"Would you like some of this bun?" he asked some time later when they had reached the open road. "I saved you half."

Lark sniffed, sure she'd rather starve.

"I don't see why you're so angry," he said, taking a huge bite of the rejected bun. "I was fast asleep. I didn't know she'd come to my room, or climbed into my bed. You must know I did nothing to encourage her for we were together all last evening. Did I say anything to her? Even smile at her? How can I be to blame?"

To Lark he sounded not only self-righteous but petulant and she vowed not to reply. If he did not know what he had done to offend her, she would not tell him. And it had nothing to do with the maid's trying to seduce him. That had been shameful, yes, but in thinking it over she knew it had not been his fault. But to call her Lark! She stiffened again just thinking of it. She would never forget it. She doubted she could ever forgive him.

On through the bright September morning they drove, passing villages and small towns until they reached Wilmslow. Every time Byrn stopped to rest the horses, Lark climbed down and walked away from him, and not once did she say a word.

Byrn pleaded with her several times, but finally he took refuge in a sullen silence. There was nothing more he could say. Nothing he could do. He did not know why Lark was carrying on so. Surely she knew he had not asked the maid to visit him. If he had, wouldn't he have made sure the door was locked?

It was then he remembered the door had not had one; how hard it had been getting to sleep when he was worried about thieves coming in to rob him, even murder him. No doubt that was why he had been sleeping so soundly this morning, and why he was still so tired. His eyelids felt grainy and he could not stop yawning, but he knew he had no chance for any more rest, not until nightfall anyway.

From Wilmslow they traveled on to Warrington and Wigan, where Byrn stopped to purchase a bottle of wine and some food for their dinner. He even bought a fruit tart for Lark, hoping it might sweeten her mood. To his dismay she ate it and still would not talk to him.

He had driven a way out of town, only pulling up when he saw a pretty wood. But the only one to speak to him was a little wren, and it seemed more interested in the crumbs of their repast than in him. Lark sat with her back half turned to him in stony silence.

As they prepared to leave, Byrn decided he had had quite enough. Indeed, he was angry now, as angry as she was.

As she went to get into the carriage, he said in a tight voice, "There is no sense in doing that, Miss Winthrop-Bates. We are not going anywhere until we have this out."

She looked at him for the first time since they had left the inn, and what she saw on his face made her pause. He looked stubborn and determined, and somehow she was sure he meant exactly what he said. He even reminded her of his father the earl for a fleeting second, and she did not like that at all.

When she still said nothing, Byrn folded his arms across his chest, and leaning against the side of the carriage, he went on, "I have tried to explain my side of things, and you have refused to talk to me. And this is the girl I am supposed to marry in a day or so? What a pleasant prospect for me! But perhaps you would rather I take you back? Not marry you at all? If so, you must tell me."

"You know I can't go back, not now," Lark said, stung into speech. "I am ruined, *ruined,* if I do not marry, and it is not very kind of you to remind me of that."

Then her isolation here in a strange place, and her dependence on him, as well as the unhappiness she was experiencing, overwhelmed her and she burst into tears. Her heartfelt sobs made Byrn quick to abandon his nonchalant pose to take her in his arms.

Wisely, he let her cry, just holding her close and rocking her a little without saying a word. And he did not

speak until at last she grew quieter. Taking out his handkerchief, he wiped her eyes and ordered her to blow her
nose. Only then did he say, "Now tell me. What is
wrong?"

"I can't," she whispered. "It is too dreadful."

Although his brows rose, he persisted. "But you must
tell me, Lark. We cannot go on like this, and you know
it."

She gulped, and all the hurt poured out in half-
completed sentences as she told him how he had called
the maid Lark in his sleep.

"I never thought I could ever be so humiliated," she
finished, sobbing again. "To hear you say my name
when you were cuddling that great common girl—ooh!
Look at me! Do I look at all like her? Well, do I?"

"Of—of course you don't," Byrn stammered as she
backed away and glared at him, hands on her slim hips.
"But, Lark, I was *asleep*. I didn't know who it was."

Feverishly he thought for a moment and inspiration
struck. "And I was dreaming of you, my sweet," he
added. "That is why I said your name. It was a wonderful dream, too. We were married and together in a great
soft bed with lavender scented sheets and fluffy pillows
and—no, no, you must not blush! Men do think of things
like that, you know."

"It appears to me that's all you do think of," she complained, but he could see his tale of the fictitious dream
had been a stroke of sheer genius, for she was smiling
now.

She was also scratching her arm, and he realized she
had done that a lot all morning, yes, and her leg as well.
And then he had to scratch his chest.

"Why are you doing that?" she asked.

"For the same reason you are, I guess," he said as he
took her back in his arms and kissed her cheek. "I think
we were both visited last night by something a lot
smaller than the innkeeper's daughter."

"Whatever can you mean?" she asked, looking puzzled.

"Bedbugs, my dear," he said.

"Oh, no," Lark moaned pulling away to inspect her arm, horror written on her face. "How can I be married covered with bedbug bites? I won't! I won't!"

"If we don't get going, you won't have to worry about a wedding," Byrn told her as he hustled her to the carriage. "Up you go, lady," he added lifting her to the perch. "The bites won't last forever, and don't worry, I'll kiss 'em better, just you wait and see."

Remembering one she had been dying to scratch all morning, Lark blushed. But she was happy now in spite of the insect bites. Besides, she might have expected something of the sort in that ghastly inn. But somehow, some way, they must get more money so they could avoid all such places in the future. But how?

Perhaps Drew had something with him he could sell, she wondered. A fancy waistcoat for instance, or maybe a fob or a watch. And although she could not bear to part with her Grandmother Winthrop-Bates's pearl necklet, she could certainly sell her ecru muslin gown. It had never become her, and she could not ask Drew to make all the sacrifices.

She was wondering when they would reach the next sizable town so they could sell their things when suddenly she had a brilliant idea, and in her delight, she bounced up and down on the perch.

"What have you thought of now, minx?" the viscount asked looking sideways. "Your eyes sparkle like sun on a new snowfall."

"Oh, pray do not mention snow," she admonished him. "Haven't we had enough to worry about without that?"

"Well, it is only September, and although I am sure there has been snow this far north in that month before, somehow I do not think from the weather we have been having that—"

"Oh, hush, hush," Lark said, cutting off this prosy discourse. "I have just had the most marvelous thought! Remember your friends who are climbing in the Lake

District now? We cannot be far from that part of the country and it is on the way to Gretna, isn't it? Why don't we go and find them? Surely they could lend you enough money so we may be comfortable."

Byrn's hands dropped and the team began to canter before he slowed them to a trot again. "My word, why didn't I think of that? Have my wits gone begging?" he asked himself. "Of course. Jerome will surely have the blunt. Or if he has lost in play to Reggie or Will, they can lend it to me. Let me see, now. Yes, I'm almost positive they intended to stay at an inn at Keswick near Derwent Water. It is only early afternoon. We should be able to make Keswick by dark if there are no delays."

"There will be none," Lark told him, looking militant. "We have had quite enough bad luck this journey. I refuse to consider there might be more. It would not be fair at all."

Byrn did not shake his head at this typical feminine method of handling problems for he hoped she was right. How glorious it would be to stay in an excellent hostelry, eat a well-cooked ample meal, order a good bottle of wine, even get a change of team. As they continued north, he firmly put from his mind what he would do if they reached Keswick and Haviland was not there. Like Lark, he was determined to hold bad luck at bay by sheer will.

It was almost full dark before a tired couple and an even wearier team of horses arrived at Keswick and began to ask for Mr. Haviland at the local inns and smaller homes as well that took in boarders. Neither he nor his party were anywhere to be found; indeed, it appeared he had never been in Keswick at all. Lark was not only tired now, she was hungry from the unaccustomed exercise of walking up the steeper hills to spare the team all afternoon, and she had a blister on one of her heels. At the last cottage they tried, she did not even get down but sat slouched over on the perch, barely heeding Byrn who was questioning the woman who had come to the door. She did not think she had ever been so depressed.

"Come on, Lark," Byrn said as he came back to lift her down. "We can stay here tonight. The woman who keeps the house feels sorry for you. She'll give us supper and clean beds, too."

As they walked to the open door where warm candle-light welcomed them in, a boy led the tired team to the barn.

Miss Gilly, their hostess, was a middle-aged woman, tall and lanky and homely. As she served them soup and sliced some bread and mutton, she kept up a running conversation. Going to Gretna, were they? No, no, they must not bother to deny it! It was plain to see that had to be their destination. No, no, there was no need to tell her any more. What she didn't know, she could not reveal, wasn't that so?

She urged them to have another slice of bread and butter and some of her honey in their tea as she sat down at the table with them. "Aye," she said, winking at Byrn, "your lady has a lovely face and I admit I like a good romance, I do. Only way I'll ever be likely to get next and nigh to one with this face on me," she added without any rancor.

When Byrn began to assure her there was nothing wrong with her face, she waved his protests away. "Oh, aye, lad, you may have been able to sweet talk your lady into running away with you, but I cut my eyeteeth years ago, and I know what's what. Tell me, why were you bothering to look for your friend? Why weren't you racing for the border? Isn't someone after you?"

Byrn only blushed and nodded, but the food and hot tea had caused Lark to regain her spirits and she said, "We need money. We hoped he would lend us some."

"Why, I am sure I am sorry to hear it," Miss Gilly said, patting Lark's hand. "But let me tell you a story, if I may. I've lived here alone ever since my parents died, taking in boarders every summer. I've always dreamed of seeing a couple of lovers heading for Gretna—maybe even being able to help them, but none ever came till you, tonight.

"Let me give you the money you need, and later, your young man here can repay me. I trust him, you see, and it will be something nice for me to remember, the night I helped two young people on their way to Gretna.

"And maybe, just maybe, if you don't despise it, you could name a daughter of yours Phyllis, for me. I should like to think of a dear little girl, as pretty as her mother, bearing my name."

Lark was quick to say she thought Phyllis a lovely name and she would be happy to oblige. Miss Gilly sighed and pressed her hand in gratitude.

The next morning as they set off again, richer by several guineas and with a basket packed with good food to eat on the way, Byrn complained. "Whyever did you say you would name a daughter Phyllis? I don't even like that name!"

"I would have promised to name one Marmaduke, I was so grateful to her," Lark retorted. "And we may only have sons. Even if we don't we can make Phyllis a middle name.

"Will we really be there today?" she asked next, a little shyly now. "I hope my gown doesn't get too crushed, or too dirty from the road dust," she added as she smoothed it over her knees.

But the gods who had smiled on them and led them to Miss Phyllis Gilly had turned capricious that September morning, for a few miles farther down the road one of the horses went lame. While Byrn inspected its leg, Lark looked up anxiously at the suddenly darkening sky. A cold wind was already beginning to blow from the north and her spirits, which had been so high only moments before, plummeted.

# Nineteen

The earl and Harriet left the Park in good time the morning after their arrival there. Morland told her the men he had sent out to search for their children had been on the road shortly after dawn so their capture was imminent. Harriet agreed with him, but inwardly thought she would keep her own counsel until she had Lark standing before her. The earl did not have an army of men and the border was long. And perhaps Byrn had not gone to the Lake District after all. Who could say?

She was almost sorry she had even mentioned it, for Marsh had admitted he did not know exactly where this Mr. Haviland had written he intended to stay. Might they not be wasting time trying to locate him?

They made good time after they left Morland, but even with the earl's various teams waiting for them at strategic inns for the change, they were not to get beyond the small town of Settle that first day. Harriet was amused and touched when she saw how the earl had arranged for her comfort. One of his own maids was there to wait on her, and the bed was made up with fresh sheets and pillows from Morland. There was even scented soap and soft towels for her use. The dinner served was superb as well. She wondered if he had gone so far as to hustle his chef ahead, sitting on a wagonload of delicacies right after the last dish had been sent up to the dining room the previous evening. She did not ask him, however. He might always travel in this state. After seeing Morland Park she would not be surprised. And he had been reserved today. She had caught him frowning more than once, and wondered at it.

They set off early the next day. Harriet had noticed the mornings were cooler now, and there was often a touch of crispness in the air. Whether that was due to their heading north or the approach of the autumn weather, she did not know.

The earl was silent again, the frown between his brows noticeable. Thinking to divert him, Harriet asked him to tell her more of Byrn.

He looked surprised but he said, "Let me see. I must not malign him in spite of this latest start of his, lest you think him nothing but a worthless blood. Let me say then that he is an ordinary young man with all a young man's failings."

"Come, come, you can do better than that," Harriet protested.

"I believe I told you he was only nine when his mother died. He took that hard. I was careful from then on to be there for him. I tried to guide him, encourage him without coddling him, even challenge him, all in the hope he would be a son I could be proud of. But you know, Harry, no one can make their children into what *they* want. They grow up their own way, bent on their own destiny. Haven't you found that so?"

"Yes, I have," she said, trying not to show how affected she was to hear him forget his formality and call her by her childhood name. "I suspect he is not as mature as you were at his age, though, for you did not have a father's help and guidance to ease your way."

She remembered the derelict upbringing Marsh Pembroke had endured. An absent father who had died young of his excesses, a mother addicted to opium who never seemed to know or care where her son was or what he was doing. Marsh had, in effect, had to bring himself up and in doing so had matured early.

"Turnabout is fair play, ma'am," he remarked. "What of this paragon daughter of yours Andrew loves so desperately?"

"Lark? I think the best way to describe her is to say she is practical but at the same time, impulsive."

"Ah, a typical woman, in fact," he said.

Harriet decided to ignore the challenge she heard so clearly in his voice, to contradict him if she dared. "She loves to dance and ride and go to parties. She is fond of people around her, but she hates needlework and lessons and she can't stand to be preached at. There, I have been honest with you indeed, sir. I should add she is fiercely loyal and thoroughly nice. And until this escapade she has never given me a moment's worry."

There was a long silent pause until she added, "Well, not so many moment's worry, anyway."

They both laughed, and until they reached the gray-stoned town of Kendall spent the time relating incidents in their children's lives. Harriet could tell Mrs. Kerr had been right. Marsh was proud of his son, although he would never admit it, for he called him "the young fool," or "that idiot," more often than not.

At Kendall, Harriet was again escorted to a private room in the best inn while the earl went off to question the townfolk. No one had seen anyone resembling his descriptions and he was frowning in earnest when he rejoined Harriet more than an hour later. The two stood side by side watching as the fresh team the earl had had sent ahead was backed into the traces.

"Do you still think it worthwhile to continue on our present course?" Harriet asked, almost hoping he would say no.

He nodded. "At least as far as Ambleside. It is not necessary to enter the District through Kendall. There are other roads. But if we find no trace of them in that village, I suggest we go on to Gretna without further delay."

The early morning mist had cleared by now and the sun was strong in a brilliant blue sky. In spite of her ever present concern for Lark, Harriet prepared to enjoy herself. She had never seen this part of England before, but she had heard glowing accounts of it. And who had not read Wordsworth's "Descriptive Sketches"? Perhaps they might even be so fortunate as to catch a glimpse of the famous poet on one of his long rambles.

The drive was lovely, each bend in the road revealing some new vista. After they passed through Windermere town, the road led them by the lake, its shimmering water reflecting the sky above it. The scene was so serene it was hard to believe the weather could ever turn vicious here. As they rounded another turn in the winding road, Harriet exclaimed, grasping the earl's arm tightly in her delight.

"Oh, do stop, please," she begged, her eyes intent on the view before her.

Obediently, the earl halted the team. From the road, a field stretched down to the water's edge, where a few sheep grazed peacefully. Beyond the lake itself, the mountains known as the Furness Fells thrust up in quiet grandeur, their peaks hidden in the clouds that had suddenly come to veil them. It was a breathtaking sight; Harriet knew she would never forget it.

She felt a sudden exultation that brought a suspicion of tears to her eyes and made the scene before her dim for a moment. She suspected that exultation came because she was seeing all this with Marsh Pembroke beside her and she did not understand herself at all.

"It is so beautiful," she murmured finally.

"Yes," he agreed, and when she turned to him she saw he was looking at her, not the view. The little pulse in her throat that seemed determined to betray her began to flutter again.

"Shall we go on," she suggested as he continued to gaze at her silently. It was only then she realized she still had hold of his arm and she let it go quickly and shifted slightly to put space between them.

"What a shame it is we did not think to acquire some food and drink in Ambleside. We might have had a picnic here beside the lake," the earl remarked easily.

"We might, if we were not in such a hurry to catch our wayward children," she reminded him.

"Do you know, I am getting very tired of those two. They began by being annoying and they have progressed to being obnoxious. Perhaps I won't banish Andrew to St. Kitts after all. Perhaps I'll send him around the world on a trading vessel. One dealing in hides and fish, I think."

His chatter had given Harriet time to recover her poise, although she could still feel that pulse. "I am sure you will be as glad to see him as I shall be glad to see Lark," she said. "I agree they are exasperating, but after all, they are ours."

"Given to us as partial punishment for our sins?" he asked as he set the team in motion.

There were other vistas to admire but Harriet never suggested they stop again. She was confused, disconcerted, and she could hardly wait for a period of solitude when she might reflect on what had happened to her this morning. Until then, she intended to keep her mind firmly focused on her absent daughter.

The village with the delightful name of Ambleside appeared a short time later. At the head of Windermere Lake, it was a charming place. The mountains here were larger and more rugged than those they had seen earlier and the buildings of the village fit the setting in a way that, although surely unplanned, seemed designed. Harriet thought it a charming spot; she hoped she could see it again someday when she would have the leisure to enjoy it.

Instead of resting at some inn, she asked if she might not stroll around the village. The earl was quick to offer his arm.

"Perhaps you can think of some questions that have not occurred to me, to ask," he said as they set out. "Ah, sir, if I might have a moment of your time?" he asked, tipping his hat to an elderly gentleman walking a very small dog.

The man frowned and seemed about to walk away until Harriet smiled at him. Although she did not look his way, she sensed the earl's amusement.

"We are searching for my son, and, er, his cousin," Morland explained. "We were supposed to meet them here yesterday, but we were delayed. Have you seen them, perhaps? My son is nineteen years old with dark curly hair. She is a blond, not as fair as this lady, however. They were driving a matched team of roans hitched to a black phaeton, the wheels picked out in scarlet."

"I can't say I have, sir," the elderly man told them.

"The young man has blue eyes like his father," Harriet contributed. "We are sure they came through here."

"I advise you to ask Maggie Dunne, ma'am. She doesn't miss a trick, that one. Sits in her window there and watches the world," he told them, pointing to a small cottage nearby. It did not even have a patch of garden, for its door opened directly on the street. As they looked at it, a lace curtain in one of the windows twitched across.

"Thank you," Harriet said with another warm smile. "You have been most helpful, sir, and so kind."

The gentleman swept her a bow, and she told herself she really had not heard his bones—or his corset—creak as he did so. Even his dog seemed astounded by his gallantry, for it gave an incredulous woof.

As they walked to the cottage, Morland said quietly, "How at fault I have been not to have had you with me all along, ma'am. It is obvious you have a talent for obtaining information—er, at least from the stronger sex."

Looking only ahead, Harriet replied, "Then I shall not say a word while you question this Maggie Dunne, m'lord, only observe how well you do with the weaker sex."

They had to wait after they knocked on the cottage door. At last it opened slowly to reveal a tiny little white-haired lady in a wheeled chair, peering up at them and smiling.

"I saw you talking to Fergus Fletcher," she said brightly. "Is there some way I might help you?"

Morland bowed and smiled, and she dimpled. Under

the lace cap she wore on her curls, her blue eyes crinkled
shut in her delight.

"We are looking for my son and his cousin, ma'am,"
the earl explained, and went on to tell her the same tale
he had spun for Mr. Fletcher.

"Oh, dear," the lady said. "Where are my manners?
Please come in. I am Maggie Dunne."

They stepped inside as she backed her chair and rolled
it into a tiny parlor. Harriet curtsied as the earl introduced them both.

"Do be seated," their hostess invited. "I would offer
you a cup of tea, but Jennie has gone to the market. She
is my maid, and a good girl, too, but alas, she never
seems to be about when I need her. And I suspect she
has a young man she meets, it takes her so long to do a
simple errand. Tch, tch! The young think nothing of their
duties these days, do they?"

No matter how the earl might have wanted to agree
with that statement, he held his tongue. "Now about my
son, ma'am," he said, gently returning her to his major
concern. "Is it possible you might have seen him and the
phaeton and his cousin? It would have been within the
last day or so."

She folded her hands in her lap and looked down at
them as she thought. Harriet could almost see her trying
to remember every person, every animal, every cart and
dray and carriage that had passed her window.

"I might have," she said at last. "You must understand
I am not always at the window no matter what Fergus
says. Hmmph!

"But I do admit it gives me an interest, crippled as I
am. There have been several carriages these past few
days. It is not as busy now as it is in the summer months
when people come from all over England. Oh, my, yes,
we are all abustle then! But there are still a good number
about, and there will be until the first autumn storm.
*That* clears them out in a hurry, and a good thing, too.
For then we can all return to our regular pursuits without
being hedged about with strangers."

She leaned forward and winked. "It's a very good thing they never discover that after that first blow there is often a spell of golden weather to surpass any other time of the year. No, sir, you may be sure we keep that to ourselves."

"Very wise of you," the earl said evenly. Harriet was sure he must be getting impatient with this garrulous old lady. For herself she could only pity her. She was so hungry for company that even if she had seen Byrn and Lark, she would have spun out the telling for the pleasure of having them here.

"Now about my son, ma'am," Morland prompted.

"Yes. Well, as I was saying, it is very possible they passed this way. A black phaeton, you say? Bay horses? Yes, I am sure I saw such a rig. And your son is young? His cousin, too? Oh, can it be they are bound for Gretna and you are in pursuit, sir? My word, I wish I had paid more attention. You may be sure I shall do so in the future."

"No, they were not bound for Gretna," he lied. Harriet wondered if he wanted to tell her that keeping more careful watch would hardly matter since he only had one rash, impulsive son and he intended to make sure he never, ever considered Gretna again.

As he rose, Mrs. Dunne's face fell in ludicrous disappointment. "Don't feel you must run away, sir, ma'am," she begged, turning to Harriet to implore her with a look to remain. "I am sure Jennie will return soon, and I would so enjoy your company."

Bending down, the earl took her hand in both of his and pressed it gently. "I am sorry we cannot oblige, ma'am, for we must be on our way," he said. "Perhaps if we pass this way again some time, you will allow us to take advantage of your kind offer? Thank you. You are very good. Mrs. Winthrop-Bates?"

As they went to the door, the old lady's assurance of hospitality was fervent in their ears.

Walking back to the inn, Morland remarked, "I do not think she saw them, in spite of what she said. She is lonesome and she wanted us to stay. But we will inquire further."

They questioned a dozen people: shop owners, idlers, a shepherd visiting the village, even some children. Only one person thought he might have seen the couple they sought, but he, like Mrs. Dunne, could not be positive.

Back at the inn, the earl ordered tea while they discussed what they were to do next. Harriet tried to keep her disappointment from showing as she busied herself making the tea. For some reason she felt close to Lark here. Would she have that sensation if Lark had never been here at all? Or was it only that she was indulging in wishful thinking?

As they sipped their tea, the earl's agent was announced.

"What news?" Morland asked abruptly.

"They are not at Gretna, nor have they been, sir," Mr. Goodwell said. "No one has seen them, either. Sam has been asking all along this route, and there has been nothing."

"We've found much the same. Very well. Return to Gretna and keep watch there. They cannot be far away. I depend on you to keep Byrn from participating in any marriage ceremony. Mrs. Winthrop-Bates and I will travel on and spend the night at an inn in Penrith. Arrange that as you pass through, please. We will join you in Gretna late tomorrow morning."

Later, as they themselves left Ambleside, Morland said, "I can see you are depressed, ma'am. You must not be. We are very close to them now, and I do assure you they will come to our net tomorrow or the day after at the latest."

"I sense we are close, too, sir. But I admit I am frustrated. I feel as if I am being mocked, led here and there while someone, something—laughs at me."

"Fate you mean?" he asked. "Have you ever considered how strange it is that we are on our way to Gretna together at last? That it took twenty years after the trip was first proposed to you for you to finally agree to it? Don't you find that ironic, ma'am? I do!"

Harriet wished he had not mentioned that long-ago time; after his first outburst she had been grateful he had pretended he had forgotten it had ever happened. She wondered what made him refer to it now.

"I have been trying to forget," she said when she realized he was waiting for a reply. "And I thought we agreed never to discuss it again."

"So we did. But no matter what we agreed, you must admit the past will always be part of our memories. And whether we speak of it or not, it refuses to be disregarded. Behind the pleasantries we exchange, it waits to be examined and discussed. All those things we never said to each other whose omission we can only regret now, clamor to be revealed at last. And those things we *did* say and regret even more, beg to be forgiven. I hurled several harsh accusations at you at our last meeting, madam. You may have forgotten them; believe me, even after twenty years, I have not."

"If it will make you feel better, know I forgave you for them long ago, m'lord," Harriet told him, staring straight ahead at the road that wound upward as they traversed the Kirkland Pass. Her throat felt so tight she had trouble swallowing.

"Yes, I forgave you with all my heart," she heard herself repeating, and knew she had never said anything she meant more. "I hope you in turn forgave me for all the pain I know I caused you.

"But enough of this, enough!" she added, pounding one gloved fist on her knee in her agitation. "I warn you I do not intend to discuss the matter again. Let this be an end to it!"

She was so distressed she could not help how abrupt she sounded, but he had driven her to the end of her patience. She was surprised therefore to hear his amused chuckle, so surprised, she turned and stared at him.

"So," he said, as if to himself, "Harry is not dead after all."

He must have heard her gasp, for he explained, "I goaded you to that display, and I did it deliberately. You see, I wondered if you had changed as completely as it appeared. You seemed, as Mrs. Harriet Winthrop-Bates, the perfect conventional lady. You were calm and serene and well-mannered. Such an elegant widow, concerned only with the proprieties. All proper and prim and prudent with as much fire to you as a frigid old dame of ninety. You were boring, in fact.

"But I had to wonder if your transformation was as complete as it appeared."

He turned and glanced down at her and smiled, his expression a caress before he added, "I can't tell you how reassuring it is for me to discover that at least something of my Harry still exists."

# Twenty

Since Harriet was incapable of responding to this remark, it was just as well the earl changed the subject, pointing out a particularly handsome prospect and the remains of a road the Romans had built here long ago.

A short time later, approaching another steep rise, he suggested they get down and walk to spare the horses. Harriet was glad to do so, for while he led the team he would not be able to see her on the other side.

She was thoroughly confused, her thoughts disjointed. Could it be those remarks of his had been made with some other purpose in mind than just to goad her into reacting, perhaps? Had she only imagined the tenderness in his voice when he spoke of "his Harry"? Surely he could not love her still! No, that was not possible. It was only curiosity on his part, it had to be. Or was he hoping she would betray herself into admitting she loved him and always had? But I don't love him, she thought fiercely, pausing for a moment to catch her breath. The road was very steep and they had quite a way to go before they reached the top.

*Oh, I admit I loved him more than life once, the way any young girl loves for the first time. Completely and with a whole heart, forgetting everything and everyone else. But it was a consuming love that burned so brightly it could not last. I married another man, bore his child, lived with him in harmony until his death. And I hardly pined for Marsh Pembroke all those years.* Because you kept yourself busy, her conscience reminded her. And because you would not *let* yourself think of him.

Harriet knew how these days together had taxed them

both. Surely when this business of Byrn and Lark was resolved and they were free to go their own ways again, life would return to normal. She felt a sudden stab when she recalled how he had described the woman she had become in that "normal" life. Prim, he had said. Proper. Boring.

How dare he? she asked herself, but knew she was only trying to scare up some resentment against him to hide behind, much as she was hiding now, behind a horse's flank.

But was it possible he did love her then? Want her as he had once? But we can't go back, she argued silently. There was no way to return to the young people they had been. Life had intervened.

He knows that as well as I do. Besides, he asked me if I were going to marry Douglas now I was free to do so, at the inn in Bury St. Edmunds. He would hardly have done that if he had any feelings left for me himself.

They had reached the top of the rise and stopped to catch their breaths. Harriet saw a small beck tumbling down the side of the fell to the valley below, and a few farms scattered about there. They looked like a child's building blocks on a deep green carpet.

It was with the greatest reluctance she rejoined the earl in the carriage to begin the descent to Ullswater, the lake that lay just south of Penrith where they were to spend the night. To her relief, Morland seemed preoccupied with his own thoughts, and she was free to indulge in her musings without interruption. And as she did so, the last time she had seen Marsh Pembroke twenty years before returned to her mind in vivid detail.

Douglas had not been there. She remembered he had not come to Pembroke House nearly as often the older they all became. Because he could not bear to watch Marsh and me together? she wondered.

It had been much the same time of year, only early October. The trees were just about to turn while the nights were chill, the days rich with a dreamy sort of completion. The fields were heavy with crops and even the bees droned more slowly as if to savor this golden time before the winter storms began.

She had come to their meeting place in response to a note he left for her tucked under a special stone in the garden path. They always communicated that way, since he was forbidden to visit the house. She remembered she had gone to meet him with dread, for only the evening before her parents had informed her they intended her to marry a James Winthrop-Bates. In vain she had pleaded with them to spare her, told them she could not, would not marry a stranger. And finally, in desperation, she had revealed her love for Marsh and his for her. She would never forget her mother's piercing screams, her father's tight-lipped white face, nor the terrible things they had said to her. And in the end, she was forced to bow to their will. She was only seventeen. She owed them her obedience and she knew she had no other choice.

Of course there had been another choice. She could have run away with Marsh, but in doing so she would have divorced herself not only from her family, but from any hope of decent society in the future. And at the time, she had not had the courage to dare such a move, nor did she think their love strong enough to endure the punishment of exile.

He had been waiting for her near the cave in the woods, tossing pebbles into the stream to disturb the trout there. His face lit up in a smile of welcome when he saw her that tore at her heart, and he crushed her in his arms and kissed her before she could say a word. It was then she had begun to cry.

"What is it? What is wrong?" he had demanded.

"My parents told me last night they have betrothed me to another man," she admitted. She cried out with pain as his hands tightened on her arms. He released her at once.

"No, they can't do that!" he exclaimed. "You are mine. You have always been mine, Harry."

Her tears continued to flow and she sobbed as she shook her head. "There is nothing we can do, Marsh,"

she told him. "Nothing to change things. They have decided. And when I told them I loved you, my mother had
a fit. Indeed, we had to summon her maid to her, and a
doctor. And my father! It was dreadful the way he glowered at me, dreadful—"

"We will run away," he interrupted. "Today, right now
if we have to. We'll go to Gretna and marry there. They
can't stop us!"

"How are we to do that? We have no money, no carriage or horses. They'll catch us in a day, and then where
will we be?"

"No, they won't. We'll leave after dark and canter
through the night, hide during the day. You'll have to
wear breeches, but you won't care for that, will you,
Harry? And I'm sure I'll be able to find enough money
in the house. My mother must have some tucked away.
Huh! She probably will notice *it's* gone before she
misses *me*.

"You'll have to take one of your father's horses; I'll
ride my gelding. Do you think you could steal some food
from the kitchen? And don't forget a warm cloak and a
blanket."

"Marsh, stop!" she said, grabbing his arm and shaking
it. "I can't go with you. I can't. And if you only thought
for a moment, you'd see how impossible running away
would be. They would find us and we'd be shamed."

"You don't love me," he said, his voice flat now, and
his brows knit in a mighty frown. "Oh, you've always
said you did, but when things get difficult, your love is
nowhere near strong enough, is it? I would dare anything
for you, risk ruin, disgrace. But you . . . ! You have only
been a silly little girl pretending to be in love. And I
don't mean enough to you, perhaps I never did, for you
to defy your parents.

"I think I hate you now, Harry."

"Oh, no," she sobbed, clutching him tighter. "No, you
don't hate me! And I do love you, I do! But I can't do as
you ask, I can't."

"Coward," he said. She had never heard such scorn,

such fury in anyone's voice before. "Stupid little coward, swayed by convention and what everyone will think. Go to your betrothed then. I wish him joy of you!"

He had left her at a run, tearing through the woods with no regard for the branches and brambles that whipped around him. Now Harriet wondered if perhaps that was how he had received the scar she had noticed over his left eyebrow in London. But deep in remembering, she could only see how at the time she had sunk down on a log and cried as if she would never stop. But of course there are only so many tears, only so much grief and remorse.

Eventually she had returned home, become the dutiful daughter her parents demanded, gone on with whatever life had in store for her.

She had learned from one of the kitchen maids that local gossip said Marsh had gone wild, drinking heavily, seeking fights, and sleeping with any girl who would have him. Only two months later she had heard of his marriage. She knew her mother had as well, for one evening she had begun to speak of it. Something she must have seen in her daughter's face, however, made her change the subject quickly, and Marsh Pembroke was never mentioned again.

His elevation to the peerage and the old title of Earl of Morland had come a few months after his marriage. His uncle, the former earl, and his three sons had all drowned crossing the Channel from France where they had been visiting distant relatives. Their ship had been caught in a gale and all hands were lost. Some of the bodies washed up on various beaches, some were never seen again. The earl's and his sons' bodies had been found so there was no question about the succession.

Preparing for her wedding which was to take place in the spring, Harry wondered if her parents were sorry they had been so adamant about Marsh Pembroke. Surely his ascendancy to an earldom must have rankled. But she realized from various remarks her father made, it wouldn't have mattered if he had become king. He was a ne'er-do-well, one of the dissolute Pembroke clan, and as such no title or honor could make him a jot better than he ever had been in Mr. Fanshaw's opinion.

She sighed and shook her head.

"Was that another of your heartfelt sighs I just heard, ma'am?" the earl said and she was recalled to present time and present company with a jolt. "Don't worry. I have no intention of asking you about it, so you may be easy."

"You may ask if you care to," she found herself saying, then wondered wildly who was putting words in her mouth. "I was only thinking that although there is nothing we can do to change the past, there is nothing to stop us from regretting it either. Isn't that so, m'lord?"

When he made no immediate reply, she felt exultation welling up in her again. He could not call her coward now, she told herself. And for the first time in a very long time, she had said just what she felt, and she was not sorry she had done it either.

He drove to the bottom of the hill they were descending before he said, "That is true, ma'am, and it is most perceptive of you to realize it. You may be sure I have also been regretting the past. I look forward to discussing the matter with you in more depth this evening after dinner, when I do not have my hands so full of reins."

He sounded almost amused, and Harriet wanted to ask what he meant by that statement. But instead, she only inquired the name of the fell to their left. The earl obliged, but she was not misled. He had every intention of discussing her remark. She wondered what she would say to him when he did.

They arrived at Penrith in excellent time to discover Mr. Goodwell had all prepared for them. The same maid was there to wait on Harriet and there were even some fall flowers in a bowl on the table in her room. She lingered over her dressing for dinner until finally she had to go down to the private parlor and join him. And she told herself, whatever came of this night, she would be ready for it.

It seemed an age before the covers were removed, a decanter of port and two glasses set before the earl, and the servants were bowing themselves away.

"I wonder where they are tonight, Lark and your son," Harriet said before he could take control of the conversation.

"Very close. Not in Penrith yet, however. Goodwell inquired, and I've had a man watching ever since."

"When do we leave for Gretna in the morning?" she persisted, and wondered at his little half smile.

"Shall we say nine? You seem uncommon anxious to come up with my young scoundrel and your wayward daughter, ma'am."

"Well, of course I am," she retorted. "Haven't we been chasing them over the better part of England for almost a week now?"

"Have you thought how you are to punish her?" he asked idly before sipping his port.

Harriet stared down into her glass. The deep ruby liquid had a heady aroma, but she was neither seeing nor inhaling it. "I have no idea," she admitted. "I can hardly beat her, and as for withholding new gowns or telling her we cannot live in town, well, there has never been enough money for those indulgences anyway."

"I thought as much," he said calmly and she wondered why she had admitted her poverty so openly. "I take it Mr. Winthrop-Bates did not leave you well before with the world?"

"No, he did not. He seemed to have no sense about money matters, and invariably invested in projects that were doomed to failure. And no one, not even his man of business, could get him to change his mind once it was made up. His failures occurred so often, it was almost as if a wicked fairy was intent on his ruination. And ours. Lark's portion is saved, and I have my grandmother's bequest, but there is nothing else left. I even had to sell the estate to pay his debts."

"What was he like, besides unlucky?"

"Why, what can I tell you? He was kind to me in his fashion and he adored Lark. She was not born until we had been married almost three years, and he had begun to despair of ever siring a child."

"Did it matter she was a girl?"

"Not a bit of it. He loved her wholeheartedly from the day she was born."

"When he heard that bird."

"Yes, from then. Of course he did want a son, too, but it was not to be. But what of you, m'lord? Tell me of your life if you would be so good."

He poured himself another glass of port before he began, and for a moment after, he stared into the fire as if to find the words he needed there. Harriet sensed he was about to make a confession, and knowing Marsh, she knew how hard it would be for him.

"I married Annie Combs shortly after I left you that day in the woods. I think I went a little mad when you refused to run away with me, and I did things I should not have done. It was almost as if I were trying to do away with myself, but as you can see, the gods were obviously not through with me.

"Annie was sure she was pregnant. As it turned out, she was, with Andrew. But it didn't matter either way to me. In my eyes, she was as good as any other since I could not have you. And in her arms I could forget you. Briefly."

Harriet held her breath, sorry she had asked him. Still, he continued, and she could do nothing but listen and ache for him.

"I didn't deserve her, you know," he remarked, pushing his glass in slow circles on the scarred table. "She tried so hard to be a good wife to me. And when I became earl, although she hated it, she tried to be a good countess, too. It didn't work. The servants despised her because she never got anything right and she couldn't seem to learn. And she was common, uneducated. But she did love me to distraction, I'll give her that. There was nothing she wouldn't do for me. But you know,

Harry, when I wasn't bored by her, I was embarrassed. I'm ashamed of that now."

He rose to go to the window and look down at the street. "I did mourn her when she died. I knew I had never deserved such a rich outpouring of love as she gave me when I had none to give her in return. And I tried not to feel relieved she could no longer keep me tied to Morland, too ashamed of my wife to introduce her to society or even the local gentry.

"Tell me, Harry, did you love your husband?" he asked, turning to stare at her.

"Why—why, I was fond of him, yes. He was not a bad—"

"No. I didn't ask if you were *fond* of him as you might be fond of the color blue, or a particular food, or a certain flower. I asked if you *loved* him."

She hesitated for a minute before she lifted her chin and said, "If you insist, no, I did not love him."

"I see. I cannot tell you how you have relieved my mind."

She rose from the table and he came back to her, to stand close before her.

"Since we are getting such an early start in the morning, I would like to be excused now," she whispered.

He traced the outline of her face slowly before he took her chin in his hand and looked deep into her eyes. For a moment, she was sure he was going to kiss her, and just the thought of it so unnerved her, she felt her knees begin to quiver.

But he did not kiss her. Instead, he said softly, "Go to bed, Harry. There is always tomorrow. Yes, keep that in mind, my girl. There is always tomorrow."

At the door she paused, reminded of something. "But I thought we were going to discuss what I said this afternoon about regretting the past," she said.

He smiled at her, a singularly sweet smile that made him seem years younger. "But my dear Harry," he said, throwing out his hands in astonishment, "isn't that just what we have been doing?"

# Twenty-One

Harry had looked puzzled when she left, and Marsh Pembroke was still smiling when the door closed behind her and he was left alone. But of course she was confused, poor sweet, he thought as he stretched luxuriously.

His thoughts went back from this past week when they had been together almost constantly, to the London Season just concluded. He had begun badly with her, calling and telling her that her daughter was not good enough to be Countess of Morland. Ha! Compared to Annie Combs, Lark Winthrop-Bates was a princess. But he had been angry, still angry with Harry because for all those years he had not been able to forget her. And when she had come to join him in that insipid little parlor of hers, he had been stunned. Somehow he thought she would have shown her age more. At seventeen she had been a pretty girl; now, in maturity, she was beautiful. And he could not help remembering she could have been his, if she had dared. Thinking back on those twenty years without her—his loneliness, his unfortunate marriage—all, all unnecessary but for the want of a little courage, he had lashed out at her in his coldest, most sarcastic way. And when he saw he had wounded her, he had been glad.

But such vindictiveness could not survive. All through their children's entanglement, he had continued to call on her. It had not been at all necessary he do so, for he could have sent Andrew away the first time he learned of his infatuation with the girl, couched his order in such a way the boy would not have dared to disobey. He had had that power but he had not used it. No, he realized now he had deliberately prolonged the affair, even spun it out, so he could see her, speak to her, be near her.

It was also evident why, when he had observed her with Viscount Webster, he had been angry. It was so obvious Douglas was in love with her still. And who could blame him? While they were all in London he had studied them secretly and been relieved when Harry did not appear to return his friend's love. But when they had first started to search for the runaways she had smiled at Douglas as she thanked him for his help, become choked up with emotion. That was why he had asked her if she intended to marry the man, even felt obliged to beg her not to hurt him. He remembered now how defeated he had felt at the time. Defeated and yes, bitter.

Morland leaned his elbows on the table and pushed his hair back from his temples with both hands. Only when he had watched her admiring his Copley drawing, had he realized he loved her as well. Not the way he had as a boy, with a passion and possessiveness that made it impossible for him to keep his hands from her, but with a disciplined man's deep lasting ardor to set things right for her in any way he could—to protect her, cherish her. And although he felt sorry for Douglas, he meant to take her away from him if he could. There were two of them, and only one could have Harry. Someone had to lose. He was determined it would not be he.

It had been awkward. He knew he could not woo her while they were preoccupied with the chase. He did not want her to be uncomfortable in his presence either, as surely she would have been if he had tried to make love to her. And so he had held his tongue. And with every sign of her growing trust and returning affection, no matter how minute, he had been elated. Every tentative smile, every blush, a barely concealed gasp, the moments of unguarded conversation—even the way she had grasped his arm when she saw the scene near Ambleside recalled the old Harry. But the old Harry had not truly appeared until he had goaded her to it. "Enough!" she had said. "Let this be an end to it!" she had ordered, as impetuous as a girl. He had almost crowed in triumph that he had forced her out of that shell she had grown in order to present herself to the world as a proper, staid widow with a grown daughter.

Ah, yes, the daughter, he mused, frowning now. He would have to do something about her. Of course, if she and Andrew could convince him they were really in love, as he and her mother had been, then there was nothing for it but to agree to the marriage. When Andrew was twenty-one and Miss Winthrop-Bates nineteen, he amended. In the meantime, Andrew could go to St. Kitts, see something of the rest of the world, and gain some much needed maturity, and his betrothed could attend an excellent finishing school and learn some of the propriety he was about to insist her mother discard.

Still, he admitted he would much rather the future Countess of Morland had not been named for a *bird*. Ah, well, he told himself as he rose to seek his bed at last, one can't have everything, can one? And having Harry would make up for all the rest.

"Well, here's a to-do," Byrn said as he straightened up from inspecting the horse's leg and looked up at Lark where she sat huddled on the perch. "He's gone lame all right. He'll take us no farther."

"What are we to do?" Lark asked, determined to be calm.

Byrn did not answer. Instead he threw his hat on the ground and stamped on it in frustration.

"What on earth are you doing? Have you gone mad?" Lark demanded.

"Damn-damn-*damn*!" he swore. "Why me? Why now? We were so close to winning through. *Damn*!"

"I realize you are disappointed, but I must ask you to moderate your language, sir. I am a lady, after all."

"Oh, let me alone," he muttered, and her brows rose in indignation.

He paced up and down beside the rig and did not look at her as he said, "We cannot go on in the phaeton. I'll leave it here. You can ride the sound horse, I'll lead the lame one. There should be a village somewhere ahead. Even if there is not, we'll be able to get help in Cockermouth."

"But what of my clothes?" she asked. "I can't just leave them."

Byrn managed to control his temper but he was feeling sorely tried. "We'll have to. That large portmanteau is too heavy. As for those silly bandboxes, how are you to manage them astride? You don't even have a saddle. Do try for a little common sense."

Lark glared at him. "Why can't we tie everything to the lame horse?" she asked, trying to sound reasonable.

"Because he's done in. We've used these beasts hard all these days. They don't have much left, and I'll not be responsible for killing them. Lord, my father would have my head if I were to do such an infamous thing."

"I hardly think just carrying two little bandboxes, even the portmanteau, would kill them," Lark argued, but he was not paying any attention to her for he had gone back to check the lame leg once more. Well, I guess I know what is important to him, she fumed. And if he were any kind of a gentleman at all, he would have offered to carry my portmanteau himself. After all, it only took one hand to lead a lame horse.

She climbed down from the phaeton and said, "You'll have to help me up. But before you do, get my portmanteau from the boot. I'll not leave my Grandmother Winthrop-Bates's pearls behind for robbers to find, and I must have another gown and my pelisse."

She saw him open his mouth in protest, but she gave him such a withering glance of scorn, he went to do her bidding without another word.

Lark wound the pearls around her neck for safekeeping, donned the pelisse, and tucked her other gown under her arm. It was not very secure, but it was the best she could do.

The wind was rising now and her skirts whipped around her legs when Byrn lifted her to the horse's broad back. Perched sideways, she grabbed a handful of mane to steady herself.

"All right and tight?" Byrn asked politely. She only nodded slightly as she continued to stare straight ahead. She thought she heard him mutter something to himself, but she ignored it. Men, she thought. Men!

It was a long, uncomfortable morning. Lark's mount discovered it could shake her off if she relaxed for only a second, and it managed to do so twice. She decided to walk instead, only to discover the blister she had acquired yesterday made that a painful alternative. Barely half a mile farther on, she was mounted again. To add to her other woes, she dropped the spare gown several times. When this happened, Byrn had to pick it up for her. Finally he asked why she had brought it at all.

"Because it is going to rain. Just look at those clouds. And I won't be married in a sopping wet gown, all shivers."

"Well, we'll be a fine pair, won't we? You in your dry gown, I in my wet coat and breeches."

"You should have thought of that before we abandoned the phaeton," she told him, sounding smug.

Byrn set his mouth hard. He was doing the best he could, wasn't he? But Lark! It seemed to him she thought only of herself and her precious clothes. Had she ever asked how *he* was doing? How *he* felt? No, she had not. She had only complained and whined when she wasn't being sarcastic. Oh, he admitted that occasionally she had shown signs of the old Lark he had loved so much, but in the main, she had been more a burden than a joy.

His heart sank. He was committed. They had to marry. He had no choice in the matter, none at all. He could only hope and pray that once restored to a more normal existence, her temper would improve. He had not suspected she was such a shrew, in fact he was amazed at how different women could be from one moment to the next. And if he had known before what he knew now, he would never have proposed to her at all. Women, he thought. Women!

It began to rain shortly thereafter, just as Lark had predicted. It was a hard, driving rain, too, and they were soon wet through and shivering in the cold wind.

On and on they plodded, the lame horse slowing them considerably. Byrn concentrated on putting one foot ahead of the other while he tried to cheer himself by thinking how close they must be to some kind of shelter.

It was Lark who called his attention to a croft ahead, hard by the side of the road.

The shepherd who answered their knock seemed amazed that anyone would be out in such weather, but he was quick to offer them his hospitality and soon they were installed before a blazing hearth holding hot cups of tea. Lark leaned back against the hard settle, letting Byrn and the shepherd discuss the problem. She barely heard the man promise to bring the phaeton to his farm, and care for the horses until their return from Gretna. She did manage to stir herself when she learned Cockermouth was only five miles farther on, and the tavern keeper there had a gig he sometimes hired out.

An hour later, the rain stopped and some weak sunshine lit the interior of the poor croft. Lark was still wet, but she was glad to be on her way again, even in the back of a rude cart, sitting on a pile of straw. As the shepherd's old horse lurched into motion, she had to grab the side of the cart to keep her balance. Across from her, Byrn stared off into the distance, frowning.

Lark inspected him with a critical eye. His clothes were still as damp as her own, his cravat a travesty, and his hair blown into tangles now he had discarded his ruined hat. He did not look a bit like the bridegroom she had once dreamed of, waiting for her at the altar. And the way he was glowering hardly improved his appearance. Still, she had to wonder whether she would look any better herself when the fateful moment came. She certainly did not feel very bride-like.

The journey to Cockermouth passed with little conversation. Fortunately the clearing weather held, although far to the north additional clouds could be seen massing again on the horizon. Lark eyed them with loathing.

As soon as the shepherd pulled up before the tavern, she was quick to leave the cart, and while Byrn spoke to the owner, she visited the necessary and tried to smooth her damp curls under her sodden bonnet.

She thought Byrn looked a little easier when she joined him again, and when she saw the horses being led from the stable she knew why. They were hitched to an ancient gig that showed in a few places it had once sported bright yellow paint.

"How long will it take to get to Gretna?" she asked Byrn, for she had noticed the gig had no hood.

"Three hours or a little more," he said. "But if it begins to storm, we can stop in Carlisle for the night. I told this fellow we might not be able to return his gig for a couple of days."

He paused then and came closer to say, "I'm sorry, Lark. Sorry this wasn't easier for you, smoother somehow. I did try, you know."

"I know," she said just as softly. "It's all right, Drew. You couldn't help a lot of what happened."

Fortunately the shepherd interrupted them before Byrn could get angry again, for hadn't she as good as said there was a lot he could have?

Only a few minutes later, behind a sway-backed pair of the sorriest horses Lark had ever seen, she and her betrothed set out on the last part of their journey. Some women exchanging gossip over a picket fence pointed to them and laughed, and a handful of little boys chased after them making rude sounds of derision. Lark fumed silently. She kept her head high although she was sure her face was as red as Drew's. Someone should write a book about eloping, she thought darkly. If girls knew even half the horrid things that could happen, they wouldn't be so eager to throw their caps over the wind-

mill. She was reminded that very few did, and this
knowledge depressed her so, she could hardly keep her
composure.

For a little while she thought of her mother, wondering where she was and what she was doing. She regretted hurting her and causing her to worry more than she
could say, and if there had been any way to erase the
days since she had run away, she would have snatched at
the chance.

Of course, the way things had turned out, she and
Drew had had no choice. His awful father, the evil earl,
would have separated them forever if they hadn't run
away.

Her eyes widened. Could she honestly say now, such a
separation would have broken her heart? she asked herself. Now, when she had been with him so constantly,
seen him more plainly without the handsome polished
appearance and manners of the London beau he had always seemed? She darted a glance at him where he was
wrestling with the team, one of which was determined to
walk to Gretna while the other was equally set on a fast
canter.

He was swearing again under his breath, and with his
hair every which way, he looked more a wild man than a
gentleman. She supposed she should object, but she really didn't care. In fact, she was so sore from riding on
hard, uncomfortable surfaces in wet clothes, she was
tempted to join him in a few of the choice oaths she had
learned from him.

They reached Carlisle at three in the afternoon. They
were very hungry for they had forgotten to purchase
food for the journey and there had been no place along
the way to stop and get some. Several sharp words had
been exchanged on this subject, Lark wondering why her
escort had been so dim-witted as not to have provided
something so necessary, and Byrn declaring he did not
know why everything had to be his responsibility. Surely
she could have mentioned it, back in Cockermouth,
couldn't she? He, for one, could attest to the fact she was

hardly reticent whenever there was even a hint of trouble. These pleasantries effectively ended the little rapport that had begun to build between them again, and they ate a hurried meal at a local inn in identical, injured silence.

As they left the inn and took their seats in the gig again, neither noticed the man standing back in the shadow of a large carriage at the side of the yard. And so intent was he on brooding over the dismal future he was sure to face as a husband, Byrn paid no attention when the fellow rode past them on a handsome chestnut and headed at a gallop for the border and Gretna.

# Twenty-Two

After staying overnight at Penrith, Morland and Harriet drove to Gretna, arriving well before the noon hour. It was not a pleasant day. Harriet had eyed the dark clouds ahead in the north with some trepidation. She recalled the earl saying this part of the country could be dangerous in wet weather. She was concerned for Lark. Where was she? And was she all right? Had that benighted boy seen to her comfort and care? When she mentioned her concern to the earl, he only laughed a little and said she might be easy.

Harriet wondered at his mood. It seemed almost light-hearted, which she thought hardly appropriate under the circumstances. It continued to bother her they had had no sign of the runaways. Surely with all the earl's men searching, something should have been discovered by now. Yet here was Marsh Pembroke, whistling if you could believe it, the picture of unconcerned elegance.

She wondered how he managed to dress himself so well without the services of a valet. For herself, she was becoming very tired of her small selection of gowns.

"I am glad you wore the green one today," he remarked as if he had read her mind. Harriet gasped.

"It is my favorite for it at least attempts to match your eyes, ma'am. Not that it is successful. I doubt even emeralds could best their brilliance."

Disconcerted, Harriet thanked him for the compliment.

The village of Gretna was an unprepossessing place. Situated at the head of Solway Firth almost amid the marshland there, it consisted of a few cottages, a church and manse, and a large inn. It was raining hard when they arrived and Harriet was delighted to scurry into the inn to get dry and warm again.

To her surprise, the earl did not join her there. Eventually she went to the window to see what he could be doing. She had a problem discerning him at first through the driving rain, but at last she saw him at the stable door, deep in conversation with one of his men.

She leaned closer, her breath misting the pane until she had to wipe it away with her sleeve. Perhaps the man had brought news of the runaways? Perhaps he knew where they were? Oh, do come and tell me at once, Marsh, she begged silently.

But the earl made no move to enter the inn. Instead, he accepted a large umbrella from one of the ostlers, and set off down the village street.

Disappointed, Harriet retreated to a chair by the fire, wondering where he could be going as she did so.

It seemed an age before she heard his footsteps in the hall, and she was on her feet when he knocked and came in. He was smiling still.

"You have news? Someone has seen them?" she asked.

"No, no one. But I beg you to remain calm. They have not been here. The minister, a Mr. Elliot, says he has not married anyone for the past ten days. Of course that may change at any time."

"I am sure I don't care if it does, as long as the couple is not my daughter and your son."

"In honor of our success, I shall ignore that provocative remark."

"You seem uncommon cheerful this morning. I wonder why that should make me feel so uneasy?"

"Don't concern yourself," he told her. "Perhaps I am cheerful because we have reached Gretna before our tiresome children. Among other reasons."

"But how can we be sure—really sure—Gretna was

their destination even now?" Harriet demanded, wringing her hands and pacing the floor in her agitation.

He put his hand on her arm to hold her still. "Trust me. We can be sure," he said. "My men have all reported and there has been no sign of the elopers at any of the border villages from here almost to the North Sea. They are coming here, Harry. In fact, I expect to see them before nightfall."

She stared up into his arresting blue eyes, serious now with conviction, and for a moment she was unable to move. His hand was warm on her skin—she wondered it could feel so right there. He did not take his eyes from her face and she was helpless to look away as they inspected every bit of it to linger at last on her lips.

He smiled gently as he released her and stepped back. "Look," he said, indicating the window, "the rain has stopped. Would you care to take a stroll and inspect the place?"

"Yes, let us go out. It will be something to do to pass the time," she agreed, picking up her pelisse. He took it from her and put it over her shoulders. Harriet could feel his breath on the back of her neck. It was as warm as his hand had been. She had the strangest urge to lean back against his chest so he would have to put his arms around her. Confused, upset even by such a bizarre whim, she went to the mirror to don her bonnet.

The village was soon explored as they picked their way around puddles left by the storm. Harriet shivered as the cold north wind set her skirts to dancing. What sun there was was often lost in clouds; it looked like it would rain again shortly.

"Well, what do you think of Gretna?" the earl asked as they reached the outskirts and turned back.

"It is hardly a romantic spot," she said.

"Strange, your reaction. Now I myself feel its aura strongly. Just consider how many happy couples have married here. Doesn't the very thought give you pause, Harry?" he asked, his voice teasing. Not waiting for her reply, he went on, "And here I thought women the more sentimental sex. Can it be I was wrong? Of course, I doubt I would have appreciated it when I was twenty. Not as I do now. So simple and plain, yet perfect for its purpose right down to the inn where the newlyweds may retire to, er, consummate their union."

Confused, Harriet pretended to study the place again. The clay houses were old and in need of repair, the church was ordinary, and the few small shops, mean. Only the inn seemed prosperous, abustle as it was with activity.

"Perhaps it will grow on you," he said. "Let us hope that is the case, Harry."

Her eye was caught by an approaching horseman. "Look there, Marsh," she said, glad for the interruption. "Isn't that Douglas riding in?"

He stared through narrowed eyes before he waved. Tired, wet, and mud-spattered, Viscount Webster trotted toward them and reined in, a frown on his face.

"Have you any news, Douglas?" Harriet demanded, releasing the earl's arm to move closer to horse and rider.

He dismounted and whistled for an ostler before he answered.

"I'm sorry to say I do not. Nor had any of your men I met along the way, Marsh," he said. "And you? No sign of them at all yet?"

Harriet shook her head, trying hard not to cry. Marsh could tell her she had nothing to worry about, but where, oh, where could they be? Perhaps they had been set upon by highwaymen—they were little more than children, after all. Perhaps they were lying murdered somewhere, their possessions even now being hawked in the thieve's den in London called Clare Market. Perhaps that was why no one had seen them all this time.

She made herself stop thinking of such things as they walked to the inn. She must not give in to panic. She must trust Marsh was right.

"Will you forgive us, Harry?" he asked, and she became aware of them again. "Douglas needs to clean up,

and there are a few things I would say to him. We shall
join you shortly."

When they came to the parlor later, she wondered at
Douglas's grim face. She even noticed there was a white
line around his mouth before he turned away to take the
glass of wine the earl had poured him. *But of course he
is only tired, she told herself. What a dear, good friend
he is to go to all this bother! I do love him so.*

The three sat together comparing notes of their travels
and telling of their disappointments. Eventually, the men
settled to a game of cards. Harriet alternated between
watching and standing guard at the window to stare
down the road that led to Carlisle. A hearty dinner was
served about mid-afternoon when there was still no sign
of the runaways. Harriet had to force herself to eat, and
even so, the earl had more than a word to say about her
lack of appetite.

The dishes had been cleared away and she was once
again at her post by the window when she cried out and
leaned forward to peer through the glass at the strange
vehicle that was approaching the village. "Marsh, come
quickly," she said over her shoulder. "I am sure this must
be Lark and your son."

She sensed him behind her, Douglas as well.

"Why, yes, I do believe you are right. Here are our
wandering little gypsies at last," the earl said in such a
quiet voice it sent shivers up her spine. "I wonder if they
will come to the inn first or go directly to the manse?"

As if in answer, the gig stopped at the inn gates.

"They appear to be arguing about something," Webster remarked.

"My, my, not even wed yet and quarreling already.
Ah, now they are coming here. I suspect the lady won
that argument.

"Well, my dears, I suggest it is time we ourselves
went to the manse."

"But why?" Harriet asked. "Why should we do that?
Why don't we just confront them here? Surely there is
no need to humiliate them before a stranger."

"Mr. Elliot already knows of the situation, Harry," Morland told her as he put her pelisse over her shoulders and handed her her bonnet. "Come along, now. I don't want our runaways seeing us just yet. And yes, I have a reason for it. Trust me."

"You seem to be asking me to trust you a great deal lately, sir," she complained, but she put her bonnet on and let him lead her from the room. A silent Viscount Webster followed. To her surprise, the earl went down the servants' stairs at the back of the house to a side door. Harriet strained to hear Lark's voice but she could not distinguish it from the general rumble that came from the taproom.

Mr. Elliot, the minister, was a spare man with white hair and a twinkle in his eye that made a mockery of the stern lines on his face. He bowed them into a parlor and asked them to be seated before he left them with only the ticking of a mantel clock to keep them company.

"I demand to know what is going on here," Harriet said, suddenly uneasy for no reason she could name.

"Control your impatience, Harry. It is a surprise," Morland told her. "I am sure the children will be here soon. I suspect your daughter wanted to freshen up before the ceremony and that is what is delaying them."

To an impatient mother it seemed forever before the knocker sounded. Harriet rose from the chair she had been perching on uneasily, to stare breathlessly at the door. She had never been separated from her daughter for such a length of time in all Lark's seventeen years—it seemed an age to her. Behind her, the earl lounged against the mantel, much as he had been so wont to do in her little house in London.

The door opened and the Reverend Mr. Elliot ushered a solemn, frowning couple inside before he shut the door behind them and went away.

"Sir!" Byrn exclaimed, turning white as he caught sight of his father.

Harriet steeled herself for the confrontation to come. It was just as well she did, for when Lark saw her, she gave a glad cry and flung herself into her arms. Over her shoulder, Harriet looked in astonishment at the earl.

"Oh, Mama," Lark sobbed, the tears streaming down her cheeks, "I cannot tell you how glad I am to see you!"

"It does not appear you have been a very successful lover, Andrew," the earl remarked in an aside to his wary son.

"Oh, Mama, it has been just *horrid*," Lark rushed on, oblivious of the others in the room. "He didn't bring enough money—I've been so hungry! And he *snores*, Mama, he does!

"I've been so wet and miserable, jounced about in smelly old carts—and he even dared to tell me to *hush* when I tried to talk to him. And then there was that awful shed and it had rats! And I was bitten by bedbugs at that inn where he called the maid who climbed into bed with him by *my* name, Mama, if you can believe such an insult! What's almost as bad, he preaches constantly, as if I were a child. And he likes his horses better than he likes *me*, Mama. He does, he does!

"Today he insisted I leave all my clothes back in the phaeton because he *claimed* the team could do no more—and I have a blister on my heel the size of a shilling, and it *hurts*!"

Over to one side of the room, trying to stay detached from this unusual reunion, Viscount Webster struggled manfully to keep his expression noncommittal. The earl's face was impassive as well, although Harriet was sure she caught a glimpse of amusement in his eyes.

"There, there," she murmured, patting her daughter's back and trying not to look as shocked as she felt at this long recital of misfortunes.

"You snore? How could she know that?" the earl demanded, still speaking so only Byrn could hear.

"We had to sleep out one night in that shed she mentioned," his son confessed. "But there weren't any rats there. Lord, if that isn't just like her, exaggerating all the time."

He seemed to sense his father was waiting for something further for he added, "I've not made love to her, sir, if that is what concerns you. I promised her I wouldn't till we were married."

"I cannot tell you how you have relieved my mind, Andrew. Thank God you remembered you are a gentleman. But I believe I must question you about this maid who, er, got into bed with you, I believe Miss Winthrop-Bates said? How could she possibly *know* that?"

Byrn flushed. "I overslept, and she came to wake me. While she was in the room, the maid came in. Lark hid, and, er, you know, sir . . ."

"I believe I can picture it well enough," his father said dryly. "It was perhaps unfortunate you called the wench Lark."

"Unfortunate! It was a disaster! But I got through it, eventually."

"One hardly dares ask how," Morland murmured.

Byrn leaned closer to whisper. "I was asleep, snoring again, *she* said, when it happened. I told her I'd been dreaming of her."

A look of genuine admiration crossed the earl's face. "Ingenious, my boy, ingenious," he said. "As for your liking your horses more than the young lady, didn't I tell you you were too young to marry?"

"But there is nothing else we can do," Byrn said in a despairing voice. Then he drew himself up when he noticed Lark was listening now from the safety of her mother's arms.

"We have been together day and night all this time. Lark will be ruined if I do not give her the protection of my name."

"Oh, I hardly think such a dire sacrifice need be made," his father said carelessly. Lark gasped, sure the evil earl meant to leave her, in the eyes of the world, a soiled spinster.

"But how can it be avoided?" Byrn argued. "Even if none of us say a word, somehow news of things like this does get around."

"Very true, but in this case what will get around is that

you and Miss Winthrop-Bates, along with our dear
friend Viscount Webster, traveled here in our company.

"You see, the young lady's mother and I had decided
on a whim some days ago, to marry at Gretna. You came
along to serve as witnesses. It is a trifle eccentric, of
course, but I assure you no one will think a thing of it.
Earls are not only entitled to be eccentric, they are expected to be, no doubt due to their exalted rank."

# Twenty-Three

There was absolute silence in the room when he stopped speaking. Harriet stared at him, completely stunned. His son seemed dumbstruck as well, and as for Lark, she was so pale she looked as if she would collapse if her mother let her go. Only Douglas Webster was unchanged. In his place by the wall, he never took his eyes from Harriet's face.

"Do close your mouth, Andrew," his father said. "You look as if there is nothing in your head but air.

"As for you, young lady, release your mother. Go hang on a chair, or even Andrew if you must. He's about to become your brother, so no one can say nay to that."

"Now see here, Marsh," Harriet began, recovering both her voice and her poise at the same time. "How dare—"

"Give me a moment, my dear," he interrupted with a warm smile. He turned to the two runaways. "It is true the marriage I mention is my most fervent wish, and it also has the advantage of solving a great many problems. But tell me, are you still determined on your original course? I must say I have seldom seen any couple who appeared less in love, and less well-suited, than you two. Is it possible I am mistaken? *Do* you want to marry still?"

As the gentleman his father had reminded him he was, Byrn could hardly bring himself to admit he did not, but when he saw Lark shaking her head so vigorously, he flushed and said, "Well, if she doesn't care for it, I am sure I don't either. I was only trying to do the right thing."

"Sometime later, when we are alone, we will have the opportunity to discuss what the right thing would have been. I look forward to it," the earl told him, his voice cold now. Looking uncomfortable, Byrn subsided.

"Douglas wants a few words with you, Harry, and I have deferred to him," the earl said, turning to her again. "Come along with me, you two. There is a parlor across the hall where you can wait until you are summoned. And don't start arguing," he warned as he held the door for them. "I have had quite enough of you and your escapades. It would be unwise—most unwise—to try my patience further."

The door closed behind the three and Webster came to stand close to Harriet, his eyes searching deep.

"Did you know, Harry?" he asked quietly. "Did you suspect Marsh was going to do this?"

"He—well, he did make me wonder if he cared for me still, by some of the things he said, how he looked at me these past two days. But he never gave any indication he wanted to marry me," she told him. She still looked shaken, yes, and angry as well, but he saw something else in her expression that made him bow his head and close his eyes for a moment.

She reached out to him. "Douglas, please, I—"

He put a big hand over her mouth. "No, Harry. I can't say it is all right for I love you, too, but you don't have to say anything. There isn't anything you could say, anyway. And you can't make it easier for me. I guess I have always known deep inside you could never be for me. You've belonged to Marsh heart and soul since we were children, and now you will be his at last, in truth. Tell him he had better be good to you, or he'll have to answer to me."

"Oh, Douglas," she cried, throwing herself into his arms and weeping. For a moment those arms closed fiercely around her before he set her free.

At the door he checked before he turned and said, "I

must beg you to excuse me from being a witness, Harry. I fear I am not that noble. But you will have your youngsters—they will suffice. I'll wait back at the inn."

Harriet wondered why he did not ride away immediately. She wondered as well why she had not told him she had no intention of marrying Morland, no, not even to save her daughter's reputation. But she forgot him and Lark and everything else when the earl came back and shut the door behind him. The sight of him looking so pleased with himself angered her, and she had to clench her fists by her side to keep from striking him.

"How could you, Marsh?" she demanded.

"I know," he said simply. "It was very bad of me, arrogant, in fact to announce our marriage in public before I knew you would have me. Becoming an earl has not made me any humbler than I ever was, I fear. I am sorry."

"How could you do such an infamous thing?" she rushed on, ignoring this handsome apology. "What is my daughter—your son—to think of us? It would serve you right if I refused to ever see you again! I am not some insignificant female to be had on a whim of yours. And you needn't think you have only to cock a finger to have me running to your arms. The very idea!

"Furthermore, I resent being used to draw attention from our children's escapades. And even if I were insane enough to agree to marry you, it would not be here of all places! No, this time you have overstepped all bounds, sir. I am most displeased."

"No, you're not. You're furious," he told her, grinning till she ached to hit him. "Ah, Harry, Harry! What is wrong with marrying at Gretna? It's legal, and people do it all the time."

"Runaways—young people eloping to escape persecution or to make a coming child legitimate. People who are already outcasts of society. How would it look for two staid, settled, middle-aged people like us to follow their example? We would become a laughingstock. And who would ever marry Lark then, with such a hey-go-mad mother in her background?"

His grin faded. "I do wish you would forget your daughter. I have, Andrew as well. And although I am of course desolated I must contradict you, madam, I am not the least staid or settled, even at forty. And no one laughs at whatever I chose to do."

"And that's another thing," she went on, ignoring most of this speech. "There is no way in the world I could tolerate being called 'madam,' in that cold, disapproving manner you have acquired. I hate it. No, Marsh, I won't marry you, I won't!"

"Will you marry me if I promise never to call you madam again?" he asked meekly. Harriet shook her head.

"Then I shall just have to make love to you until you are convinced," he murmured, although to Harriet's profound regret he did not take her in his arms.

His deep blue eyes burned into hers as he said, "Listen to me now, Harry! I do not propose marrying merely to draw attention from our tiresome children, and I think you know that. Nor do I care what the world thinks of me—or of you. The only person whose good opinion of me I value, is you.

"I want to marry you because I must have you beside me, and I have no intention of taking no for an answer, not this time. We have lost years, we must not lose another minute! I love you, Harry. I love you more than I ever could as a boy. Please, darling, for my sanity and all my future happiness, say you will marry me—here—now!

"And you may be as sure as you are of the changing seasons that I will love you with all my heart and soul and strength for the rest of our lives.

"And if Gretna does seem a bit rakish to you—although I intend to begin changing your ideas of propriety—we can be married again in the chapel at Morland when we return there. I would like that, and two ceremonies would assure me you were mine at last.

"Say yes, Harry, say yes!"

She smiled and he began to relax. "I am not so deranged as to agree to marry a man just to keep him sane and happy," she told him. "However, I admit I might do so for my own state of mind. You have been very eloquent, sir. I find I believe you."

He took her hand and raised it to his lips, his eyes still intent on her face. "You may always believe me, Harry. I could never lie to you."

He drew her down close beside him on a sofa, but still he did not take her in his arms.

A little startled at her boldness, Harriet said, "But why don't you kiss me, Marsh? Don't you remember that is how all our quarrels ended when we were young?"

"Of course I do. And as I am sure you are aware, I cannot wait to kiss you. But I am afraid that must be postponed for a short time." She looked a question, and he added, "You see, I must get you married to me quickly. I fear still you might change your mind! Besides, I am not sure our children can be trusted to preserve the fragile truce they are now enjoying. Not for much longer, at any rate, and if I begin to kiss you, it will be a great deal longer."

"I was shocked at the way they spoke of each other. Do you think they were ever really in love?"

"I think they were more taken with the idea of it. Of course, we helped. Oh, yes, by trying to keep them apart, we fanned the fires nicely and gave them the thrill of feeling persecuted. If I had known, I would have arranged for them to be constantly in each other's company. Still, I expect they will feel a pang or two every once in a while. Those pangs won't last."

"I hope you are right," she murmured, reaching up to touch the scar over his left brow. When she asked if he had acquired it running away from her that fateful day they parted, he laughed and said, "I am tempted to take a leaf from Andrew's book and say yes because it would sound so romantic, but alas, I cannot. I came a cropper jumping a horse over a fence. It was all my fault, too. I crammed him, poor beast.

"But let me tell you what I plan to do. Andrew is going to leave here tonight for Oxford where he will stay until Christmas. I may, mind you, I *may* allow him to return home at that festive time, but only because he is to sail for the West Indies right after the New Year.

"And if you approve the scheme, I have prevailed on Douglas to invite your daughter to pay a month's visit to his younger sisters in Derbyshire. That will give us time to investigate a number of excellent finishing schools where, it is sincerely to be hoped, she can be taught to be more of a lady and less of a madcap. Of course it is entirely your decision."

"I do approve. I wondered what I was to do with Lark. I knew I couldn't send her back to my mother—oh dear, I almost forgot! Mother said she wouldn't speak to me ever again if I married you."

He thought for a moment before he shook his head. "Well, that would be grand, but I do not rely on it. She will be sure to forgive you eventually, but never me. And I have no desire to see the woman who kept you from marrying me all those years ago. Later, you can visit her if you like, but you must go alone."

He rose then and drew her to her feet. For a moment he held her close to his heart, his face buried in her hair. She heard him groan and then he whispered, "Come, my dear. Let me call Mr. Elliot and the children. I fear if I do not, almost immediately, I am in great danger of forgetting my main purpose here."

A few minutes later, the simple ceremony was performed and the certificate of marriage filled out. The couple were attended by two strangely silent, even perplexed young people. But even if either one of them had wanted to voice any opposition to the marriage, they did not dare. They were on their best behavior, for they knew their futures were about to be decided, and their punishment meted out.

Lark shyly wished the newlyweds happy and Byrn

gave Harriet his most elegant bow along with his best
wishes. She wanted to hug him, he looked so much like
his father at the same age. And she was determined to
spend some time with Lark before she left for Derbyshire, reassuring her about her future. There was a lost
look in her eyes her mother did not care for. But alas,
this familial harmony was too good to last.

"I suppose Freddy Colchester will be calling on you
just as soon as you get back to London," Byrn said
stiffly to Lark as they all walked back toward the wel-
coming lights streaming from the inn windows. "It's a
very good thing for you, my girl, our journey to Gretna
will be hushed up. For I assure you, if I told him some of
the things I've learned about you, he'd never want to
marry you."

"Little you know," Lark said smugly. "Why, he asked
me if I would even before we left town, so there! And I
might just accept him. Unlike yourself, *Freddy* is a gentleman. *He* would never treat me as you have, and furthermore—"

From where they were walking behind, Harriet could
hear Lark's voice rising and she would have interrupted
except for the pressure of the earl's hand on her own.

"That will be quite enough from both of you," he ordered, his voice cold. As the two fell silent, he added,
"And whether you marry this Freddy, miss, or indeed,
anyone else, is not for you to decide. Not now, it isn't."

A confused Lark stared over her shoulder at him and
he added, "Can it be you have forgotten I just became
your stepfather, and as such, your guardian? My consent,
as well as your mother's will be necessary before any
marriage of yours can take place. And right now, we do
not consider you of an age to wed. You appear to have a
great deal of growing up to do first."

Forgetting himself, Byrn began to chortle while his in-
dignant new stepsister could only sputter her indignation. A quick glance at the earl's face showed Harriet he
was silently congratulating himself on a chore neatly accomplished. Hiding a smile, she pressed his hand so he

would know how much she admired his adroit handling of the situation.

She forgot her troublesome daughter and her new stepson however as Marsh looked down at her, all his love for her writ plain in his intent blue eyes. She did not even wonder why her heart gave that funny little skip that was becoming so much a part of her. Instead, she wondered how long it would be before they could decently be alone together.

As if he knew only too well what she was thinking, the earl smiled and bent to whisper so only she could hear, "Soon, Harry. Very soon. Trust me to see to it."

She stared up at him, wondering if the delighted anticipation she could feel flooding through her was obvious. But strangely, she did not care. Feeling as giddy as any eighteen-year-old, she prepared to discard the lady who had been Harriet Winthrop-Bates to become, once again, simply Marsh Pembroke's Harry.